Dear Patron: You are invited to make a brief signed or unsigned, after reading this novel. may help other readers in their book select as negative comments are requested.)

LOVE ALL

LOVE ALL

A NOVEL

CALLIE WRIGHT

HENRY HOLT AND COMPANY NEW YORK

Henry Holt and Company, LLC
Publishers since 1866
175 Fifth Avenue
New York, New York 10010
www.henryholt.com

Henry Holt® and ® are registered trademarks
of Henry Holt and Company, LLC.

Library of Congress Cataloging-in-Publication Data

Wright, Callie.
  Love all : a novel / Callie Wright.—1st ed.
    p. cm.
  ISBN 978-0-8050-9697-2
  1. Families—New York—Fiction.   2. Family secrets—Fiction.
3. Cooperstown (N.Y.)—Fiction.   4. Domestic fiction.   I. Title.
  PS3623.R528L68 2013
  813'.6—dc23   2012039044

Henry Holt books are available for special promotions and premiums.
For details contact: Director, Special Markets.

First Edition 2013

Designed by Meryl Sussman Levavi

Printed in the United States of America

1   3   5   7   9   10   8   6   4   2

Love All is a work of fiction. All of the characters, organizations, and events portrayed in this novel either are products of the author's imagination or are used fictitiously. This work also includes various references to a real novel, *The Sex Cure* by Elaine Dorian, which was published in 1962. However, in *Love All* the author has used the characters and events portrayed in *The Sex Cure* fictitiously.

TO MY MOM AND DAD

LOVE ALL

1994

PROLOGUE

In a bizarre coda to parenthood—played out at the advanced age of eighty-six—Bob Cole had been recast in the role of needy newborn, and just as Joanie had for their daughter forty-odd years ago, now his wife got up with him, trailing Bob to the bathroom and standing sleepily outside the door to chat. At midnight, she was there describing the spring blooms she anticipated any day now: Hadn't he noticed the crocuses already leafing, marking the place where their violet flowers would soon skirt the stems of the tulips? It was possible that the soil bed didn't get quite enough sunlight, she admitted, which likely meant that not all the bulbs would come up, but still it would be something new this year, not the same old daffodil mix they'd always done.

Bob had never planted a flower in his life, but Joanie would have him believe he was as integral to the goings-on of their household as he had been when he'd run his own insurance agency, paid the bills, and treated his wife and daughter to weeklong summer vacations at a furnished cabin on the lake. His revisionist wife: if Joanie still thought of him as that six-foot-tall man with a full head of hair, she seemed to have forgotten his erstwhile propensity for a few pastimes less wholesome than gardening.

At four A.M., Bob again slid out from under the covers and this time Joanie didn't stir and the bathroom light didn't rouse her, and Bob was pleased to think that she was so deeply asleep. How tired she must be, how completely exhausted from all this tending. Twelve years her senior and their age difference had never felt more pronounced.

From the window above the toilet Bob could see down to the backyard, where Joanie's flower bed was cast in gibbous moonlight. The crocus leaves were jutting through the snow, just as Joanie had described, mapping a pattern so complex that Bob wondered if his wife had plotted it out on paper before laying spade to soil. When had she found the time? Soon the sky would shade salmon pink and they'd begin their day with coffee and orange juice, eggs and toast, and a grapefruit split between them. After breakfast, Bob would read the paper in his recliner by the kitchen while Joanie did the dishes; late morning, she'd heat soup for their lunch while he napped in his chair.

In the early afternoon they'd go for a drive up the scenic lake road or through the winding farmlands of Cherry Valley, routes without destinations, the luxury of being old. Joanie piloted Bob's Buick, touring them through the countryside they'd both grown up in: past six-mile point, where Miller's Pioneer Restaurant had been their Sunday-night destination when they were first married, then cresting Mount Wellington, with its bird's-eye view of the lake. In the winter Bob could see straight down to the swimming area of Camp Chenango, where he'd been a vanguard sailor as a young boy; in the summer the seasonal Springfield Hill Road carried them over to Route 33, and they drove alongside muddy farm fields lined with plastic sheets holding down feed or bales of hay.

In the late afternoons their granddaughter, Julia, occasionally stopped by with her friends, and these visits were plainly the highlight of Joanie's week. She plied the kids with molasses cookies and lemonade, while Julia, Sam, and Carl spoke in a private language they found so funny, it had the power to drop even the towering Sam to the floor. Had Bob ever been so young? Not that he could remember. Certainly if he'd managed to bring home a girl at the age of fifteen he wouldn't have been playing board games with her in the sitting room.

When the diuretics had finally done the work for his heart, Bob felt his way back to bed and soon dropped into the seal-clubbed slumber of children, that impenetrable state in which his heart could quietly rest while he slipped into a dream. This time he made his way to the country club, to the great lawn beneath the brightly lit clubhouse, where a horn section was beginning to chop out the first notes of "Rug Cutter's Swing."

From the end of the dock, he heard a soft splash followed by a man shouting, "Now look what you've done," then the reverberations of the diving board. A silhouetted set of tuxedo tails beat the air like wings.

"Should we join them?" a woman asked, and Bob looked left and saw a head of cropped blond hair, a face he'd nearly forgotten, her cheek shadowed by the collar of his own suit jacket draped over shoulders that were otherwise bare.

Bob jerked awake to find daylight edging the linen curtains in the bedroom and tinting the white cotton flaxen. He was not just thirsty but parched, desperate for a glass of water.

"Joanie," he whispered.

Next to him, his wife lay supine, eyes closed, and anyone might have thought she was asleep except that she rarely slept on her back, usually on her left side, curled vigilantly toward Bob, a habit she'd developed early in their marriage.

Bob touched her cheek, then quickly pulled his hand away. He pushed up on his elbow and lowered his good ear to her chest, but his labored breath was an amplified rasp in the otherwise silent room.

"Joanie?"

He patted her cheek—slapped her, really—then took her by the

shoulders and shook her until her nightgown bunched over her clavicles and wadded at her neck. She was tangled in the sheet, the chenille
bedspread, the wool blanket she insisted on right through summer,
and when he tried to lift her, to force her upright, their nest of bed-
ding tugged her down.

Bob glanced at the phone on Joanie's nightstand—should he call
Dr. Brash? 911? From his own edematous lungs, could he breathe air
into hers? A vitality that had eluded him for years brought Bob up to
his knees on the bed and found him pushing Joanie's hair off her face,
then placing his mouth over hers. He exhaled without count, inhaled
without rhythm, and when his breath grew short, he rubbed his wife's
frail chest until he was reoxygenated, ready to start again.

And he would have gone on indefinitely—better to be dead than
to be left here alone—except that he suddenly remembered Joanie
had not gotten up with him the second time in the night. The realiza-
tion that it had likely been hours, that his own consciousness was not
inextricably linked to hers, that the moment he understood her to be
gone was not in fact the moment he had lost her, slipped over him like
a noose. In fifty-four years of marriage, Bob had never anticipated
having to live without his wife and yet here he was already well into
his first day.

Bob studied Joanie's mouth, her jaw set, her lips pulled into a faint
grimace: a look he'd been given hundreds of times but not in many
years. While he had been dreaming of one in a long succession of
marital betrayals, Joanie had been perpetrating her own. Not divorced
but widowed—she had left him after all.

He'd have to call someone eventually, but Bob wanted no part of
whatever came next. It occurred to him that this might be the last
time he'd ever be alone with his wife and he wondered if the fact of
her death precluded the possibility of her hearing him, should he have
a few things to say.

It took him a moment to get going. He seemed to have lost his
voice. He couldn't remember how he had spoken to his wife, then he

could remember—not the easy rapport of the last twenty years, but Bob talking a mile a minute to outpace the heavy silence of Joanie refusing to ask him where he'd been the night before—and he quickly opened his eyes to dispel the image of their younger, unhappier selves.

Wearily, he sank to his elbow and let his face hover above Joanie's. He stroked her cheek with the back of his hand, then kissed her temple. He wanted her back; he tried to memorize her—wavy white hair curled behind her ears, high cheekbones, sun-spotted skin—but Bob's memory played tricks on him.

Yesterday he'd found Joanie in the study with a photo album open on her lap, documentation of one of those long-ago family vacations at the cabin on the lake. The album's protective cellophane bulged over each yellowed Polaroid.

"What are you looking at?" he'd asked.

She pointed to a photograph in the middle of the page: Bob and Anne standing in the shallow water near the gravelly shore. Bob's gingham bathing trunks were damp against his muscled thighs, the cord tied in a neat bow beneath his flat stomach. Anne clung to Bob's shoulders with exaggerated hilarity, her arms crossed around his neck, her feet wrapped around his waist, her baby-toothed grin just visible above his bright blue eyes.

"Remember the rain that summer?" asked Joanie.

But the sky in the photograph was utterly cloudless and Bob's bathing trunks were faded, as though he'd spent every day of the vacation watching their five-year-old daughter paddling around the end of the dock.

"It looks nice," he observed.

"That was the only sunny day." Joanie tapped the photo. "You took Annie swimming right before we had to return the keys."

Selective memory, Anne would call it now, and Bob thought of his grown daughter, who wouldn't hesitate to conduct an unofficial inquest into her mother's death and find him guilty in every way. What had happened to that little girl who'd held on to his neck for dear life? What had happened to the grandchildren who'd stood on chairs in the kitchen next to Joanie in Bob's old dress shirts so that they could roll out dough, sprinkle flour, measure sugar by the tablespoon? Now Teddy was a senior in high school and Julia was almost driving and Bob couldn't remember the last time one of them had spent the night. It was Joanie who had kept track of the kids' birthday parties, concerts, awards ceremonies, sporting events. She'd organized every-thing, and Anne would never let him stay in this house without her, but where else could he go?

Only three days ago, Anne had invited Joanie and Bob over for an early dinner and their son-in-law had been so distracted during the meal, so jumpy—up for another bottle of wine, down for a third glass of it—that Bob had grown exhausted just watching him.

"Something's going on with Hugh," Joanie had commented on the drive home.

Going on.

It was the same thing she'd once said about Bob, and she'd been both right and wrong—though through it all Bob had loved his wife.

Now he laid his head next to hers and took her hands in his. They'd attended two or three funerals this year alone and yet he couldn't come up with a single prayer, one proper snippet of grace to deliver over his wife's body. He might've wished her a safe passage or told her he'd see her soon, but he ran up against an age-old failure of imagina-tion. Still, he could appreciate a sense of calm Joanie might enjoy from having an entire day off: no breakfast to fix, no bed to make up, no old man to worry about. And there would be people she'd want to see. Her parents; her beloved grandmother, Rose; Nora Ames and Pearl Olsen, childhood friends; her sister, Ellie, killed in a car acci-dent only months before Joanie and Bob had met; and Joanie's high school sweetheart, Cope Ward, starting quarterback, homecoming king, the spitting image of Robert Taylor.

There were so many ways a life could go. If Cope hadn't enlisted, melting in the Alabama sun at Fort McClellan while Bob, ten years older, settled in back home. If Bob's crush, Josephine Gibson, hadn't hastily married Frank Flag the night before Frank had boarded a bus bound for Kelly Field in Texas, a kid who'd never been on a plane but was eager to learn to fly. If Frank hadn't been practicing maneuvers in the mountains of New Mexico when, a month later, a windstorm churned up under his wings, requiring an emergency landing and sending him home an injured man. If Josephine hadn't been so loyal— she and Bob had quietly courted while Frank was away, but all that had to stop now. And if Bob hadn't gone to the hospital to say goodbye to Josephine, he might never have seen her: that lovely young nurse tending to the white bandages that seemed to cover Frank everywhere.

"Bob," said Josephine. "I don't think you know my friend Joanie."

Short chestnut hair, dark eyes, skin the color of the inside of an almond. Bob had waited for her to offer her hand but she was too busy spinning out gauze like cotton candy, so he studied her fingers, long and slightly tapered. The back of her neck formed a cleft at the nape when she leaned over with her silver shears, her pink lips pressed in concentration.

"Be good," said Josephine, no longer a lover but a friend, already slipping into her role as Frank's wife, while Bob, who had never been faithful to any woman, silently promised that he would.

1

Tuesday morning Hugh crept out of the house at just after six o'clock wearing a dark fleece jacket and a wool ski hat yanked low over his brow. On Beaver Street, Eric Van Heuse, Teddy's former Biddy Basketball coach, was out collecting his newspaper, while the Erley children, three doors down, had corralled their overweight tabby on the front walk, fencing the cat with their legs and giving him a push toward their house. If Coach Eric waved, Hugh didn't see it. He'd hunched his shoulders to the sun and trained his eyes on the ground.

Normally, Hugh happily stopped to talk to every person he met. His wife and children's irritants—busybody neighbors and the absence of fast food, respectively—were Hugh's raisons d'être. He was a long-standing member of Save Our Lake Otsego and the Cooperstown Chamber of Commerce; he faithfully attended school-board and town-council meetings; the Seedlings School cosponsored soccer and Little League teams; and Hugh rode on a float in the nearby Fourth of July parade. Today, however, he was keeping a low profile.

He had been up half the night reading about factors influencing memory acquisition in young children, and for a certain boy, visual reinforcement, in the form of Hugh's face, had to be avoided. Dressing like a cat burglar, taking a roundabout route to work, hiding in his office, and generally steering clear of Graham Pennington, age five, would be Hugh's tactical offense against the sharpening of any fragmentary memories in the child's mind. Two weeks had passed since the hospital-room incident, which would work to Hugh's advantage: with any luck, Graham had already forgotten that he'd encountered his preschool principal beneath his mother's spread legs.

Hugh unlocked the school at six thirty and was relieved to find it exactly the way he'd left it a week ago. Someone had been as careful with the rooms as he was. Lights turned off, play rugs prepped for morning play, the playground raked, and the toys put away. Everything was fresh and ready to go. Mrs. Baxter had even primed the coffeepot in the tiny teachers' room so that all he had to do now was flip the switch to set the grounds brewing.

It had been a somber week since Hugh's mother-in-law had unexpectedly passed, long days filled with funeral and interment plans; cleaning out and listing his in-laws' house; and installing Bob Cole in their guest room for what looked to be a permanent stay. It was Hugh's opinion that his father-in-law—eighty-six years old, with congestive heart failure and a walker—belonged in the Thanksgiving Home. Hugh's wife, however, disagreed. It had been a long-standing plan for Anne's mother to move to 59 Susquehanna when her father passed, and now Anne argued that they had to extend the same invitation to her dad. Never mind that Joanie, a spry seventy-four-year-old former nurse who baked and cleaned—a welcome addition to any household— had been positively winning in comparison to Bob. Never mind, too, that Anne herself could barely tolerate her father. It was the right thing to do, she'd persisted, and more to the point: What would people think of her if she didn't?

At six forty-five, the Seedlings School staff began to arrive. First was Mrs. Baxter, a retired Cooperstown Elementary School secretary who had taken over Seedlings' administrative work five years back. She drove a light-blue Oldsmobile and had light-blue hair and called all the kids Sonny or Girlie, which sent them into spasms of laughter. Close to seventy, she had ambitiously made the leap from electric typewriter to PC and now pecked out Excel spreadsheets and printed up dot-matrix birthday cards for Hugh and the teachers at the appropriate times of the year.

"Mr. Obermeyer." Mrs. Baxter nodded. "Welcome back."

"Thank you. Coffee's perfect." Hugh raised his mug to her: #1 DAD! Julia had given it to him for Christmas.

Mrs. Baxter shrugged off her blazer and hung it in the closet, then removed her brown-bag lunch—always egg salad on wheat with a bag of potato chips and a Sprite—and placed it in their compact refrigerator. "Is this yours?" asked Mrs. Baxter, holding out a half-empty yogurt cup.

"No," said Hugh.

"One of the girls," said Mrs. Baxter disapprovingly, meaning Cheryl, Melanie, or Priscilla, the teachers at Seedlings. "You should speak to them about not picking up after themselves."

"Absolutely," said Hugh, who was hardly listening.

"There is one thing I wanted to mention," said Mrs. Baxter.

"Great," said Hugh. "Let's schedule a sit-down. Maybe before lunch."

Mrs. Baxter frowned, started to speak, but Hugh was saved by the arrival of Melanie and Priscilla, who commuted together and looked so much alike—blond highlights, capacious laps—that the parents constantly confused them. The kids didn't: Miss Melanie was the nice one; Miss Oak, the meanie.

"Hugh!" said Melanie, wrapping him in a hug. "How're you holding up?"

"Pretty well," said Hugh. Then, "Anne's father moved in."

Priscilla grimaced, and Mrs. Baxter gave her a tut-tut.

Last to arrive, always late, dashing in closer to seven than Hugh would've liked, was Cheryl Landon, whom Hugh had hired away from the Wallace School, in Manhattan, to teach Seedlings' pre-K. She was the illustrious engine of the Seedlings train, while a rotating cast of sweet assistant teachers—local college students receiving course credit for interning at Seedlings two days a week—were the bright red caboose.

"One minute," said Cheryl, sailing past the teachers' room with a plastic storage bin and three wrapping-paper rolls. "I just have to drop off my stuff."

Hugh tracked her with his eyes, alert for signs of disbelief, disappointment, even disgust, because if Graham Pennington had told anyone about his principal's untoward appearance during hospital visiting hours, wouldn't it have been his beloved prekindergarten teacher? Not only was Mrs. Landon warm and affectionate, capable and fun; she was also host to a weekly show-and-tell, with a progressive emphasis on the *tell*.

Cheryl reappeared in the doorway with an apology for her tardiness and a kiss for Hugh's cheek.

"We missed you," she said, squeezing his hand.

Hugh and Cheryl fell in line behind Melanie and Priscilla as they all made their way to the main entrance. It was almost time for early drop-off, almost time to greet the children.

"Anything happen while I was gone?" Hugh fished.

"Nothing," said Cheryl. "Your school is a well-oiled machine."

At seven o'clock, they stepped into the bright sunshine to greet a carpool line that was ten deep and already snaking around the block. Priscilla directed traffic, waving mud-splattered Subarus and Toyotas and Tauruses up to the curb, while Melanie and Cheryl helped the boys and girls out. The early-drop-off program featured an alternative start time for children with working parents, moms and dads who were mid-commute and didn't have time to bend Hugh's ear about his personal leave. Not so with regular drop-off. In an hour and a half, Hugh would be mobbed by stay-at-home moms lingering in the Seedlings hallways for the chance to shell Hugh with prying questions. What exactly happened to poor Joanie? Was Anne just devastated? And would his kids eat a tuna noodle casserole? Massive stroke; she is; and unlikely; but these were not the questions that had been keeping Hugh awake at night.

Last week Hugh had been summoned home to care for his bereaved family just as Graham Pennington returned to school from his convalescence. Now there were only ninety minutes left until Hugh came face-to-face with Graham and his mother. Would the boy remember what he'd seen? Had Caroline told anyone what she and Hugh had done? In the two weeks since Hugh had pushed her Indian-print skirt up over her hips and slipped her cotton panties down, he'd thought of little else but Caroline straddling his lap, the sunlight glinting off her unshaven knees. But as much as Hugh wanted to revisit the moment, he was also frightened by it—he could lose his school, his family— and even as he smiled at the early drop-offs and waved goodbye to their parents, he was mentally scouring his past, wondering how it had come to this.

* * *

Hugh had not explicitly set out to teach preschool. After college, he'd studied for a master's in education with an eye toward lecturing high school honors students at elite private schools in Boston, New York City. True, he had been drawn to education, but how, precisely, he had ended up running a preschool was a bit of a mystery even to him. He'd had plenty of time to plumb his psyche for an answer—during every school tour, at least one parent asked him why he'd wanted to "open a day-care center." The best he'd come up with so far: "I thought I'd get in my two cents early."

A more honest answer might've been that it had taken Hugh a long time to grow up, and he could still access those childhood feelings of being utterly lost in the social jungle of a school playground. There were clear rules in Hugh's preschool. No hitting, no spitting, no throwing the sand. Be nice to your friends, use your words, and always wear your listening ears. Seedlings' rule book was a blueprint for blossoming—kids needed all the help they could get, and Hugh remembered how hard it could be to choose a direction and go.

Hugh's capacity for decision-making seemed to have shorted out around the age of ten, when his brother, George, had slipped through the ice in the creek behind their rented ski cabin, and Hugh's parents had more or less followed their firstborn down. Reeling from the loss, they'd sent Hugh to boarding school, then summer camp, then college, until eventually he'd found comfort in the predictability of it all. Hugh was used to school: syllabi, reading lists, and course catalogs; orientation, registration, reading periods, and final exams. He was accustomed to the schedule of Labor Day to Memorial Day followed by summer internships and peppered with brief Sunday-night phone calls home. Hugh had even stayed on after his college graduation to work in the admissions office, conducting information sessions for potential applicants, until the dean politely informed him that he was no longer a recent graduate and it was time to move on. So to complete the circle Hugh had gone to graduate school for a master's in education, but even he could see that something was missing, that he was missing something—adventure, chance, hunger, thirst. He was on a conveyor belt of September to September and he was too afraid to get off.

* * *

When Hugh met his wife, at a party in Cambridge during his final year of graduate school, he'd been impressed first by her self-confidence, then by her beauty. Newly single—having recently broken up with a cellist who waited tables—Hugh had accepted an invitation from an old boarding-school friend to a wine tasting at his apartment, and the night of the party Hugh showered and shaved and put on his best outfit, then headed across the Charles with a bottle of Cold Duck. He hadn't been thinking: when Hugh saw that he was the sole hippie element in a sea of blue-blazered men, he quickly returned to the entryway to ditch his belted cardigan.

"You're not leaving," he heard behind him—less a question than a command—and he turned, flustered, and found himself looking into the bluest eyes he'd ever seen.

"No, I'm just—this sweater." Hugh tried to shrug it off his shoulders, but the belt had knotted.

The woman extended her hand, introducing herself as Anne Cole, and Hugh reached to take it. She wore a striped oxford shirt tucked into a tweed skirt, and brown boots with platforms so high she rose to meet Hugh's eyes. Silently, Hugh admired her manicured nails against his olive skin.

"I like your sweater," said Anne. "You should wear it. Unless you're hot. Then you should take it off."

Hugh smiled. After weeks of hemming and hawing with the cellist, he appreciated Anne's straightforwardness. "I'll wear it," he said.

Hugh offered to get her a drink, and at the self-tended bar he filled two glasses with red wine, then joined Anne in the corner she had carved out for them.

"Are you at HBS?" she asked, accepting her glass. "I haven't seen you at the law school."

"BU," said Hugh.

"Law?"

"No," said Hugh. "Education."

Anne smiled and said, "I always loved school."

Anne was a second-year law student at Harvard (where Hugh had failed to gain admission both as an undergraduate and as a graduate student, despite his meandering legacy—maternal uncle, paternal grandfather) and seemed destined for litigation. Having known him for less than five minutes, she argued that a master's was a half degree; that he should immediately switch to a doctorate program; that he should rethink his "inchoate" thesis; that he should call her friend at Harvard, who would be happy to talk to Hugh about careers in education—and then she opened her purse and flipped through a tiny black book, rattling off the home phone number of the adjunct professor.

Hugh felt alert, shocked to life. In a matter of minutes, Anne had more assiduously evaluated his professional goals than any guidance counselor who'd come before her. Five more minutes with this beautiful woman, and he'd have his whole life sorted out. He nodded attentively as she told him about her plans for internships and the fields of law she liked best.

"What are you doing next summer?" she asked.

"Isn't it November?" said Hugh.

"Right," said Anne. "Sorry." She blushed, tugging at her ear, and Hugh realized suddenly that this woman with the straight black hair and blue eyes of Superwoman was attracted to him. An editor of her law review, and she was trying to impress *him*.

Usually, Hugh relished a slow pace with women. Unlike most of his friends, who went straight to bed with their dates, Hugh had enjoyed the antiquated ritual of selecting a time, picking a place, presenting a lady with flowers, and taking her out for dinner. But after the party, Hugh led Anne back to her apartment on Central Square, where she let him undress her and turn her this way and that. He had never been so aroused. Through Anne's eyes, Hugh appeared confident and strong, more sure of himself than he could ever remember being. He knew things she did not, and she was willing to be taught.

From that first night they were always together. Within a month, Hugh had moved out of his apartment and into hers, called her adjunct-professor friend, and applied to Harvard's PhD program for the fall.

Weekends, they explored the city, just the two of them, riding the T to the North End for lasagna or to the waterfront for clam chowder and beer. Anne picked the movies, while Hugh picked the restaurants, then at night they had hungry, possessive sex, each of them feeling lucky to have found the other.

But by late January, Hugh was ready to see some friends. They were in bed reading—Anne with a mystery, Hugh with a magazine and a six-pack of beer—when Hugh found himself skimming, flipping the pages without seeing the words. It had suddenly occurred to him that he and Anne had not yet been out with another couple. Was that possible? In three months? Most of his friends had gone home for Thanksgiving and Christmas, while Hugh and Anne had spent the holidays together in Boston; then there were papers, exams. But now they were nearly asleep at nine o'clock on a Saturday night, and if ever there was a time— Hugh looked up from his magazine to discover three empty beer bottles on his nightstand, the fourth in his hand.

"Hey," he said, flopping onto his stomach. He reached under the covers and ran a hand up Anne's naked leg.

Anne scooted down toward him without taking her eyes off the page.

"You know what we should do?" asked Hugh.

"Hmm?"

"Throw a party."

Anne glanced up from her book.

"A Valentine's Day party," Hugh went on, slipping his fingers under the leg band of her underwear.

"Valentine's Day?" asked Anne. She blinked, then quickly looked back down at the page, and Hugh realized he might have hurt her feelings. He was her first real boyfriend; maybe she'd been hoping for dinner à deux.

"Yeah," said Hugh. He climbed on top of his girlfriend and she had no choice but to abandon her book. "Like for lovers." He kissed her, feeling hugely turned on, but Anne only pecked his lips.

"You don't want to?" he asked.

"Have sex or throw a party?"

"Right," said Hugh, smiling, and before Anne could argue, he lifted her shirt over her head and kissed her again.

Anne capitulated to the party but let Hugh handle the arrangements. Over the next two weeks, he sent out invitations and collected decorations, cleaned the kitchen and the bathroom, straightened his desk and paid two outstanding bills. Hugh had always wanted to host a party but secretly he'd doubted that anyone would show. Now, with Anne in his corner, Hugh hardly cared if theirs was a flop. He'd drop Jim Croce on the turntable and they'd slow-dance alone.

The morning of the party, Hugh presented Anne with a dozen long-stemmed red roses, and the smile on her face and the brightness of her clear eyes buoyed him. He believed he knew how to make her happy, and she him. But later, while Hugh ran around topping off their guests' champagne glasses and passing plates of heart-shaped brownies, Anne only watched from the couch.

"Aren't you having fun?" he'd asked, circling by.

"I am," she said. She held out her empty glass and let Hugh refill it.

"Did you meet Albert and Linda?" Albert's girlfriend was a lawyer and Hugh had thought she and Anne would hit it off.

"I think so," said Anne. "The blonde?"

Hugh took her by the hand and pulled her into the mix. He introduced her to his classmates, to his friend from the record store, to an old girlfriend who was now dating a hairstylist. He presented Anne to a social worker in need of legal advice, then watched with pride as she settled in, found the rhythm of her legalese, and appeared to enjoy herself. But ten minutes later she was in the kitchen, getting a jump start on the dishes.

"Anne," said Hugh irritably when he tracked her down.

"What?" She plunged her hands into a sink full of suds.

Maybe he should've asked her what was wrong. Maybe she should've told him. Instead, Anne remained with her back to him, her black silk skirt gently sweeping her knees. It was their first real fight and neither of them seemed to know what to do, so they did nothing. Anne finished the dishes while Hugh waltzed back out to his party, and in the morning Hugh put away the dishes while Anne vacuumed, and all was apparently forgotten without either of them having said a word.

In March, Hugh was again rejected from Harvard, but by then he was nearly finished with his master's program and had been offered a one-year fellowship in the mayor's office. It was as good a place as any to spend a year. Anne's job would take precedence when she graduated next spring, and Hugh hoped for San Francisco or London, someplace he had never been. Tokyo, Beijing, Kuala Lumpur. He'd teach English as a second language. They'd ride bicycles to work.

Then Anne was pregnant, and their choices narrowed considerably. From the outset, there was no question in Anne's mind that they would keep the baby. Such an ambitious and strong-willed woman (with tens of thousands of dollars in student loans) might not have seen this as the right time to procreate, but Anne was nothing if not convincing. She was twenty-six; he, twenty-eight. They were financially stable, living together, and likely to marry. A baby had always been part of the larger picture, Anne argued, and Hugh—whose larger picture had recently included the possibility of living in a tree house in New Zealand—agreed fatherhood could be considered an adventure, too.

Before Anne began to show, she was lobbying to move home to Cooperstown. Her father had a close friend who was a partner at a small law firm in nearby Oneonta; she could be running the firm in ten years, she said, and without all the clamoring and grinding and face time normally required of new associates. Plus, in Cooperstown they'd have her mother, Joanie, a former nurse, to sit for the baby, and Hugh would be free to take a job. Although Hugh couldn't imagine what he would do in an upstate New York town of two thousand people, he did like the idea of living near the Hall of Fame.

The single possession that George had bequeathed him was an autographed 1957 Ted Williams card, and the fog that enshrouded Hugh's memory of his brother—indeed, of his entire early childhood— seemed to lift when Hugh thought about baseball. He pictured the two of them seated at the right and left hands of their mother for the Red Sox home opener, an afternoon game, mid-April, and a workday, certainly, or their father would have been with them and they would not have been forced to wear their jackets on that almost-warm day. George—eleven years old and with only eight months left in this world—held his prize baseball card in his sweaty hand. Their father had warned him that an autograph would devalue it, but George was ready with his ballpoint.

Red Sox versus the Yankees, a pitchers' duel; both teams went scoreless until the bottom of the fifth, when the wooden 0 was finally pulled inside the Green Monster and replaced with a triumphant 1. Between innings, George darted to the left-field line to peer down at Ted until the usher tapped him on the shoulder and sent him back to his seat. Two more scoreless innings, then a home run, Yankees, who added two more runs in the ninth to go up 3–1 and ensure another at-bat for the Sox. It was George's last chance, and without asking permission he bolted from his seat and charged the wall. "Hey, mis- ter," he called, cantilevering at the waist and stretching out his arms like an angel, pen and card in hand. "Would you mind?" And maybe because Hugh had it all wrong—it wasn't the middle of an inning; it was batting practice, it was warm-ups, it was the last out of the game— or maybe because Ted sensed what Hugh and his mother could not— that this boy was ethereal and his brief life must be made great—the Splendid Splinter jogged over to the wall and reached up with his left hand and signed.

Hugh would take this card to Cooperstown, a shrine to a shrine.

In May 1976, they rented a two-bedroom apartment across from Clancy's deli, where Hugh stopped every morning for coffee and doughnuts before strolling Teddy the quarter mile to his grandparents' house. Joanie and Bob, soon to be rechristened Nonz and Poppy, waited at the kitchen door to swoop out and take over the handles on Teddy's stroller, rocking him backward up the three-step stoop and sucking him into their rich-smelling kitchen. "Have fun," Joanie would call. "Good luck," she'd say, as though there was some enterprising thing that Hugh was off toiling at. In fact, he would often just return to the apartment and watch TV until it was time to collect Teddy at three. He tried to see his situation as a phase—*When your mother and I first moved to Cooperstown . . . When you were just a baby*—but really he had no idea what came next.

It was Joanie who sold Hugh on the one-story brick building with an abandoned playground out back and a FOR SALE sign in front: the old community center that had burned two years before and been rebuilt elsewhere. A new house had gone up on the lot where the gymnasium had once stood, but the separate property of the rec hall, less than a tenth of an acre, was still on the market.

"You should buy it," Joanie said, jiggling Teddy on her hip. "You need something to make you happier here."

Anyone could see that Hugh was floundering. He'd had friends in Boston, and Anne to occupy his time. Now his wife worked up to six days a week, ten hours a day, and when she was home, she wanted only to curl up in their apartment and watch TV. Mornings, when Hugh dressed Teddy for the day, stuffing the baby's chubby legs into his tiny denim overalls, Hugh could not find himself in the room. He saw the changing table, the hamper of dirty laundry, the diaper pail that needed emptying; he saw Teddy's tonsure, a ring of light-brown fuzz circling his pate; he saw his son's cornflower eyes, bright and expectant—but where was Hugh in this scene? "People get married and have children," Anne had said. "That's what they do." And Hugh had agreed, and here he was, except that he wasn't really. Not really.

Now Joanie said, "Picture it. You could have a little school. Maybe not a *high* school, exactly, but something." She passed Teddy to Hugh, as though she were introducing them. "Like for this guy," she said.

Hugh slipped his hands under Teddy's arms, felt the weight of the boy on his shoulder; he touched his child's chin with his finger, wiping a bubble of drool from Teddy's soft skin.

Hugh borrowed the money for the down payment from his father-in-law, who was only too happy to see Hugh gainfully employed. When Seedlings opened, in September 1978, Teddy's baby sister, Julia, was the same age Teddy had been when they'd first moved to Cooperstown—a fact Teddy proudly repeated to his new classmates, six "twos and threes" comprising the first class at Seedlings. Back then Hugh had been head teacher, assistant, and principal all in one.

With a new sense of purpose and an expanding group of friends, Hugh began to feel settled in Cooperstown. Where he had grown up in the ersatz community of dorm rooms and dining halls, Hugh delighted in knowing that Teddy and Julia would come of age organically, roaming the village on their bikes, learning to swim in the lake, with grandparents and neighbors and friends acting in loco parentis to make sure they didn't get lost along the way. This small-town safety net stretched beneath all of them: not only did Hugh and Anne have each other for guidance, they had Bob and Joanie; their neighbors at the Cooper Lane Apartments; Sheila McMann, the real estate agent who had found 59 Susquehanna Avenue for them when they'd outgrown their two-bedroom apartment on Brunlar Court; Pat Byrne, their contractor, and his wife, Nancy, a maternity nurse at Bassett Hospital, who had helped deliver Julia.

But while Hugh was falling in love with Cooperstown, he did wonder if, for Anne, moving here hadn't been a mistake. She wouldn't reach out to her high school classmates, many of whom still lived in the village. She wasn't eager to accompany Hugh to their neighbors' cocktail and dinner parties. She argued with him about joining the country club—Anne hadn't been a member as a child, why did they need it now? She worked ungodly hours in a town twenty-five miles away, and Hugh couldn't understand why she'd suggested moving back if she was only going to spend all her time running away.

"It wasn't my idea," Anne confessed. "My mother asked me to."

This was just after Julia was born. Teddy was having a sleepover at Nonz and Poppy's house, while Hugh and Anne, exhausted, had gone to bed before twilight with Julia breathing softly in her bassinet at Anne's side.

Anne rested her head on Hugh's chest and traced his ribs with her finger. "Maybe we could go back to Boston," she said, "or try somewhere new." Virginia. California. She poked him and said, "Kuala Lumpur."

Hugh could feel her wet cheek against his skin and he wiped her tears but hesitated to respond. The truth was, he didn't want to leave. Even Anne would have to agree that their lives here made sense. The Seedlings School was growing and Anne was set to make junior partner that year. Without Poppy and Nonz to care for the kids, Julia, at least, would have to start day care. And in some ways Anne *was* happy here—that very morning, she'd let Teddy play "jungle gym" on their bed, then helped him hold a bottle for Julia while all three of them leaned against Hugh, cradled in his arms.

But in other ways, Hugh knew something was wrong. His desire for an extended community, outside their home, beyond their nuclear family, upset her. It had been the same way in Boston. Anne didn't need to host parties or join clubs, and she seemed to resent that Hugh did. But in Hugh's experience it was risky to have only one person to depend on—what was so wrong with making friends? Anne brushed off these kinds of questions. *Nothing's wrong with it*, she'd said, though clearly something was, because the more Hugh reached out, the more Anne withdrew, until sometimes they went entire days—early to school, late home from the office—without even seeing each other. In the mornings, Teddy and Hugh dropped Julia at Nonz and Poppy's house, then walked to Seedlings while Anne drove to her office in Oneonta. Whenever one or the other still asked, they always agreed that they were happy in their work, happy with their children. Good, good. Everything was good, but not really, not entirely, because now Hugh had done the unthinkable—the thing he had vowed never to do— and he couldn't defend it because he couldn't understand it. Hugh thought of himself as an upstanding family man, a devoted father, and a good husband, but Hugh wasn't the same person he'd been when he married his wife.

* * *

Back in his office after the carpool line emptied out, Hugh chased two Advil with a sip of coffee, then swiveled away from the many phone messages and unopened envelopes on his desk blotter. The picture window in Hugh's office showed a playground teeming with children in light spring jackets already unzipped beneath warm red faces, the girls toiling at the monkey bars while the boys stormed the small grass yard, kicking and throwing foam balls. In his week away, Hugh had truly missed Seedlings. Conceived in his mind, born of his labor, his preschool was his third child, and it would stay with him long after Teddy and Julia had gone.

Hugh recalled watching his children on this very playground thirteen, fourteen years ago. He had never been totally comfortable having them as students—what if he favored them or, alternatively, gave them a doubly hard time? In fact, he'd observed them closely in the years since for signs that he'd scarred them at an early age. So far he hadn't spotted anything too worrisome.

His recent activity with Caroline might change that, should it come to light. Hugh could hardly bear to think of hurting his children—it would be reason enough to forget what he'd done. But Teddy was eighteen and Julia just two and half years younger. In a matter of months they'd be leaving for college, returning only on holidays and for a few weeks during the summer. It occurred to Hugh that the main act of parenthood was almost over. Soon he and Anne would be in a side tent, thinking longingly of their kids.

Teddy was affable and popular, a second-semester senior who had been recruited by Oneida College to pitch for their Division I team. Although Teddy's grades weren't very impressive, lingering in the low eighties no matter how hard a time Hugh and Anne gave him, Teddy's pitching arm more than compensated for his report cards. Even as a child, when school had been about pictures hung on refrigerators and gold stars in place of grades, Teddy had spent his energy on the playground, organizing grand competitions of kickball and kick the can. But Teddy's strengths were also his weaknesses: he knew his comfort zone and he hesitated to leave it. Theoretically, it was a good strategy—look before you leap—but because Teddy hardly ever leaped, he had limited exposure to failure, and because he'd rarely failed, he was often afraid to try. Still, Hugh couldn't help being charmed by his sought-after son, though he did have concerns about Teddy's character. He was vain, moving easily—and possibly irresponsibly?—between girlfriends. They called at night and Teddy would give muted one-word answers or, worse, make Hugh say he couldn't come to the phone.

Julia, fifteen, was wry and clever and almost nothing like her brother. She was smarter than Teddy, no question, and spurned her brother's high school grandstanding for more intimate clusters of close friends. Occasionally Hugh did worry that Julia was isolated. Her best friends, Sam and Carl, were good kids—it wasn't that—but Julia hid behind them, in a way. They had their own language, which no one understood, and parent-teacher conferences often ended in complaints that Julia and her friends were exclusive to their detriment. It was an odd thing, really. Teddy was only too happy to explain how weird everyone thought his sister was, but you couldn't convince Julia of that. As far as Julia, Sam, and Carl were concerned, they were the only people worth knowing.

The latest Julia problem was this business about not trying out for her high school tennis team. It was a decision made more ridiculous by the fact that she continued to show up at the practices, hanging around the courts while Sam and Carl ran the drills. Hugh couldn't understand it. Julia had taken tennis lessons at the country club, been promoted through the skill groups right alongside her sporty brother, and consistently earned a spot in the club finals, losing only to a pixie whose Prince Junior was a cudgel against Julia's second serve. And now suddenly she'd given up the sport. Anne's opinion was that it was up to Julia. If she didn't want to try out, that was her choice. "You're always prodding the kids," Anne had said. "They're almost adults." Maybe so. But Julia needed a push, and Hugh had privately decided to give her one.

At eight thirty, he slunk from his office and stationed himself in the small vestibule to the side of the teachers' room—the supply closet—where he could observe the flow of traffic, unseen. It was a temporary solution. He'd have to come out eventually, but not until he was certain of avoiding Graham Pennington and his mother. Hugh watched and waited. Soon parents and students began to stream by: mostly moms, some dads; mostly with one child, some with two.

Hugh sensed Caroline before he saw her, felt his body thrill to the sound of her voice asking Graham if he'd remembered his lunch box, then to her scent—soap and turpentine and a hint of Earl Grey. She was standing less than ten feet away—the cuffs of her jean jacket turned back, her brown hair knotted loosely on top of her head. Hugh held his breath as Caroline passed, ushering Graham into Mrs. Landon's classroom, then turned back toward the exit alone.

Hugh remained frozen in his hiding place for another five minutes, until he saw Barry Klawson—Julia's tennis coach—charging down the hallway with his nephew in tow. Familial duty: at the last second, Hugh fell into step beside them, clapping Klawson's shoulder in a friendly hello.

"Mr. Obermeyer." Klawson stopped to offer his hand but Hugh steered them on. "Debbie's at her aerobics class this morning," he said.

"Right, right," said Hugh. "Jace, it must be so nice having your uncle bring you to school."

The boy buried his face against his uncle's work jeans, his legs scissoring in time with Klawson's.

"I realized," said Hugh, "I think you know my daughter, Julia, from the tennis team."

Klawson stopped outside Miss Melanie's classroom. "Jace," said his uncle, "go in and say good morning to your teacher. I'm right behind you."

Klawson stuffed his hands in his pockets. Thick, muscular arms, paint-splattered jeans: Barry was a Klawson of the overpriced Klawson's Hardware on Main Street, where Hugh had spent fifty-seven dollars yesterday on cleaning supplies for his in-laws' house.

"Julia's mother and I are concerned that she didn't try out for the tennis team," Hugh began. "I wondered if maybe she'd talked to you about it."

Klawson shrugged. "Not really," he said. "Though she keeps showing up."

"Right," said Hugh apologetically. "She has a hard time with . . . well." Julia would kill him if she knew he was having this conversation with her coach. She would see it as a betrayal, but Hugh saw it as parenting. Hugh leaned close to Klawson and said, "I know she didn't try out for the team, but I wondered if maybe—I wondered if you could ask her to."

"Well," said her coach noncommittally, "I've already made cuts. Our first match is Thursday, and the lineup's set."

Hugh nodded and rubbed his chin as though he were reconsidering. "I know this is asking a lot, and I really don't want to put you in an awkward position, but if it happens that there's an exhibition match or something . . ." Hugh sighed. "She wants to play, but she'll never tell you that."

"Okay," said Klawson, "but, like I said, I already cut people. And technically there's an alternate who should get first chance at any exhibition matches."

"I see," said Hugh. Then he surprised himself by saying, "You know, not too far down the road Seedlings is going to be expanding. One or two new buildings, probably. I keep meaning to get over to the hardware store to talk to your dad about ordering supplies."

Klawson regarded Hugh, and Hugh thought he saw the man's eyes narrow but he couldn't be sure. In any case, he was in with both feet. "It'd be a big order, more expensive, I know, to do it locally, but what's it all about if we can't help each other?" Klawson cocked his chin and Hugh forged on, wondering if he'd lost his mind. "Maybe I could come down to the store this evening and talk to you and your dad."

Klawson's eyes locked on Hugh's. "Yeah?"

"Sure," said Hugh.

"Okay." Klawson nodded slowly. "And maybe I could talk to Julia about an exhibition match."

Hugh nodded faintly, then whispered, "Away from her friends, if you can manage it."

They agreed to meet at six o'clock, shook once, and Klawson left to join Jace at the tactile station, the boy's fingers deep in a lump of Play-Doh.

Dizzy, unsure what he'd done, Hugh turned on his heel and froze when he saw Caroline standing at the main doors, waiting for him. There were still several mothers between them but by eight forty-five all would've cleared out, which left Hugh about two minutes to decide what to do. His stomach dropped. His pulse hammered in his ears. Anne had once called him "adecisive," and it was an apt description, but in his mind Hugh pictured himself crossing the hallway, cupping Caroline's breast under her jean jacket and pinching her nipple through the soft fabric of her T-shirt, a fantasy he'd spent a week trying to squelch. He'd had crushes before, but nothing this all-consuming, nothing this potent.

Imperceptibly, Hugh began to drift: one step toward her, one step toward his office. Thirty more seconds and they'd be alone together. But just as Hugh started to speak, to say he was glad to see her, to ask her how she'd been, Caroline turned and beat a retreat. She smiled sadly, held open the front door, and followed another mother out, leaving Hugh to wonder what decision had been made.

2

Easter Sunday, the last day of spring break, we all piled into the car to help Poppy pack his bags. It was a short drive from our house to 122 Chestnut Street, but no one spoke. Dad drove while Mom rested her head against the window; Teddy reached between them to change the radio dial; and I pictured Sam and Carl with their families, barreling up the highway toward home. So far there'd been only one postcard from Sam, written his first night in Myrtle Beach: *Dear Jules, I got a speeding ticket trying to make it to the Corner Cone before 8. Carl and this random girl Megan said I could make it in 3 minutes if I went 30 in a 10. What a bunch of tardmores. And we never got the ice cream. Guess what I was going to order?* Mint chocolate chip, but that didn't begin to answer the questions. Had he kissed her? Hooked up with her? Megan. Not so random that she didn't have a name.

At my grandparents' house, I touched everything: bottles and brushes, curlers and soaps, moisturizers and powders; I stroked the curtains, the needlepoint pillows, the terry-cloth robes in Nonz and

Poppy's closet; I hefted the silver, splashed the perfume, and drank from the crystal, my senses alive to the possibility of Nonz.

Less than a week ago, I'd walked over here from 59 Susquehanna to spend the day with Nonz—everyone else I knew was out of town: Katie, Em, Sam, and Carl in Myrtle Beach; Paige and Hilary skiing in Utah. Only Teddy's friend Dave, who'd made me a mix tape in January—heavy on the Smiths—had called to say he was around, but I wasn't hanging out with Dave. I already missed Sam and Carl and preferred my grandmother's uncomplicated company.

Nonz sat at the kitchen table in her coral reading glasses and denim apron and read aloud from a cookbook while I measured, mixed, chopped, and stirred, in a game we'd been playing for years. "Eight tablespoons unsalted butter," she began.

"Oatmeal cookies."

"Did I say oatmeal?" Nonz peered down her freckled nose at the cookbook, then back up at me. "Three-fourths-cup sugar."

"Shortbread," I guessed, opening the bag of sugar.

Her eyes were the same nut-brown shade as mine but I couldn't read them. "Two ounces unsweetened chocolate, roughly chopped," said Nonz, and if she was changing the recipe mid-game, I didn't care. We were passing time, baking a pan of double-fudge brownies on Nonz's last day on earth, it turned out, and here were the brownies now, half eaten and covered in cellophane.

Early morning, the day of her funeral: I'd stamped muddy foot-prints at the edge of my grandmother's grave. A weak slant of sun lit the grass between Nonz's plot and the brick church, and I looked up at the steeple, shielding my eyes. I'd be back here in four hours with my family, with Father Armstrong, with ashes to ashes and Nonz's casket, my grandmother inside, but for now it was just me, silent dawn, and the graveyard cast in first light. I closed my eyes and saw the Easter-egg hunts of my childhood, flamingo-pink and lime-green shells sprouting like mushrooms on the graves. I turned 360 degrees, taking in the redbrick church, the ivy-covered fence, the dirt parking lot, the marble headstones falling like dominoes toward River Street, and it seemed impossible that Sam and Carl weren't here to consecrate this.

Our friendship had been lacquered to stone in coded slitters we'd made up at Nonz and Poppy's card table. *Mayhi* translated as *extremely*. *Farm* was a slitter for the F-word. *Tardmore* was *more retarded*, and *OPs* were cigarettes, i.e., Official Purchases, e.g., Which tardmore's turn is it to file up to the cash register for the OPs? We smoked our OPs in covert nunneries hidden from the collective eyes of Cooperstown, reinforcing our fortress with a language no one else spoke. *Provides, professional*—cool. *Perkins, piece of ass*—sucks. 122 Chestnut had been our capital, the card table our courthouse, and here at my grandparents' house, over rounds of Pay Day and Bargain Hunter, we'd laid out the laws of the land.

A backgammon set; five pairs of khakis; four green highball glasses; two rakes; a push mower; a broom with straw bristles; a lamp shade with a silk fringe; and a toaster oven—these were the things that went back in the house.

A beetle collection; a TV set; five pairs of khakis; a hat stand; a trombone; a steamer trunk; a set of sheets; a nightstand with matching headboard; and an unopened bottle of Glenfiddich—these were the things that went into our car.

While Teddy and Dad tied Poppy's headboard to the station wagon's ski rack, I tracked Mom to Nonz's side of the dismantled bed. She looked lost, hugging a worn paperback to her chest. I read the title upside down. *The Sex Cure.*

"Where'd you get that?" I asked.

"I found it under the mattress," said Mom.

Which is where I kept my journal and Teddy kept his Victoria's Secret catalogs. If you wanted to hide something, under the mattress was apparently the place to do it.

"Can I see it?" I asked.

Mom handed me the book and I studied the cover. *For the rich, beautiful women of the suburban fast set, young Dr. Justin Riley had a favorite prescription.* I'd heard of *The Sex Cure* but I'd never seen a copy—even I knew about the rumor that a prominent family in town had bought up all the copies, then ended the print run. Our town's greatest secrets aired at the hands of a pulp-romance writer in 1962.

"Professional," I said, backing into the hallway with it before Mom could think to say no.

* * *

Monday morning, Poppy's first with us, I found my mother at the kitchen sink, rubbing the lapel of her gray blazer with a wet paper towel. Her dark hair fell forward across her face, hiding her blue eyes. When she was little, Mom looked like Snow White. Now she said she had to "work at it," with a lipstick shade called Maraschino and a hair rinse called Brunette Express, but Sam and Carl had said they'd still farm her, which was like, okay, a compliment, but also mayhi Perkins.

"Where'd Dad go?" I asked.

"Nonz and Poppy's house," she said, bringing the blazer to her nose to sniff. "He's cleaning all day." She checked her watch. "Dad?" she called.

I followed her gaze to the den, where Poppy had kicked back in my father's recliner. It felt like a holiday, having him here, and I couldn't quite believe he was never leaving.

"What would you like for breakfast?" asked Mom. She ran down the list of things she could cook quickly before work. Number one: cheese toast.

"What?" asked Poppy.

"Cheese toast," Mom repeated.

"It's Perkins," I volunteered.

"Julia, please. Dad—I'm late for work. Raisin bread?" Mom scanned the cupboard, then closed the pantry door and flung open the fridge. "Milk? Mustard?"

I knew Poppy hadn't slept. Around three o'clock I'd seen the glow from his TV flickering on the floor in the hallway between our rooms, and I'd crept out of bed to listen but the volume was off and Poppy wasn't making a peep. So I'd waited, watching myself in the full-length mirror on my wall: light-brown hair to my shoulders; eyes like pennies; a tiny mole on my left cheekbone, high like Mom's and Nonz's. Stretching my sleep shirt down over my chest, my breasts flattened softly. According to Sam and Carl, size didn't matter so much as having them; like collectors, they were interested in all shapes and sizes.

Mom shut the refrigerator and swiveled to the bread drawer. "Toast?" she called. "Toasted graham crackers?"

"I'll make him something," I offered. I clapped once and Poppy turned to me and I said, "We're out of eggs, we're out of orange juice, and we've never had a grapefruit in this house that I remember."

He allowed me to toast him a piece of raisin bread topped with butter and sprinkled with cinnamon and sugar, then I got him set up with the *Today* show and went upstairs to haul Teddy out of bed.

Cooperstown High School was a one-story brick building at the end of Linden Avenue, built the year after Mom had graduated from the original school on Glen Avenue. The hallways stretched out worm-like through three playing fields, twisting and growing every time a wing was added, and Teddy's homeroom was smack in the middle, across from the main office. By the time we arrived everyone was already reciting the Pledge of Allegiance, led by Mr. Steinhoffer over the PA.

There was a rule at CHS that if you missed homeroom you couldn't participate in after-school sports, so every morning Teddy and I went through the charade of me confessing to Teddy's home-room teacher that it was all my fault we hadn't high-stepped it for a more profit arrival.

"Save it," said Mr. Hershey as soon as I began. "I don't understand a word you're saying. Have you two ever thought of leaving for school five minutes earlier?"

Teddy smiled his killer smile, his black hair sleep-swirled. My brother had our mom's eyes, and though he was tall like her, he was also broad like Dad. Teddy's only visible blemish was a thin scar through his left eyebrow, courtesy of me, from where I'd stabbed him with my scissors when we were kids. I'd been slaving over a birthday card for Dad when Teddy grabbed a black crayon and signed his name in cakey block letters. I could still see his grin, like we were both in on the joke, and then there was blood running over his eye, drizzling the carpet. Girls loved that story, Teddy had told me, and it was true that Kim was always touching the white line in his brow, pressing it with her fingers.

In homeroom, as I slid into my desk between Sam and Carl, Mrs. Boulanger made a show of marking me tardy, but it didn't matter that I was late. My friends were on the tennis team—Sam at second singles and Carl as an alternate/team manager—while I was only a disgruntled groupie.

"Hey," said Sam, face plastered to hand, elbow nailed to desk. Fresh from Myrtle Beach, his nose and ear tips had begun to peel and his buzzed blond hair was bleached white. A tan line from his Syracuse cap crossed his forehead an inch above his eyebrows, but Sam was mayhi tall—6 feet 3½ inches—so when he stood, no one would be able to see it.

"How was it?" I asked.

"Profesh." Sam spoke into his hand, mashing the word.

"It provided," said Carl. His copper curls flopped over his eyes and he pushed them back, revealing loads of new freckles. Carl was the boyish image of his mom, who still spoke in a gentle brogue though she'd moved to America with her family thirty years ago, when she was fifteen. Older girls loved Carl's hair and freckles. They were always saying what a hottie he'd be when he grew up. For now, Carl looked like a red-cheeked cherub, topping out near the bridge of my nose at an even five foot three.

Half of Cooperstown went to Myrtle Beach for spring break—the half that didn't include my family, because Mom couldn't take a week off from work. Carl went with his uncle's family, and Sam went with his dad, stepmom, and six-year-old half brother, Curtis. This year, Sam's dad had said I could go with them, but my parents thought it was an imposition, even if Sam's dad said it wasn't.

I looked around our homeroom at the tan faces, the peeling noses. The girls had returned with locks of their hair wrapped in brightly colored string, tiny silver charms—a fish for Renee English, a turtle for Stacey Michaelson—dangling from the ends. With only eighty kids in our grade—four homerooms of twenty—most of us had been in school together since we were five years old. Occasionally families moved away, occasionally new families moved in, but mostly the fabric of CHS didn't change. Stacey and Sam had gone out for three months at the beginning of the ninth grade, and the three stalks of lavender and sea-foam thread now streaking her blond hair made me certain that I'd missed something in Myrtle Beach, certain that everyone had tried something new. Nicky Rivera—who used to skate up to my front door in his Vision Street Wear hat and balance on the back wheels of his board so that its vibrant belly was bared for all the world to see—now wore a T-shirt that said COED NAKED MYRTLE BEACH VOLLEYBALL, and I thought back to the ninth-grade home-coming dance, when Nicky and I had made out behind the high school gymnasium, while Sam slow-danced with Stacey, and Carl helped Izzie Adams run the concession stand. So far this year there hadn't been any new talk of crushes.

When Mrs. Boulanger dismissed us from homeroom, Sam and Carl and I went out to our nunnery behind the propane tank just off school property, crossing the unlined football field side by side. We'd been gone for only a week but it was like returning to a different world. Already there was green grass on the fields and tiny yellow buds on the trees and sunlight that did more than create shadows, that actu-ally felt warm.

Sam pointed to the OPs and I forked him the Marlboros, then

offered Carl a Camel and took one for myself. Sam flicked his topless mermaid, lighting us up.

Since the sixth grade, when our class had moved from the elementary school to the combined middle and high school, the three of us had spent so much time together that we'd started to sound alike, mimicking one another's speech patterns, a language that morphed and evolved even as we spoke it—we heard words in class, then poached them; or made them up, then tweaked them and mispronounced them, then forged on. When we'd read *Hamlet* in the ninth grade, Sam latched on to *Get thee to a nunnery* and repeated it whenever he needed a cigarette, until we were all saying it, until we had a slitter for the places where we smoked our OPs.

But just now no one spoke. The cool breeze blew across our faces and lifted my windbreaker at the hem. Sam puffed through squinty eyes, turning his back to the wind to exhale. His lips were dry and flaking, like they'd been sunburned, or kissed too hard. The summer after ninth grade, Sam had started taking Accutane, and it wasn't like an overnight thing but by September his skin had turned from swollen red to milky white, and I'd begun to notice things. Sam's eyes changed colors, shading from sea green to midnight blue. He had a small bowtie-shaped birthmark below his Adam's apple, like he was always dressed up, always fancy, ready to go. When he buzzed his white-blond hair, I ran my fingers first with the grain, then against it, until something between us shifted and I quickly pulled away.

Sam and Megan. I knew I'd get him to tell me eventually, but not here.

Beside us, Carl scuffed the soles of his worn Adidas across the dewy grass and made a footprint with his right foot near the base of the cement shed next to the propane tank. Then he lifted his left foot and stamped his sole above and to the side of the first print. We watched and smoked. Carl worked quickly, clipping his OP between his lips and putting both hands in the grass to balance while he made the last footprint, shoulder height, and it looked like someone had walked up the side of the building. The sun was already drying the first footprints, so it was good for only a moment, but still we'd never thought of it before.

When the warning bell rang, I flicked my OP into the grass and Sam crushed his out on the sole of his shoe, then he and Carl fell into place beside me as we drifted slowly back toward the school.

"How was your week?" asked Sam.

My face felt hot and my eyes started to burn. "Nonz died," I admitted. "And Poppy moved in."

"Are you kidding?" asked Carl.

I shook my head.

Sam asked when it had happened and I said, "Monday night. Right after you left."

"Jules," said Sam softly.

Maybe he wanted to say he was sorry or that he wished he'd been here. The truth was, Nonz had died and I'd half-expected both of them to feel it eight hundred miles away.

"That sucks," Sam said finally, and Carl, whose dad had died when we were six, said, "Yeah, I hate shit like that," and then the bell rang for first period and Carl and I high-stepped it so we wouldn't be late for Mr. Robin's pre-calc.

Mr. Robin had zero tolerance for us, especially Carl, who sometimes seemed to have Tourette's, he had such a hard time being quiet. We'd both been given assigned seats at the beginning of the school year: I was front-row center so Mr. Robin could keep an eye on me, while Carl was back-left, a halo of empty seats circling him so that he wouldn't be tempted to talk. Mr. Robin rolled a stub of chalk between his thumb and pointer finger, waiting for us to settle. His white hair stood up like a cock's comb and his kelly-green sweater-vest was tight over his barrel chest; he looked like a tropical bird.

As soon as Mr. Robin started the lesson, I stopped listening. I was jittery; I wanted something, but I didn't know what. Not to be stuck in pre-calc, not to be trapped at home. Even the nunnery that morning had felt foreign-ish. A week ago, Nonz was alive and Sam hadn't heard of Megan of Myrtle Beach. I wondered what Poppy was doing with the run of our house. Maybe getting into my journal, although he wouldn't understand a word of it: too many slitters and Code Reds. Dad had offered to take an extra day off from work to meet with the realtor, and now he was over at 122 Chestnut polishing and waxing and getting it ready to put on the market. There were a hundred things I'd forgotten to request from that house—Nonz's curlers, Poppy's boar-hair shaving brush, the bobby-pin box I'd used for collecting stray toenail clippings when I was a kid—and for the rest of math class I pictured Dad tossing out Nonz and Poppy's things as fast as I could dream them up.

When the bell rang I slammed my notebook shut and filed into the hallway ahead of Carl.

"Chuckie?" he called, catching up.

I looked over Carl's head to where Teddy was leaning with his back against the wall, his arms around Kim Twining.

"Who the fuck's 'Chuckie'?" I asked.

"It's a slitter for OP."

"Since when?"

"That's what we called it in Myrtle."

I was already sick as shit of hearing about Myrtle. "You can't have a slitter for a slitter," I said. "And chuckie's a terrible slitter."

Carl shrugged. "Is Poppy really living with you?"

"Right across the hall."

"What's he going to do all day?"

"Watch TV. Think up ways to annoy my mom."

"I like Anne," said Carl.

Carl liked my mother because she bought anything anyone wanted at the grocery store, as long as it was on her list. You could put a bald eagle on that list and she'd surely come home with one. Meanwhile Carl's mom could hardly remember a gallon of milk.

"Yeah, well, your Fruit Roll-Ups came in, you'll be glad to know. But poor Poppy went without grapefruit for the first time in his life."

"Tell him to put it on the list."

Carl peeled off for the science wing, leaving me in the hallway with my brother. Sometimes I cut through the library just to avoid Teddy. At school, he had a way of speaking to me without actually seeing me, calling out, "Hey, sis," while searching wildly for his friends to witness this act of brotherly love.

"Jules," Teddy said now, saluting me like a total tardmore. His entourage orbited, then moved off down the hall like a solar system, my brother the sun.

Second period Sam and I had gym class. I hadn't participated in PE since September, when a note from our school nurse had entitled me to sit out the girls' lacrosse unit due to a contusion on my shin. "It's always something with you," Miss Horchow had said, filing my note in her attendance binder. Chest pains, growing pains, muscle spasms, cramps. I'd found a medical dictionary in the reference section of our school library and had symptoms to spare.

Now I dropped my math notebook on the bleachers and settled in while the girls went outside for Frisbee golf and the boys suited up for dodgeball in the gymnasium. If my parents had known about this arrangement they would've ended it, so at the dinner table at night I described my PE units in great detail, telling them about Hope Crowley cross-country skiing into a tree and Barbara Kowski backswinging her indoor hockey stick into Angela Mink's nose. Who cared that I made it all up? Gym grades didn't factor into our GPAs, and an F in PE seemed a fair price to pay for more time with Sam.

There was no question Sam could've been a super-pop like Teddy, but either he didn't care or he didn't see it. He was smarter than most of the super-pops but not quite a striver; he played soccer in the fall and tennis in the spring, but he wasn't a jock, either. For some reason, Sam seemed to like being saddled with Carl and me.

"Hey," said Sam, collapsing on the bleachers two rows below me. We had only seconds to talk before his dodgeball game began.

The fluorescent gymnasium lights flashed on Sam's hair and I resisted the urge to pet him. He'd changed into a fresh set of gym clothes—black Umbros and a T-shirt that said SECOND ANNUAL COOPERSTOWN SOCCER KICK—and I inhaled deeply, dizzy from the smell of his detergent. When he leaned over to tie his Sambas, I spied his swimsuit tan line above his boxers, and I wondered if Megan had seen it, too.

On the gym floor, Mr. Yonkey bounced a single red ball and tooted his whistle to call the boys over. Sam didn't move.

I took a deep breath. "So?" I said.

"What?"

I rolled my eyes. "Megan."

Sam shrugged. "Nothing happened, really. Carl and Wylie and Doug just said I should go for her."

Effing Carl.

"We kissed," he admitted.

"Like once?"

My heart thudded in my chest as Sam looked down at his hands, then back up at me.

"Like a few times."

"And?"

"And what?" asked Sam. "It's not like I'm going to write her or anything. Why do you care, anyway?"

Yonkey blew his whistle and said, "Move it, men!"

"I better go," said Sam. He looked back once, then Q-Berted down the bleacher seats to join Yonkey on the gym floor.

In my math notebook I drew three connected circles, a Venn diagram for our friendship, a chain-linked triumvirate for Sam and Carl and me. Where Carl and I overlapped was in the way we made room for each other in our lives, our front doors always open, and in our mutual adoration of Sam. We courted his affections, and when we couldn't have him, which was often enough, we always had each other, and in that way Carl was my best friend. Where Sam and I overlapped was in the way he reached under his desk during history class to lay notes folded in the shape of right triangles on the very top of my knee, and in the way he used a pen during study hall to draw random images—a pine forest, an open book, our lunch monitor's shoe—in dark-blue strokes on the soft underside of my arm. At the heart of our three-way union was the language we had created, our mother tongue, but with one thousand words at the ready, I still couldn't tell Sam that I had missed him while he was gone.

* * *

Before the final bell of the day we were in Sam's Badass Scirocco Scirocco, tearing out of the parking lot at top speed, just ahead of the school-bus traffic. Tennis didn't start until three thirty and we had minutes to kill. First stop, Stewart's for snacks: pork rinds and Dr Peppers and fifty-cent gumballs from the Titan Big'un machine, then on to my house, where we could catch the first half of *The Jenny Jones Show* before practice.

Our house was a Victorian two-story at the base of Bassett Hall, which had been an orphanage when Poppy was a kid, then offices for Bassett Hospital. Next to Bassett Hall were the tennis courts where our school tennis team played, visible from our kitchen window and also upstairs from Poppy's new bedroom.

We found Poppy in front of the TV where I'd planted him that morning. He'd traded in his plaid pajamas for khakis and a wool work shirt but was still sporting his robe and slippers, which Nonz never would've allowed, and he hadn't combed his hair or shaved or applied Vicks VapoRub to his nose.

I sat on the corduroy couch next to Poppy and nabbed the remote. "Have you ever seen *Jenny Jones*?" I asked. Every episode was about oversexed teenagers. It was by far our favorite show.

"Who?" asked Poppy.

Sam kicked back on the purple couch below the TV. "Poppy," he said, "how do you like your new digs?"

"Where's your grandfather been keeping himself?" Poppy asked Sam. He and Sam's grandfather had gone to CHS together a thousand years ago. "That man has a hat of mine."

"He says you gave it to him."

Poppy made a gesture somewhere between the okay sign and the bird.

"My God," Poppy said when *Jenny Jones* returned from commercial break.

"Looks like teen prostitutes with weight problems," said Sam. "Should be profesh."

Carl had gone to the kitchen for his Fruit Roll-Ups and now returned with the whole box. He passed one to each of us, including Poppy.

"What is this?" Poppy asked.

"A Fruit Roll-Up," Carl explained. He unfurled Poppy's and peeled off the plastic sheet for him. "You eat it."

"Poppy, no," Sam said absently. "Your teeth."

Which is what I liked about Sam: there was an ease to his presence, an okay-ness with the world. He knew what he wanted, knew how to ask for it, knew he would get it, knew what to do with it when it was his. On the couch, he crossed his legs at the ankles, clasped his hands behind his head, and scooted over until he was pressed into the pillows. I thought about how simple it must've been for Megan. She barely knew him, would never see him again, but I had everything in the world to lose.

Already I had forfeited tennis, the one sport in which I'd nearly triumphed over Teddy. We'd both taken summer lessons at the country club as kids, but around age twelve Teddy had laid his athletic prowess at the altar of PONY League and American Legion, and before long his serves lacked the laser precision of his fastballs and he was choking up on his racket as though he were gripping a big-barrel bat. The last time Teddy and I played, he'd sailed every first serve long, sliced every backhand wide, and when our hour was up we were on serve 5–4, and I'd marked it down in the chronicles of my childhood as a solid win.

But it wasn't enough to take on Teddy. It wasn't enough to play, practice, improve. Two weeks ago it hadn't been enough even to earn a place on our high school's coed varsity tennis team, which, as freshmen, Sam and Carl and I hadn't made. Throughout the winter, the three of us had spent every afternoon together, driving around in Sam's BASS, smoking OPs, playing board games at Nonz and Poppy's house. Now, with four openings in this year's lineup—four seniors graduated and gone—Sam, at least, was poised to make the team, while Carl and I might still be axed. I was good at tennis but high school boys were bigger, stronger—my fate hung in the balance and Sam hadn't even acknowledged that things would change.

In the days leading up to tryouts, while Sam debated whether he'd be number two or three in the singles lineup, I thought about running track instead. Hilary and Paige, my friends from the field hockey team, spoke of long bus rides to away meets with nothing but time to hang out with each other and the other teams. I pictured flocks of girls stretching their calves and loosening their hamstrings in the grassy center of the track while boys of every uniform ogled from the lanes. Never mind that I'd never run a lap outside gym class. Maybe I had a hidden talent—long jump, shot put, pole vault—but when I pictured myself at the javelin throw, I saw only a tennis racket in my hand.

When Sam booked an hour at the indoor courts in Oneonta and invited Carl and me to join him—he wanted to practice his serves—I lied, said I had to go shopping with my mom, and instead curled up with a book in bed. If not the track team, then maybe I'd volunteer at the Seedlings after-school program or take up solo rock climbing at the gym. In the end, I did none of these things. The moment for tennis-team tryouts came and I simply didn't go.

"I probably wouldn't have made it, anyway," I'd told Nonz when she called to discuss. Dad had shared the news—Sam, second singles; Carl, alternate/team manager; me, a no-show.

"But I've seen you play," said Nonz. "You're good."

I shrugged, waited.

"So this is about Sam," she said.

With anyone else I would've denied it. Until that moment, I hadn't even admitted it was true. I knew how childish I sounded and I should've been embarrassed but I never was with Nonz.

I pinned the receiver between my ear and shoulder and quietly shut my bedroom door. "Why does he want to be on the team so badly, anyway?" I asked. "The three of us play tennis together all the time."

"Sometimes people want new things," said Nonz. "It doesn't have to mean you let go of each other."

Refusing to show up for the timed sprints and elimination drills, I'd watched instead from the window in our guest room, thinking that Sam would come for me, that he would tell Coach Klawson he needed a drink of water and run over to 59 Susquehanna looking for me, but it was Carl who'd stopped by afterward to ask me where I'd been.

Now I saw empty afternoons stretching out endlessly before me. I pictured Sam and Carl on the school bus without me, traveling to away matches against other Section III, Class C public schools. Ilion, where a sign in front of the Remington Arms factory tracked the number of days since the last accident. Herkimer, from which the closest orthodontist, Dr. Caruso, traveled one Wednesday a month to a pop-up office in Doubleday Court. In Hamilton, Sam and Carl would play on the Colgate University tennis courts. In Mohawk, they'd press their faces against the bus windows to eye the runaway-truck stop halfway down Vickerman Hill. Sauquoit, Little Falls, Richfield Springs. Frankfurt, Waterville, Mount Markham. Wherever Sam was going, I wanted to go with him, but it was too late.

"Tryouts are over," I said.

"Forget it," said Nonz, dismissing the notion. "Go to practice tomorrow. See what happens."

During the next commercial Carl asked Poppy how his day had been.

"I miss having lunch," he sighed.

"You haven't eaten since breakfast?" I asked.

"Holy crap," said Sam, who ate at least five times a day.

While I made Poppy a PB&J with a pickle and potato chips and a glass of milk, Sam and Carl changed into wind pants and zipper jackets, then the three of us left for practice.

"Bye, kids," Poppy called, which made me feel bouncy, and I walked a little faster and so did Sam and Carl and then we were almost running for the courts.

"This is why I always say, 'Ride the bus.'" Coach Klawson pointed to Sam, then Carl. "Just ride the bus with the rest of the team." He shrugged. "Not complicated, right? Julia," he said, zeroing in on me. "You're not even on the team, and now you're preventing my players from being on time. Give me five laps."

"Nice going," said Alan Forrest, rotating his racket by slow half turns with a rhythmic flick of his wrist.

I jogged the perimeter of the fence in my jeans and moccasins, keeping one eye trained on Claw. During the preseason practices before spring break, he'd grudgingly tolerated my presence on the hill overlooking the courts and even let me squeegee the baselines before practice began, but with the official season under way, Claw seemed to have pegged me for a nuisance. Nonz would've told me to talk to him. Certainly that's what Dad had advised. But the lineup was set. The best I could hope for now was co–team manager, helping Carl fill empty ball cans with water for the real players to drink from, and I didn't want to be Sam's water girl.

Technically CHS tennis was a boys' team, but because there was no corresponding girls' team, Title IX mandated that girls be allowed to try out for it, though hardly any did. All the tennis teams in our athletic conference worked this way, with anywhere from zero to two girls playing with and against boys whose skill levels ranged from "possible college competitor," like our captain, Evan, to "backyard player," like Alan Forrest, whose unorthodox ground strokes produced such dramatic sidespins that his returns occasionally bounced back over to his side of the net.

This year in our singles slots were Evan, Sam, and the German exchange student, Friedrich, whom we called Danke Schoen. In the doubles slots were Phillip and T.J., cousins who had been playing together since they were kids; and Alan and Doug, starters on the varsity football and basketball teams, who'd had convenient openings for spring sports. Alan and Doug were new to tennis, and with thick necks hammered into their shoulders, they looked wrong for the part, but they were athletic and quick and they'd beaten out Carl for a spot in the doubles lineup, and they might've beaten me, too.

After my penalty laps, I starfished on a patch of dry grass in the sun at Carl's feet and we watched Sam hit approach shots on Court 1. Seven out of his first ten went long. "Adjust your backswing," I called, and Sam shortened it up, and the next ten were perfect.

"What are we doing this weekend?" asked Carl.

"Who knows? We have four more days of school before then and I have detention tomorrow."

"We could try to get the goods."

Four wine coolers between us—that's what it took Carl and me to get drunk.

"Okay," I said.

"Policy," said Carl. Then, "Want to come over tonight? We can study for the math quiz."

"Is Sam going?" I asked.

"Doubt it," said Carl. "He's at his mom's."

Sam's mom lived in Index, twenty minutes outside town; his dad's house was just down the block from Carl's. They'd bought him double sets of everything—two pairs of sneakers, two tennis rackets, two Nintendos—but still Sam forgot stuff when he switched houses, so there was at least a chance he'd be by Carl's.

On the court, Sam practiced volleys with Danke Schoen. He stood with his knees bent, his right arm extended like a sword. Two weeks earlier there'd been snow on these courts and Claw had hauled everyone up here with shovels from his family's hardware store to clear off months of crusty slush. Doug had taken a chunk out of the baseline on Court 2, leaving a black divot that now glinted in the sun.

I thought back to last summer, to the strip-poker tennis game that Sam and Carl and I had invented: whatever logos and labels we were wearing became our sponsors, and each time we lost a round-robin match we had to remove two items of clothing. Carl and I had arrived in track pants and sweatshirts, extra socks and wristbands, wilting in the August humidity, while Sam had made no special effort at all. In his Nike shorts and Nick Bollettieri T-shirt, he'd stripped us down until I was wearing only a sports bra and shorts while Carl wore his boxers and one sock and Sam stood on the other side of the net, fully clothed.

"OP," I announced, shaking off the memory, and Carl and I skirted around behind the Womb, the miniature yellow school bus that Claw used to transport the team between school and practice. Carl lit us up and I inhaled deeply. Above us the sky was cartoonishly blue and I thought about summer, no school or practice, just Sam and Carl and me.

"Claw's coming," said Carl suddenly. I took a mind-numbing drag and mashed my OP on the Womb's tire. Carl did the same and we hopped out from behind the bus in time to catch Claw peering around the bumper.

"What're you two doing back here?" he said, smoothing his running pants. He was tall with orange hair and green eyes that went squinty when he was annoyed. "Were you smoking?"

"No," I said.

"Yes," said Claw. "Carl, go get your racket."

Carl took off for the courts and I started to speak but Claw touched my shoulder and said, "What's the plan here?"

I said nothing. The two things I wanted most in the world were here at Bassett Hall, and I was afraid I could have only half of either of them: not Sam's girlfriend but his water girl; not a team member but a team manager.

"You can't just hang out with the team all season," said Claw.

On the courts at the bottom of the hill, Sam hit backhands: crosscourt, crosscourt, down the line. I was terrified of the things he wanted—the things I wanted, too. Girlfriend or random girl? Hanging out or just a kiss? Sam was a train zooming by and I couldn't see my way on.

"So?" said Claw.

"I don't know," I said.

Claw shook his head, thinking I was being sarcastic, and it occurred to me that there are very few people who can hear us the way we want to be heard.

* * *

After practice, Sam and Carl came back to my house to pick up the Badass Scirocco Scirocco. It was still light out and we squeezed onto my porch swing, kicking off with our right feet, catching the ground on the way back with our left. Carl brought up the idea of getting the goods, and we agreed to take the BASS out Friday night and drive up Route 28 until Sam found a clerk willing to sell him our Seagram's Wild Berries and his Natty Light. When the sun started to set, we swung without talking, the only noise a creak from the chain on Carl's side that fired up when we pushed off. The last light cast our shadows across the painted porch floor, stretching Sam's head to the opposite railing, and when we saw my mom's car turn onto Susquehanna, we pushed harder, nearly tipping at the apex.

Mom waved as she shut off the engine, and all three of us waved back.

"Kids," she said, hauling out her briefcase. "Time to say your good-byes."

We let the swing glide to a stop.

"See you tomorrow," said Sam, pushing off my thigh and the armrest as he rose, and a shock bolted up my spine.

I followed Mom into the house, narrow and long with two stair-cases. Walking front to back we passed the living room, my mother's study, and finally the kitchen, which fed into the den where Poppy was asleep, TV blaring, a blue light flickering over his skin.

"There's Poppy," I said.

Mom said nothing, only drifted back to the kitchen.

"What are you making?" I asked.

"I don't know," she said. "I haven't had a second all day." She glanced through the pantry. "Sloppy Joes?"

"Here," I said, returning the seasoning mix to the pantry. "Let me."

Mom drank white wine while I made a green salad with Nonz's mustard vinaigrette and spinach quesadillas. The quesadillas were fry-ing when Teddy and my father walked in.

"Hey, old girl," said Dad, kissing my head. He wore khakis that were frayed at the hem along with his old running sneakers—clearly not a workday. An unidentifiable orange splotch had stained the pocket of his button-down shirt: Play-Doh or Gak. It had probably been there for ages.

"What's the occasion?" asked Dad, pointing to the quesadillas.

"Poppy's here."

We all peered into the dark den, where Poppy was snoring.

"How's he doing?" Dad whispered to my mother.

Mom shrugged.

"He watched *Jenny Jones* with us today," I said.

"Nice, Julia," said Teddy, but what was his problem? At least I'd been here.

"He liked it, okay?"

"That show's total trash."

"Kind of like Kim Twining?"

"Hey!" said Dad. "No fighting."

Which was our cue:

Teddy said, "Crisscross, applesauce."

I said, "One, two, three, eyes on me."

Dad said, "Okay, okay." He pushed his wire-rimmed glasses up on his nose, the portrait of a school principal. It just so happened his was a preschool. "Now it's time to play the quiet game."

At the dinner table, we fell into our places—Dad at the head, Teddy against the wall across from me, and Mom to my right. Our table was the sanded and polished nine-foot barn door from Poppy's childhood farm, which he'd saved and gifted to my parents when they moved back to Cooperstown. We tended to cluster at one end of the table but Poppy plunked himself down at the other head of the table—the foot, I guess—far from the action and the food.

"Poppy," I said, waving him over.

"I can't squeeze back there," he said. "This'll be fine."

"Yeah, but Poppy." We had a way of doing things—we had an end of the table where we sat—and everyone who came to dinner, which was mostly Carl and sometimes Sam, sat in the seat across from Mom.

"Why don't you switch with me?" said Mom. "I'll go next to Teddy."

"I'm fine, Anne."

Mom put up her palms as though she'd run into an invisible wall. If it weren't for my father, we would've spread like roaches to eat alone in our favorite holes. Mom preferred the kitchen island, stooped over a legal brief. Teddy and I liked to split the purple couch, careful not to touch. Who knew what Poppy liked—he seemed miserable at our dinner table and given the chance probably would have scurried off to the TV in his room.

"So," Dad began, "any second thoughts about the tennis team?"

"No," I lied.

Teddy launched into a detailed description of his knuckleball, offering his sock for a demonstration, but Mom said no.

Suddenly Poppy cleared his throat and said, "I had no lunch today."

"You did, Poppy. PB&J, remember?" But he wasn't talking to me.

Mom apologized for not leaving him a sandwich and said she'd go to the grocery store tomorrow, but Poppy only shrugged.

"I don't want to put you out," he said.

"You're not putting me out, Dad. I'll get some of those soups Mom buys and whatever else you like."

"I don't know how to fix all that," said Poppy.

Mom took a deep breath and exhaled slowly, and I wondered if she was wishing Nonz were here as much as I was. The last time Nonz and Poppy had come over for dinner, he hadn't had any problem sitting near us and when he'd needed something from the kitchen he'd walked right in and found it.

"Dad," said Mom gently. "Hugh and I both work."

Poppy pushed his plate away.

"Now you're not eating," Mom observed. "You just said you were hungry."

"Never mind," said Poppy. "I'll be fine without."

"Jesus, Dad—"

"Anne," my father warned, and Mom shifted her gaze to him.

"What, Hugh?"

"Nothing," he said. "Let's try to be calm."

God, did he never learn?

" 'Let's?' " Mom repeated. "This isn't preschool, Hugh. My father is an adult and if he can dish it out he can very well take it."

Dad wiped his mouth and made a show of putting his napkin in his lap, carefully smoothing it so that he didn't have to actually look at my mother when he said, "No, you're right. You're absolutely right. I just thought it's his first day—"

Mom threw up her hands, frustrated. "Why is this my fault?"

I glanced at Teddy, who was picking a cuticle on his thumb.

"Anne," said Dad.

"I'm exhausted!"

Her blue eyes, normally clear, were bloodshot, small pouches bagging under the lower lids. Suddenly Mom covered her face with her napkin, sour cream brushing into her hair; I'd never seen her cry and quickly looked away.

Dad jumped up from his chair while I scooted mine back. "Come on," he said, helping Mom up. She was only a few inches shorter than he was but just then she looked like a child.

When they were gone, Teddy tossed his napkin on the table and in five long strides he was at the back stairs, climbing them two at a time.

Minutes passed. Poppy and I didn't speak. Outside, it was nearly dark.

Poppy picked up his quesadilla and bit. His teeth chomped through the thin tortillas, wood knocking wood. My parents still hadn't come back to the table and neither had Teddy, who flung himself out the front door soon after leaving me with Poppy.

"Why don't you and Mom get along?" I asked.

Knock knock knock.

"Poppy?"

"Huh?"

"Why don't—"

"We get along fine."

I cleared the table—though technically it was Teddy's turn—using my knife to scrape my mother and brother's food onto my father's plate, then stacking them all on mine. I reached for Poppy's plate but he said he wasn't finished.

I carried the dishes to the kitchen, where it was so dark I had to feel for the counter. I started to turn on the lights, then changed my mind. Teddy had the right idea. I left the dirty plates in the sink and headed for the front door.

Outside a cloud had swaddled the moon and the streetlamps barely lit the sidewalk. I walked down Susquehanna to Chestnut and over to Leatherstocking Street, where I entered Carl's house through the backyard.

"Hey," said Carl. "I thought you weren't coming over."

I eyed his plate. His mom went to a widows' support group three nights a week and tonight she'd left him a feast to go with his TV.

"What is all that?" I asked.

"Steak, fries, Dr Pepper. We're celebrating my return from Myrtle Beach. There's more of everything in the kitchen. Bring the ketchup," he called after me.

I served myself two steak strips and a handful of fries, but I wasn't hungry.

"Where's the ketchup?" I called, pawing through the refrigerator.

"Cabinet," said Carl.

"Right." In my house, ketchup was in the refrigerator but maybe it was like peanut butter and could go either way. I shut the fridge and opened the first cabinet next to the stove: spices, a pepper grinder, and a large orange pill bottle.

I turned the bottle and read the label:

Mary Matthieson
Hydrocodone/Acetaminophen 5mg/500mg
Generic for Vicodin
Take 1 tablet by mouth every 4–6 hours as needed for pain
Quant: 20
Refills: 0

Carl's mom had been depressed since Carl's dad died, but last spring things had gotten much worse. Carl had moved in with his uncle in Richfield Springs for two weeks, right in the middle of the school year, and he probably wouldn't have told us why except that Richfield Springs was fifteen miles from Cooperstown. Sam didn't have his license yet, and we wouldn't stop hounding Carl about how we were going to hang out after school when he was living two towns away.

"Why can't you just stay at Sam's dad's house?" I'd asked.

"I can't," said Carl, for about the fifth time.

"He won't care," said Sam. "We can take over the basement."

"Where's your mom even going?" I asked. She worked at a bank on Main Street, and I'd never known her to take a single day off, much less two weeks.

Carl didn't answer.

"Did she actually *say* you can't stay at Sam's dad's?"

"I'm supposed to stay with family," said Carl. He looked deeply uncomfortable, refusing even to make eye contact, fidgeting helplessly in his seat.

"Why?" asked Sam, and finally Carl leaned forward, hands palming the table, and told us that his mom had OD'd on Vicodin, okay, then he pushed away from the table and disappeared, leaving us with his bowl of tomato soup and Otis Spunkmeyer cookie, untouched.

I shook the bottle. Full. The name at the bottom of the label was Michael Tremont, DDS—a dentist in Utica whom lots of people in Cooperstown went to. Maybe Carl's mom had broken a tooth while Carl was in Myrtle Beach. Maybe she'd lost a cap or undergone a root canal, but I wondered if Dr. Tremont knew about last spring.

Two cabinets over I found the ketchup. Back in the den, I handed Carl the squeeze bottle and he squirted it directly onto his fries.

"You're not supposed to do that," I told him.

"Do what?"

"Squirt ketchup onto your fries."

"Why not?" he asked.

Because if you were ill mannered enough to smother your French fries in ketchup, Anne Obermeyer liked to say, you should at least have the decency to use a fork—but I didn't repeat this to Carl. I wondered what it would've been like if Carl's dad were still alive. He'd died when we were in the first grade, long before Carl and I had become friends. On the nightstand in Carl's bedroom was a framed photograph of the two of them at one of his T-ball games, taken ages ago. In the picture, Carl's dad was leaning over him at home plate, his hands covering Carl's on the handle of the bat. I'd once asked Carl if he remembered that day and he'd said almost, he almost did.

"Why are you staring at me?" he asked.

I settled next to him on the couch and tucked my legs under the blanket. "Carl," I said, "what happened between Sam and Megan?"

He held a French fry in midair, then set it back on his plate. "I don't know," he said. "Not really anything, I don't think."

"Sam said they kissed." Carl shrugged and I turned to face him. "Did you see it?"

"There was this boardwalk by the beach—I saw them down there. She was pretty Perkins, to be honest."

"Really?" I asked.

"I don't know," said Carl. "She was okay. Do you want me to quiz you?"

"No."

"Come on," he said, poking my ribs. "The quiz is Wednesday. Quadratic formula." Carl pushed his math book onto my lap, then pointed to the equation and said, "Memorize it."

But I couldn't concentrate. His first night in Myrtle Beach Sam had written to me, and I wondered now if he'd been trying to tell me something, not about speeding tickets or random girls named Megan but about possibility.

"Carl," I said quickly. "Did they sleep together?"

"Jesus," said Carl, his cheeks flushing. "I told you, I don't know." He stood up, knocking the blanket off us. "Why does it matter?"

When I didn't respond, he disappeared into the kitchen and I heard his silverware clattering in the sink and his plate shuttling across the counter, but I didn't go after him. He was angry, or annoyed, but I was thinking about how Sam had touched my leg on the porch swing after practice and how he was home now. If not Megan, someone else; if not Myrtle Beach, Cooperstown. My chest tightened while my pulse raced ahead, counting out the hours till homeroom, history, then seventh-period study hall. I'd offer Sam my arm and he would ink my skin with a thousand blue lines.

3

Hugh couldn't remember the last time he'd left school in the middle of the day, but after his run-in with Caroline he acted on an impulse that told him he needed fresh air, a brisk walk, and a lobotomy. Back in his office, he grabbed his ski hat and gathered the mail from his desk and didn't stop when Mrs. Baxter rose from her desk and called his name.

At the Doubleday Cafe, Hugh waved to one of the owners, then to Randolph DeVey, a local lawyer whom Anne couldn't abide, sitting alone in front of the mute jukebox. A trio of Yankees fans in matching caps drank coffee at the bar; it was too early for tourist season but still a few found their way. Hugh recognized the older couple in the window seat from church, and they nodded to him, and Hugh returned the gesture, then continued to watch them for a moment. The woman held her coffee cup with both hands, making knots of her knuckles, while her lanky husband stared resolutely out the window. Neither spoke. Something about the way the woman worried her cup reminded Hugh of his mother. Ten years ago his father had lost a short battle with lung cancer, and three months after that, his mother had followed his father into an early grave. Yoked together for more than half a century by a common sorrow, theirs had been a marriage of loss, not love, and it made Hugh sad to even think of them now.

He took a seat at a table for two near the back of the restaurant.

"You want to see a menu?" asked Missy, leaning across Hugh's table to lay down a set of stainless-steel silverware.

"I guess not," said Hugh. The specials were chalked on the wall. Hugh consulted the board, scanning for his breakfast. "What's the omelet?" he asked, squinting.

"Cheddar and bacon."

Hugh shrugged. "The omelet, please, and coffee."

"You got it." Missy turned and walked to the kitchen, her generous backside swinging in her black pants.

"Nice day," said Randolph from across the room. He had the *Daily Star* open in front of him alongside a mug and four empty creamers.

"Beautiful," Hugh agreed. He shuffled through the stack of unopened mail he'd brought along, then placed it on the table and proceeded to ignore it.

Hugh's problems were reproducing at rabbit rate, and in his estimation they all led back to his wife. If Anne worked in Cooperstown, Hugh might have called her right then and the two of them could've met away from the house and everything the house seemed to bring with it: Anne's father, a broken faucet in their bathroom, an infestation of flies in their basement. All of these things needed tending to, and Hugh supposed that's what life was mainly about but, frankly, he needed a time-out from his life. When, for example, had he started noticing waitresses' backsides?

"Brewing a fresh pot," Missy called from the bar. "Gorgeous day," she said.

Already spring, soon to be summer, and school would be out for the season. Hugh would be free to can beans and pickle cucumbers, play high-handicap golf on the nine-hole course at the north end of the lake, grow tomatoes in his backyard. Maybe this summer he really would get started on expanding Seedlings. He'd take seriously his meeting at Klawson's Hardware this evening. He'd write down figures instead of just pretending to do math in his head. Building a larger school would mean more work—taking out a loan, hiring and training teachers—impinging on Hugh's relatively relaxed schedule, but with Teddy off to college in the fall and Julia soon after, what else would he have to occupy him but Seedlings?

Hugh watched Missy pour his coffee. She had been a waitress at the Doubleday since it'd opened, and Hugh had never seen her anywhere outside the restaurant—he wasn't sure she even lived in Cooperstown—but she was such a fixture here that he felt like he knew her.

"Do you live in town?" Hugh asked when she brought his coffee to the table.

Missy produced a teaspoon from her apron. "Milford," she said. "I drive in early and get back late. Might as well live here, I guess." She laughed and Hugh smiled. He wanted to keep her talking but he couldn't think of anything appropriate to ask. She didn't wear a wedding ring, he noticed, and he wondered if that had always been the case.

"Omelet'll be right up," she said, and Hugh nodded and thanked her and watched her walk away.

"Read the paper yet today?" Randolph held up the Oneonta *Star*.

Hugh smiled. "Not yet. Anything interesting?"

"A few of my clients are in the police blotter, but that's to be expected. How's your wife holding up in the big city?"

"I don't even pretend to know what she does over there," said Hugh.

Randolph stood and collected his briefcase and newspaper and walked over to Hugh's table. "I heard Anne's mother passed away," he said. "Terrible business."

"It is," Hugh agreed.

"Give her my best."

Hugh nodded and Randolph turned, crossed the restaurant, and stepped gingerly onto Main Street, shielding his eyes from the sun.

When Missy set Hugh's plate in front of him, Hugh said, "You want to join me?"

He had not expected her to say yes, but she shrugged and pulled out the chair across from him.

"I'm on break," she called back to the kitchen. Then, to Hugh, "Mind if I smoke?" Missy produced a pack of Pall Malls from her apron and struck a match from a flimsy white book. Waving the cardboard match to extinguish the flame, Missy inhaled and exhaled, and Hugh, not wanting to offend her, resigned himself to the smell of smoke on his clothes.

Missy said, "You run that school up on Mill Street, don't you?"

"That's right," said Hugh.

Missy smiled good-naturedly, tiny lines circling her mouth and creasing her forehead. She was not unpretty.

"They say it's a good school." She gestured with her cigarette. "Seedlings?"

"Seedlings," Hugh confirmed.

"I don't have any children. Nieces and nephews, but they're in school over in Milford."

Hugh nodded. "We have a few kids from Milford. About one or two in each class."

"How much does it cost to send them up there?"

It was Anne who'd first warned Hugh about this kind of question. In her estimation, Missy wasn't weighing the cost of tuition against the quality of education; she was preparing to judge. And given that there were few other private schools in the area, any amount of tuition was bound to seem absurdly high. So Hugh generally tried to answer without really answering: "It's hardly any more than day care" or "We run the school for as little as we possibly can." But for some reason he revealed to Missy that tuition was "about five thousand a year."

Missy whistled loudly and fell back in her chair as though she'd been pushed. "Five thousand for one child?"

Hugh shrugged, hands clenched under the table.

"Wow," said Missy. "Rich people, huh? Must be the doctors' kids."

Hugh understood that Seedlings was not for everyone—it was nothing to be sorry for, he told himself—but still he felt deflated as Missy extinguished her cigarette and pushed away from the table. She scrawled a few lines on her order pad, then tore off his bill—$6.35— and slid it across the table, telling him to take his time.

"You don't have to go," said Hugh stupidly.

Missy smiled, then disappeared into the kitchen.

Hugh eyed his half-eaten omelet and decided he was no longer hungry. By now the coffee was room temperature and he took two gulps, then pushed it away. Riffling through his wallet, Hugh selected a ten and shoved the bill under the edge of his plate. Too much, but he didn't want to wait for change.

Back at Seedlings, reeking of cigarettes, Hugh passed Mrs. Baxter's desk outside his office and she neatly rose from her seat and fell into step behind him, as though they had choreographed it. He heard her clicking along in time, felt her just shy of his heels. He turned at the doorway and she nearly bumped him.

"Mrs. Baxter," said Hugh evenly.

"I didn't know you were going out," said Mrs. Baxter. She sniffed the air. "Have you been smoking?"

"No," said Hugh.

Mrs. Baxter's eyebrows went up, her forehead wrinkling.

"Can I help you with something?" asked Hugh.

"Graham Pennington's mother has been calling." Mrs. Baxter crossed her arms over her chest, clearly pleased to have purged herself of the news.

"Been calling?" Hugh's legs felt boggy.

"Once while you were out just now. Once last week and once yesterday. I tried to tell you this morning."

Hugh regarded Mrs. Baxter and held his voice steady.

"What does she want?" asked Hugh. "Did she say?"

"She didn't, but I've written down her number for you." She pointed to the stack of carbon-copy messages on his desk. "I imagine it's about her son."

Hugh barely managed a shaky "Anything else?"

"Nothing else," said Mrs. Baxter, clicking away on her blocky high heels, as focused as ever. He heard her pull out her roller chair and plug in again, and then there was the *tap tap* of her computer keys, *tap tap tap*, ninety words a minute. Priscilla had timed her.

Hugh closed his door and crossed the room to his desk. He stared at the phone, waiting for it to ring. Ears perked, he heard Melanie on the playground, calling, "Michael S. and Michael D., right now please." Then Priscilla counting, counting, recounting, finally shouting, "Brian Meyer! All the Dolphins are over here and you're still climbing up the slide, which we don't do. Up the stairs, down the slide. Please put on your listening ears." Hugh had on his listening ears. The phone would ring. He could already hear it, a shrill *brrrrrrr*, a deafening *ding-a-ling-a-ling*.

The Dolphins filed in; the Bumblebees filed in. In Hugh's office, nothing happened. While Cheryl's prekindergarteners queued up behind the playground doors, it was silent on the yard, then twenty-five children bounded out, armed with shovels and buckets and foam balls. Hugh easily picked out Graham Pennington, his giant plaster cast cradled in a sling.

Hugh squeezed his temples, trying to suffocate his thoughts, but they were popping up too quickly. He tried to reassure himself that any fragmentary memories the boy might possess of . . . well—and here, Hugh's brain fritzed, a kaleidoscopic trick of the mind whereby he was able to both see and not see Caroline's unpainted fingernail tracing his erect penis—would soon give way to the body's natural coping system: if the boy bothered to think of it at all, he would eventually decide he'd dreamed it.

Finally there was a death knell from the black phone on his desk. One, two, three. Mrs. Baxter was going to let it ring.

Hugh snapped up the receiver before the end of the third toll.

Line 1 glowed green but no one spoke.

"Caroline?" said Hugh.

"Oh," said Caroline. "It's you."

* * *

On a chilly Wednesday the week before Joanie died, Graham Pennington had slipped from the top of the playground monkey bars and landed squarely on his left arm. By the time the teachers reached him, he was sitting up in the sand, slightly dazed, and when they peeked inside his jacket sleeve, they saw a tiny white sliver of bone poking through the skin below his now-bluish elbow.

Hugh called 911 first, then Graham's mother, who could not be reached at either of her numbers—home and studio—so he called Graham's father, who was divorced from Graham's mother and worked for a bank in New York. Mr. Pennington, however, was en route home from Tokyo—his assistant promised to relay the message as soon as he landed—and the emergency contact, Graham's aunt in Troy, didn't pick up the phone.

Nothing like this had ever happened in Seedlings' nearly sixteen-year history and Hugh had been both petrified and proud. The teachers had acted quickly and professionally. They cleared the yard. They kept Graham warm and talking. When the ambulance arrived, the children pressed their tiny faces to the windows to watch the EMTs wheel Graham on a stretcher across their playground. Cheryl walked beside the stretcher, softly brushing back Graham's hair, telling him he was doing so well, everything would be fine, just fine. In the parking lot, Hugh boarded the ambulance with the boy and the crew and they took off for Bassett Hospital.

One of the technicians drove and the other inserted an IV in Graham's wrist. He did not cry, but he squeezed his eyes shut and whispered to himself until the technician said, "All done." Soon a painkiller coursed through Graham's veins and he seemed delighted to be riding in an ambulance. The technician worked quickly with gauze and a splint, hiding the wound, and the boy was a model patient. When Hugh asked him where he might be able to reach his mother, Graham rattled off a list of places—her studio, the gym, Tracey's, Beth's, the gallery, the paint store. "Et cetera," said Graham, and the technician, a young bald man with a gold cross around his neck, laughed and said, "Must be some school you're running over there."

"Here we go," he said when they unloaded Graham in the emergency dock at the hospital. Then the EMTs disappeared inside, leaving Hugh and Graham in the open bay off the main drive. Hugh's children had been sewed up and x-rayed and even splinted at Bassett, but they had never entered through the back door on a stretcher. Passersby slowed to see. Hugh wanted to tell them to mosey on, no rubbernecking please, but he understood their curiosity. Hugh himself was anxious to know what would happen next.

A nurse arrived and Graham was wheeled through the ER to admitting. Hugh produced a photocopy of the child's health-insurance card, kept on file at Seedlings, and signed the necessary forms. When that was finished, an older nurse led them to a curtained room, where Hugh helped Graham change into a yellow gown, carefully pulling down the boy's jeans and stripping his feet of their sweaty socks. The nurse cut off Graham's jacket and shirt so as not to disturb his arm. By now Graham was vaguely green and Hugh asked if the doctor would see him soon.

"Just as soon as he can," said the nurse. She closed the curtain on her way out.

Hugh smoothed Graham's hair as he'd seen Cheryl do and asked him if he wanted to hear a story. Graham didn't answer so Hugh kept quiet. He'd left instructions with Mrs. Baxter to keep trying Graham's mother—she'd be here eventually, Hugh told himself, but he was starting to feel panicky. Graham closed his eyes and Hugh fretted that the child might pass out. What if he went into shock? Could that happen to a five-year-old?

By the time Graham's mother charged into the examination room and threw her body over Graham—twenty minutes, an hour later?—Hugh was pacing the room, eyes fixed on the boy's chest, monitoring its rise and fall.

"Graham," said his mother, and at the sound of her voice Graham opened his eyes and smiled sleepily. "Sweetie? My God. Are you okay?" She enveloped him, smothered his face with kisses, and through the muffle of her hug Hugh heard Graham say, "I broke my arm."

The bone was well hidden under a mound of sterile gauze so that there was, thank God, nothing to see. Still, Graham's mother looked him over head to toe as though to make sure he was really all there, and she stroked his hair and his cheek and his torso.

During this examination of Graham, Hugh had a chance to study Graham's mother. She wore paint-splattered white carpenter's pants and a man's button-down shirt, her golden-brown hair swept into a sloppy topknot, her car keys stuffed into her back pocket. He tried to place her from the carpool line at school but couldn't get beyond the image of an old Subaru station wagon.

"Thank you," she said, turning to Hugh, and he was instantly struck.

She was not conventionally beautiful—thick eyebrows arched high over hazel eyes and her incisors gently overlapped—but Hugh couldn't unlock his eyes. A smudge of white paint crossed her reddening cheekbone and Hugh had an itch to rub the paint with the pad of his thumb, but she was looking right at him.

"I'm so sorry this happened, Mrs. Pennington."

With her left hand still on her son, she reached out with her right to shake Hugh's hand. "Caroline. Caroline Murphy, actually, but Caroline. Thank you so much for tracking me down. Hugh, right? I have to thank you. Your assistant called every store in Cherry Valley until she found me."

"Graham's been very brave," said Hugh.

Caroline regarded Graham's doctored arm while chewing a piece of gum. "How did this happen, love?"

Hugh had only just begun to say when the doctor entered the room.

He excused himself and used the pay phone in the waiting room to call Mrs. Baxter. Hugh reminded her to fax a copy of the accident report to their licensor, a woman in Albany whom he had never personally met but whose looping signatures on Seedlings' certificates of operation were as familiar to Hugh as his wife's. Anne—Seedlings' "general counsel"—would have to call Diana D. Humphries in the morning to discuss insurance, liability, and legal claims, things Hugh did not even attempt to understand.

Hugh told Mrs. Baxter he would not be back to school that afternoon, then dropped two quarters in the phone and called his wife's firm in Oneonta. Her secretary answered, a twenty-something named Alyson with a high, scratchy voice.

"Mrs. Obermeyer is in court today," said Alyson. "Is there a number where she can reach you?"

So officious. Hugh supposed that's the way she was paid to be, but for Christ's sake.

"Not really," said Hugh. He eyed the hallway to Graham's examination room. "Will she be back soon?"

"I couldn't say. Can I take a message?"

"Tell her I'm going to miss dinner tonight," said Hugh. "Tell her I'll see her at home."

In the waiting room, he read an old copy of *Newsweek*, but really he just turned the pages. The night before, Hugh had gone to sleep while Anne was still downstairs working. The night before that, she'd come up early, shaping herself to his side, but Hugh had pled exhaustion. He liked to think they had sex regularly but the last time had been six weeks ago, on his birthday in late February. They'd drained a bottle of wine at dinner and let alcohol be their foreplay, and healthy Hugh had gotten and maintained an erection, but he was out of practice—or, rather, the kind of practice he'd been doing had trained him for the quick release—and seconds after he was inside Anne, he was done.

Anne's hurt had been immediate and visible, a silent retreat to her side of the bed, but what could Hugh do? After nearly nineteen years of marriage, they still fought in silence. On a scale of one to ten, where ten was marital bliss and one was divorce, Hugh had no idea how Anne and he rated. He knew a few couples who had divorced— Caroline Murphy and her husband, for example. Hugh closed the magazine and went to see how she was holding up.

Graham's arm was broken in two places, but the surgeon—a man whose wife directed the annual high school musicals—did not sound overly concerned. He called it a "routine" compound fracture and said they would clean the bone to decrease the risk of infection, insert pins above and below the breaks, and apply a plaster cast. The main thing was to watch for signs of infection. If all went well, Graham would be back at school in a week.

Graham went into surgery at a little after five o'clock, while Hugh kept Caroline company in the tiny waiting room outside the OR and tried to distract her from thinking about her son. He learned that Caroline and Graham lived in an old farmhouse in Cherry Valley, fifteen miles northeast of Cooperstown. Allen Ginsberg used to summer there, she told Hugh, tanning naked in his satellite dish. Sounded like the right place for Caroline Murphy, beautiful not in spite of but because of her worn clothes and paint-splattered hair. Hugh could imagine what Anne might say about her, but he tried not to.

They had the waiting room to themselves but sat side by side in attached bucket seats, Hugh stealing glances at Caroline. Tendrils of hair threaded her silver hoop earrings and a macaroni necklace looped her throat on a white string. She wore an oversize man's diver watch, and Hugh was both curious and envious; he hardly knew her and wanted to know more.

"So how long have you lived in Cherry Valley?" he asked.

Caroline tilted her head and said, "Three years."

Hugh thought of his own path to Cooperstown, eighteen years ago. Anne's job, Teddy, then Julia. It wasn't that he wanted to go back; it was that he wanted to go forward, to finally go.

"What about you?" asked Caroline. "Are you from here?"

Hugh started to say his wife was, but the words caught in his throat. "Boston," he said.

"A transplant, then," said Caroline. "Same as me."

Hugh stood and pointed to the vending machines nestled between two potted ficus trees. He felt dizzy, light-headed—he needed a moment to collect himself.

"Can I get you something to drink?" asked Hugh.

Caroline said, "I'd love hot tea, if they have it," and Hugh crossed the room, conscious of the possibility that she was watching him. If the vending machine didn't have tea, he thought he would go down to the cafeteria or across town to Stewart's or to a tea plantation in India to accommodate her. Caroline's first words to Hugh that afternoon had been *thank you*, then *thank you* again—no hurt, no deep-seated anger, just genuine gratitude for his help, and Hugh was eager to reciprocate.

At eight o'clock, Graham was wheeled out of surgery to post-op. Hugh and Caroline stood beside him while the anesthetic wore off, his little body seizing against the diluting of the narcotic in his bloodstream. During the worst of it, Caroline held Graham's shoulders and the nurse held his legs and Hugh felt so guilty he couldn't look. When it was over, they followed Graham's stretcher to his balloon-bordered room on the pediatric floor of the hospital. Graham had a private room with a view of the parking lot and the rolling hills to the west of town. Hugh stood by the windows while the floor nurse set up

Graham's IV and connected a tiny pulse monitor to his index finger. He was already asleep, from the painkillers or sheer exhaustion.

Sometime after ten, Hugh touched Caroline's arm and told her he should go.

"It's late," Caroline agreed. She reached into her purse and pulled out a piece of gum and he watched her fold the sugared stick into her mouth and move it cheek to cheek with her tongue.

"Will you sleep?" asked Hugh.

"Sure." She pointed to Graham's bed. "There's plenty of room. I'll have a friend bring me a change of clothes."

"I'll come back tomorrow," Hugh offered.

In the glow of the bedside light, Caroline reached out to him and he felt her arms around his neck, and then she was hugging him. Hugh stooped and let his arms circle her. She was tiny and he could feel every bone in her back.

"Thank you for staying with us," said Caroline softly, so as not to disturb Graham. "I couldn't have gotten through it without you." Her lips brushed his ear and he let his hand find her neck, where the skin was warm and soft.

He considered staying exactly where he was, but finally he pulled away and they stood near each other, no longer touching.

"Come at lunchtime tomorrow," said Caroline. "Hopefully Graham will be awake."

Outside in the hallway the lights were too bright, and the sounds—nurses squeaking in soft shoes, phones ringing combatively—made Hugh want to retreat back to Graham's room. Tomorrow, Hugh thought. It was not long to wait.

He told himself he was doing the right thing. He promised himself he'd tell Anne about the accident on the playground. But when Hugh got home, at half past ten, Anne's car wasn't in the driveway and he found a note on the kitchen counter: *The kids have eaten. I'm going back to work for a few hours. Let's talk tomorrow.* But they never did.

* * *

That night he dreamed of the cabin in the Berkshires where, until his brother's death, Hugh had spent his childhood holidays. It was winter again, but in the dream Hugh had not seen George, only Caroline, who was naked on the rock above Reacher Falls, the air freezing but the sun-drenched shale warm against their skin. Hugh curled his body against Caroline's side, wanting to have sex, but he was overly conscious of the wind off the frozen river. He rolled away, touching his back to the stone, then pushed up against her again, cold, back and forth until Hugh woke, hard, on Anne's side of the bed.

When he woke again it was the blue hour of morning. Quietly, not wanting to disturb his sleeping wife, Hugh took clean clothes from the bureau and crept to the bathroom to dress, showering in cool water, then shaving and combing his hair in front of the mirror. Hugh had a flush of grays throughout his dark hair but he weighed the same 165 pounds as he had when he was thirty—thanks to his job, he never sat still (though he did have a bad habit of polishing off the kids' birthday cupcakes in the teachers' room). But even if Hugh hadn't physically changed since he'd married Anne, his thoughts felt unrecognizable. The dream about Caroline had thrown him. If it was simply about sex, by every definition Hugh's wife was extremely attractive, tall and trim with neat black hair and crystal eyes. But in the beginning, it wasn't Anne's careful composition that Hugh had been attracted to.

When they'd started dating, Anne had reached out for his hand whenever they'd left the apartment together, and even after Hugh had moved in with her, in a sweet display of vulnerability, Anne had continued to sleep with her childhood stuffed rabbit, Hop, until Teddy was born and she'd passed the bunny down to their son. Hugh remembered with real fondness the lazy weekends before they'd had children, Hugh reading on the couch with Anne's head in his lap or the two of them taking energizing walks from Harvard Yard to Back

Bay to Beacon Hill and home. On Anne's half birthday one year, Hugh had planned an elaborate picnic, replete with a treasure map, taking the T out to the beach a day early to bury a few of Anne's favorite things from home—a coffee mug, an inexpensive bracelet, a red pencil—for her to rediscover in the sand.

Anne had chosen him—plucked him from the wine party in Cambridge as though he were a lost lamb—and Hugh had grown confident in the warm light of her desire. From the beginning, he'd found Anne's subtle dependency charming and sexy, but from time to time, when Hugh had failed to meet even one of Anne's needs—spoken or not—she'd had a way of taking them all off the table, as though she wouldn't risk being disappointed twice. Cooperstown had only exacerbated this tendency toward self-reliance. After Anne's second miscarriage in as many years—when Teddy was six, and Julia was three—Anne had wept openly in Hugh's arms every night for a week. He'd soothed her with promises: it was enough; they had enough; they had their family, their kids, their careers. But Anne had wanted to keep trying for a third while Hugh was content with the two they had, and what should've been a difficult discussion between two people who loved each other instead became a kind of breaking point. It was hard to fathom, but more than a decade had passed since Anne had really asked him for anything. They had their busy lives, which were increasingly playing out in separate spheres—then yesterday a boy had fallen off the monkey bars and Hugh had found himself in a hospital room with a woman who could ask for his help, and he had felt excited again, turned on by his own capability. He'd remembered what it was like to need someone and be needed. Hugh pictured Caroline's eyes now, darker than his wife's, less like a swimming pool and more like the sea.

Hugh tiptoed down the stairs to the front door, then drove the two blocks to Bassett and parked but did not turn off the engine. It was incredibly early, the lights in some rooms still off and the sidewalks deserted. A doctor in green scrubs crouched at the side entrance to the

ER, smoking a cigarette. What if Caroline and Graham were asleep? What if the doctors were making their rounds and Hugh had to wait in that dreadful hallway? What if—now that Hugh thought about it—Graham's father had driven up during the night, and Caroline had gone home while her ex-husband took a shift with their son?

Caroline had said lunchtime, and Hugh decided he could wait.

At school he was anxious and wired, but he was not the only one. Mrs. Baxter pestered him with questions about the surgery, about the recovery period, about the mother who was so difficult to track down. Cheryl arrived early for once, with dark circles under her eyes, bearing homemade sock puppets for Graham to play with. The first puppet was small, perfect for a child's hand, and the second was a giant tube sock intended to fit over his cast. Priscilla had baked brownies and Melanie had bought ten sheets of shiny stickers and a sticker book for Graham. They drank strong coffee in the teachers' room and talked about how awful it was until it was time for early drop-off, time to greet the kids.

Hugh killed the morning by commissioning get-well cards from the classrooms. He went door to door, doling out construction paper and glue sticks and brand-new crayons from the emptied supply closet, which had been meant to last the rest of the school year.

"I feel terrible," Cheryl confided to Hugh while her kids cut with safety scissors.

"He's a five-year-old boy," said Hugh. "This is what they do."

Cheryl shook her head. "I've told them a million times, 'No one goes on *top* of the monkey bars. Swing, hang, but don't let them crawl on top.' They don't listen."

"Who doesn't listen?" said Hugh.

"The assistant teachers. Jackie and Amy. They were on yard duty when it happened."

Hugh ran his hands through his hair. He was too tired to process this. "Graham's fine," he said.

"Make sure he knows how much we miss him," said Cheryl. "And play puppets with him. He'll be so bored."

At noon, with the thrill of the hunt, Hugh homed in on Graham's hospital room and sailed past the injured child to greet his mother, who had changed into a floor-length skirt and a V-neck T-shirt.

"Hi," said Hugh, buzzing with adrenaline.

"Hi." Caroline smiled.

Hugh spun to face Graham, whose broken arm was enthroned on a stack of pillows. "Here it is!" he said, gesturing dramatically at the cast.

Graham looked uncertainly at his arm, then back up at his principal.

"How's the patient?" Hugh asked.

Caroline ruffled her son's sandy-brown hair, then felt his forehead. "The pain medication is making him a little sick."

Graham reached up with his good hand and held on to his mother's wrist.

"I won't stay long," Hugh promised, but Caroline shook her head.

"He's in and out," she whispered. Then, more loudly, "Graham, I think Mr. Obermeyer has something for you."

Only then did Hugh remember that in his hands he was clutching a cornucopia of pleasures for a bedridden child, and he pulled around a chair until he was sitting next to Caroline.

"Everyone at school is thinking of you," said Hugh. "Should I read some of the cards your friends made?" Graham nodded and Hugh held up the first card, a sheet of orange construction paper with glitter-filled glue lines painted down the front. When Hugh opened the card, a shower of silver and gold fluttered prettily over Graham's gown.

"Look at you!" said Caroline.

Graham smiled and clutched his mother's arm tightly over his body, fashioning a hug, and Hugh remembered with a pang when his own children had still cuddled.

Inside the orange card was a crayoned stick figure with one arm and two legs and a seven-rung ladder in the sky overhead. Another stick—the missing arm?—floated alone at the bottom of the page.

"Get well soon!" Hugh improvised. "Should we read another?"

Hugh went through each card, telling stories about the pictures in an animated voice designed to impress Caroline and hold Graham's attention against the pull of the painkillers. Graham's eyes drooped but he seemed to be following, and after the final card he told his mother, "These are all for me." She agreed that they were. Hugh placed the stack of cards on the table at Graham's bedside.

Graham beckoned for his mother's ear and she leaned in close.

"Ask him," said Caroline, but Graham protested and pulled his mother's ear toward him again.

Finally Caroline said, "Would you like to sign Graham's cast?"

Gently, the plastered arm was proffered for Hugh's signature. There were two others—his mother's and the surgeon's. So Graham's father had not been to visit.

Near the underside of Graham's wrist, Hugh indelibly inked his name at what he felt was a safe distance from Caroline's blocked letters and the surgeon's inscrutable scrawl. *Hugh Obermeyer*, he wrote and then felt ridiculous—*Mr. Obermeyer* or even *Principal Hugh* would've been more appropriate—but it was a Magic Marker, and there was no going back.

"I have more," said Hugh, holding up Cheryl's sock puppets and the stickers and a Tupperware container of brownies. But Graham had turned his face toward his mother's side and soon dropped off to sleep, her hand on his chest.

"Poor guy," said Caroline.

"I'm so sorry this happened," said Hugh. "Cheryl wanted me to tell you how sorry we all are." They watched Graham sleep for a moment, then Hugh said, "Is it okay for you to be here all day? I mean, work-wise?"

"Work-wise, it's just me. It's no problem to be here."

Hugh nodded. "Is there anything I can do?"

"Come," said Caroline. "Talk to me."

They moved their chairs across the room to the window, where they sat close to each other.

"It's funny," said Caroline, her voice low, "but I don't remember meeting you until yesterday. Obviously I've seen you—dropping off Graham and everything—but it seems strange we never spoke."

Hugh shrugged. In the waiting room yesterday they'd talked only about Caroline—her artwork, her year living on a commune, her childhood out West. Now Caroline seemed to have taken an interest in him.

"Some mothers want to talk all day," said Hugh. "It's hard to get away."

"Seedlings was my ex-husband's idea. Demand, really. I would've been just as happy to have Graham at home with me, but Richard wanted him in school and it's his call," she said vaguely. "Anyway, the school has worked out beautifully."

"I was my kids' first teacher," said Hugh. "I had it easy."

"How many kids do you have?" asked Caroline.

"Two. A boy and a girl." Hugh smiled. "They're almost grown."

Caroline said, "Sometimes I look at Graham and wonder where the baby went. He was so little." She held her hands apart the width of a sweet potato.

"He's still little," said Hugh. "He just has a big arm."

Caroline shook her head.

"What?" asked Hugh.

"Nothing."

"Come on. What?"

"It's nice to meet someone who actually stops for two seconds to listen." Caroline looked at him from under lowered lids, a touch of self-deprecation in her voice, and Hugh felt certain she was . . . not flirting, not that exactly. "You're sweet," she said.

Hugh let his eyes drop to her feet—black Converse high-tops like the ones Hugh had worn in high school. He breathed, and breathed again. He still did not look at Caroline.

"Did the doctor say how long Graham will have to stay here?" he asked.

"Till tomorrow," said Caroline. "Then we go home."

It was like watching a strand of dominoes topple: the final tile was still standing, but the pieces had been set in motion and the tiles could not help but fall.

Hugh put his hand on Caroline's leg.

"Hi," she said.

"Hi," said Hugh, and he leaned forward in his chair and kissed her on the mouth.

Now Hugh shut his eyes against the memory, a habit he'd formed two weeks ago that had left Anne asking if he needed to see their ophthalmologist. In fact his problem did feel medical, compulsive and obsessional, a movie reel running ad infinitum, a horrifying porno starring Hugh.

With complete disregard for the proximity of the nurse's station, Hugh's kiss in the hospital room had been prelude to a flurry of grasping, turning, pulling, and lifting before Caroline resourcefully thought to fashion their chairs into a makeshift settee. Quickly, without speaking, they'd hurried to undress each other, Caroline unzipping Hugh's pants, Hugh nearly dizzy with arousal to find that Caroline wore no bra. The scene had played out in extreme close-up, and it was only in Hugh's memory that a world existed beyond Caroline's skin, hair, mouth, tongue. He would strangle the memory if he could, leaving only the dream state of irrational, unconscious pleasure that he'd momentarily experienced, a pleasure so pure it had seemed preordained, as though Hugh had been moving toward it all his life. Which is to say, he would've done it. He had every intention of doing it. In fact, they almost *were* doing it—Hugh lowering Caroline to his lap, Caroline reaching to guide him in—when a still, small voice, thick with sleep, called out from across the room, "Mom?" and, without thinking, Principal Hugh leaped gracelessly behind the privacy curtain, sweeping it across its track.

* * *

Caroline's warm breath puffed through the receiver and Hugh shifted the contoured handset to his left ear.

"I heard about your mother-in-law," Caroline began. "I'm so sorry."

"Thank you," said Hugh. He drummed his blotter with nervous fingers. "I was sorry to miss Graham's first day back, but Cheryl says he's doing great."

"He's thrilled," Caroline agreed. "He was going crazy at home."

Hugh waited, but Caroline did not continue.

"My secretary said you called," Hugh admitted. "I literally just got back to the office."

"But I saw you this morning," said Caroline gently. "Remember?"

Hugh marched his fingers across his desk, then tipped them over the edge, knuckles first. Wherever this conversation was going, she would have to take them there.

"First," said Caroline, "I wanted to say that you were wonderful with Graham—coming to the hospital to visit and having the teachers call to check on him."

Hugh hadn't even known about the sympathy calls. "It was the least I could do," he said.

"Well, anyway, I do appreciate it. And I heard that your father-in-law moved in, so I'm sure this is already a stressful time."

"Thank you," said Hugh. *Already?* Hugh didn't speak. He did not even breathe.

"I might as well just say it," Caroline blurted. "Richard is looking into Graham's fall."

The nerve synapses connecting Hugh's ears and his brain shorted; the information was lost. "Sorry?" said Hugh.

"Graham's father is talking to a lawyer. I wanted to tell you myself, before you heard from him."

Hugh went rigid in his chair as the content of her words took form. "Heard *what* from him?"

Caroline lowered her voice, her lips brushing the receiver. "Graham said he was standing on top of the monkey bars when he fell."

"Caroline," he said. "Is this about us?"

"Hugh, no," said Caroline quickly. "That part was fine."

Fine: an indecipherability at best, a calculated reduction at worst; his children's catchall for every suspicion, doubt, boredom, delight, wonder, fear, and disappointment; their most obscene four-letter word.

Hugh took a deep breath, then closed his eyes and said, "Has Graham said anything about . . . ? I mean, does he remember . . . ?"

"I don't know," said Caroline. "I don't think so."

"Caroline," said Hugh, "can we talk about this in person?"

"I'm not sure," she said. "It was hard enough to convince Richard to let Graham return to school while we sort this out."

Hugh thought of Anne—liability, lawsuits, negligence—she would know what to do. But in the two weeks since the boy's fall, Hugh hadn't breathed a word about the accident to his wife.

"Can we slow this down?" asked Hugh. "Can I see you?"

Caroline seemed to consider it, then said, "Can you come here?"

They settled on twelve thirty the next day and Hugh hung up the phone.

Paralyzing half thoughts swirled through his head. A lawsuit, Hugh could not handle. If Richard Pennington brought legal action . . . if Caroline was compelled to testify . . . if the boy started to remember . . . Hugh knew enough about litigation to understand that even if they settled, everything could come out. Accidents happened—children fell—but what he'd done with a student's mother was condemnable, and if Anne didn't kill him first, the talk in town alone would close his school.

Hugh pressed the intercom button and called Mrs. Baxter into his office. He asked her to pull everything they had from their insurance agency in Oneonta. He'd stay here all night if necessary—he'd read the insurance forms, he'd review the accident report, and tomorrow he'd go see Caroline.

Hugh pictured himself as an indefensible ten-year-old watching in horror as his brother slipped through the ice below Reacher Falls. Neither running for help nor easing across the ice to try to catch George's hand, Hugh had let the great tragedy of his life wash over him. Now it seemed as if all the decisions since had been made in that single moment of indecision—but Hugh was no longer a child. He sensed something sinewy, powerful rising up in him, a long-dormant beast stretching its shoulders and hams. He felt protective not only of his school but of himself. If Richard Pennington wanted a tangle, Hugh would be ready; and if seeing Caroline Murphy again would help him to prepare, Hugh was especially game for the fight.

4

Moonlight seeped through Hugh and Anne's twin skylights, reflecting softly off Bob's dinner plate in the
darkening room. From a nearby backyard, he heard
the sounds of children shouting and squealing until
one of them threatened to tell, then it was quiet for a moment before
they began to laugh again. A dreamlike familiarity pressed Bob back
to a long-ago dinner hour with his own family, his younger brother
already excused and racing off to play while Bob remained at the
kitchen table with his mother watching him watching his peas grow
cold. He traced a knot in Anne's dinner table—the pine side door
from his father's dairy barn—and pictured the barn's gambrel roof, the
sliding great door, the shiplap siding. The hayloft had been big enough
to encompass Bob's entire childhood, from hide-and-seek with his
brother to courting Maud Corley below a dormer on the east side.

If no single memory ever told the whole story, Bob preferred to
focus on the happier times, freezing his mind at the hypersharp
vertex of a scene when everything was exactly as it should be—what
good did it do to look forward or back? Who needed to be reminded

that from that same treasured hayloft Sonny had fallen through the feed chute, dropping a full story and breaking his pelvis, or that Bob and Maud had dozed off under the dormer, waking only when the sun was already cresting the horizon and Bob's father was beginning his ascent into the loft? Bedridden, Sonny had missed a year of school and never gone back, though he'd been the better of the two Cole boys at reading and math. As for Bob's indiscretion with Maud, an unforgiving Mr. Corley had shamed the dairy cooperative into dropping Wilson Cole from its membership, and after five years of struggling on his own, Bob's father had been forced to find work in the village, a step back, laboring for another man.

But all that had passed now, and none of it could be changed—Bob saw no point in scrutinizing his mistakes. Anne, on the other hand, liked to examine everything. Even as a child she'd been maddeningly analytical, wanting to know why he waited two weeks to cut the grass—until it was nearly impossible to push the mower—when if he would only mow the lawn every week he could finish his chore in half the time. Because Bob didn't like mowing the lawn! But he'd also been enchanted by his clever and serious daughter, an altogether different sort of person from Bob. Where he had been an average student, Anne anticipated her teachers' assignments and worked ahead in her spelling book. Bob was hopelessly disorganized, but Anne laid out her clothes the night before school. His daughter did her chores without prompting and even offered to help Bob finish his, scrambling onto the roof to dig wet autumn leaves out of the gutters or slithering into the basement crawl space to open the vents for summer. It was almost as though Anne were the parent and Bob and Joanie the children and, as such, Anne was especially protective of her mother.

Out for a drive together on a Sunday afternoon, Anne might inform Bob that Joanie no longer liked going to the hair salon, therefore he needed to buy her mother a portable at-home dryer; not only that, but Anne knew exactly where to get it—Western Auto for

$10.44—and they could stop there on their way home. The next Saturday, Bob might come downstairs thinking he'd spend an hour reading the paper and Anne would cut him off at the pass, whispering in his ear that her mother's birthday was coming up and she and Bob had to get down to the Smart Shop right away to see what they had in Joanie's size. If Bob felt guilty about the cause of Joanie's discomfort at the hair salon, it was Anne's precocious grasp of her parents' marital discord that completely gutted him. His bright, perceptive daughter, who understood far more than she ought to, was not censuring him for his bad behavior but was instead trying to help him, and Bob both appreciated her advice and felt physically ill when he considered that she was only twelve years old.

But now Anne was an adult, too, and Bob was in no mood to accommodate her calculating mind. If his daughter wanted to know how he could be both hungry from lunch and unwilling to eat his dinner, here's how: he'd hardly slept the night before, and he missed his wife. After Bob had insisted that Anne make up his new double bed with a set of queen-size sheets from Chestnut Street, the extra fabric had caught at his legs all night long, keeping him just this side of REM, but at least the sheets had smelled like home. Bob pressed his head between his hands and squeezed. In the hour since their spat at the dinner table, Anne had not come back downstairs, and Bob feared he owed her an apology. Yes, he had been petulant—he could hear Joanie telling him he knew perfectly well how to make a sandwich—and yes, when left alone at the dinner table like a recalcitrant child, he had in fact cleaned his plate, but Anne could hardly expect him to run upstairs and check on her as though she were still ten years old. Bob and Anne hadn't lived in the same house since she'd graduated from high school and he wasn't sure he could bear the arrangement again.

Outside in the backyard, a white picket fence separated the lots to either side of Hugh and Anne's house. There had been a time when Bob could name nearly every family in every home in the village: the

Olsens would've been Hugh and Anne's neighbors to the left, the Jankowskis in the perpendicular house on Beaver Street, and the Beckers directly behind them on Pioneer. Now the best he could do was identify a place by what it had once been. Gone were three hardware stores, two barbershops, a shoe repair, a butcher, and a furniture store on Main Street, replaced by baseball-card outlets and souvenir shops for the growing number of tourists who found their way to the village every year.

At the age of eighty-six, Bob was straddling two worlds, and occasionally he seemed to slip into the gulf between them. Last fall, at the intersection of Pioneer and Main Streets, he'd been on his way to the post office when he'd got to thinking about a fire in the late sixties that had burned down three businesses across from the entrance to Doubleday Field—the Tower of Pizza, the Pic 'n Pay, and one other, right in between. What was the name of that place? They'd sold high-end women's clothing, lingerie in back, and as Bob pictured white tissue paper in delicate cardboard boxes, he'd failed to notice his car bearing left instead of right—following his train of thought toward upper Main Street. He hit the brakes too late, plowing into a streetlight and barely missing Brenda Corrington's granddaughter on her lunch break from Church & Scott.

After that, Bob had known what was coming. Not a humorless trip to the body shop but an end to Bob's days on the road. He and Joanie had reached the agreement the way they'd settled so many things between them over the years: in the context of another conversation altogether. Joanie had insisted that her Toyota was acting funny, then asked if she could borrow Bob's car, and even as he'd known that the keys wouldn't be coming back to him, he'd unclasped his silver ring—a retirement gift from Charlie Stanwood—and told Joanie not to adjust the mirrors; he had them exactly the way he wanted them.

Now Joanie was gone and their Buick was sold and their house was on the market. There weren't many towns where the death of one resident could downshift the overall head count, but last Bob had checked, the population of Cooperstown was hovering around two thousand, with more people leaving than coming, and the new ones that did arrive—like his son-in-law—were frighteningly enthusiastic about the place. They acted like they'd discovered Shangri-La, like there were no other small towns left on earth, like there could be no problems in a village with only one stoplight. But Cooperstown had had its share of problems, just like anywhere else.

Bob could've turned on a light or the television, but right now he welcomed the dark and the silence. He marveled at Anne and Hugh's enormous den, the four-hundred-square-foot addition to the back of the house that Hugh had commissioned when they'd moved in a decade ago. French doors, exposed crossbeams, recessed lightbulbs that must require an extension ladder to change. Anne's single touch had been an entire wall of books, floor-to-ceiling shelves with a sliding library ladder that crossed in front of the French doors and carried a curious reader wall to wall and up to the highest shelf. A gable window let in additional light above the shelves, and Bob scanned the volumes from a distance, wondering what he would find.

Hands down, the biggest scandal in Bob's lifetime had been the publication of a paperback novel in 1962. The first he'd heard of *The Sex Cure* had been at a lawn party at Stan and Betsy Cavett's house on Glimmerglen Road, on a Saturday evening in early September, the weather already starting to change. An autumnal breeze stirred the grass at their feet as the sun dropped behind the hills to the west. Joanie hadn't yet begun to dress for the cooler nights but when Bob offered her his sport coat, she said she'd rather go inside.

Bob liked the Cavetts better than Joanie did, and earlier in the evening they'd had a row about whether to come to the party. Bob and Joanie weren't members of the country club and had seldom run with anyone from the Cavetts' set, but at the vet club's annual Christmas dinner last year, Bob had been introduced to Stan Cavett, an ER resident at the hospital, and they'd gotten along well. The son of a

Catholic dockworker, Stan had graduated from the same state college as Bob, then worked his way through medical school before marrying Betsy Heath. Now he golfed with a high handicap, swam with a life preserver, played poker rather than bridge, and everyone seemed to like him all the more for it.

Stan had reached out to Bob many times that summer, inviting him to Sportsman's Tavern for a drink after work or to dinner at the Otesaga hotel. They'd golfed together on the Leatherstocking course, and Stan had toured Bob around the lake in his new pontoon boat. If they docked at the country club for a few cocktails afterward, what was the harm? Stan was inclusive, generous, and all his friends were potential customers for Bob's insurance agency.

Typically Bob stopped his memory of that night right here, with his second gin and tonic in hand, pleasantly light-headed but not at all drunk, Betsy Cavett in her fuchsia cardigan and black silk pedal pushers making her way toward him across the neatly mowed lawn. But tonight, alone in his daughter's den with nobody to see him and no partygoers left, Bob risked a look, straining for what was past Betsy's lovely blond bob: a group of guests gathering around Tom Halloway near the bar.

Bob had played golf with Tom two or three times that summer and remembered him for his remarkably deep voice and the impressive Plymouth Fury he drove, but they weren't friends. Tom worked at a bank in New York, returning to Cooperstown only for the weekends; Bob had been to New York only twice, once for business and once with Joanie on their honeymoon.

Bob took a sip of his gin and tonic, swirled the ice, then sipped again. Slowly, casually, he made his way across the lawn to join Tom's circle, positioning himself at the outer edge of the group, then asking the woman next to him, who looked to be in her early forties— Joanie's age—what he'd missed.

"Tom's going to do a read-aloud," she said, rolling her eyes.

If there was one thing Bob had learned that summer it was that every party needed a spectacle, a story to be repeated and relived in the coming days, a mythmaking stunt to keep the memory of it alive through the long workweek to the next weekend. The time Archie Wheeler had driven his Cadillac straight across Paul King's front lawn, knocking over the stone wall Paul's grandfather had built. The time Millie Foster had slapped Ruth Potter for using Walt Foster's necktie as a band for her hair. Joanie could nurse one martini all night, her lemon twist growing soggy in a pool of melted ice and gin, but Bob didn't mind throwing back a few, letting go, and he figured that's what was happening now, some new kind of alcohol-induced silliness for which Tom Halloway would be razzed on the tennis court in the morning.

"They were all at the bar by nightfall," Tom began, and everyone turned to their neighbors and smiled indulgently with raised eyebrows: this was a first, even for Tom.

"They were all at the bar by nightfall," he repeated, then, *"the Art Peevers and the John Logans and the Ted Halloways, Ridgefield Corners' gay young marrieds."*

"Uh-oh," said Helen Logan good-naturedly, elbowing Jack.

Bob felt warm bodies press against his back as both men and women—husbands and wives—gravitated toward the book. Tom signaled for silence and a hush whispered through the group, then he picked up where he'd left off. The setting: Harry Kyle's tavern, where apparently none of the characters had paid their chit.

Bob thought of his own account with Harry Kaye, owner of Sportsman's Tavern, where Bob had run up quite a tab with Stan that summer. *John Logan, Harry Kyle, Ted Halloway*—the names in Tom's book were slightly off but also completely familiar. It was disorienting, surreal, like listening to Anne read from a page of her nonsensical Mad Libs.

"Tom," said Jack Logan. "What is this?" But it was still a joke just then and the sound of their collective laughter floated up into the powder-blue sky.

Tom flipped forward a few pages. *"In Stu's bed,"* he read, pausing. "Doctor Stu Everett," he clarified, staring at Stan Cavett, MD.

No one moved, least of all Elva Hanson, Stan's mistress, who was standing near a tiki torch with her ginger hair aflame in light. Everyone at the cocktail party—save, perhaps, Joanie—already knew about Stan's affair with Elva, but they certainly hadn't imagined they'd see it printed in a book. Was it possible? In Stu's bed, who? Not Stan's wife, Betsy, but *"Olivia,"* Tom announced, and just as Bob's eyes darted over to gauge Elva's reaction, she melted away from the light.

"Tom," said his wife sharply, slipping into the center of the circle that was now completely silent. She reached for the book but he held it away from her, tilting it to catch the light off the tiki torches arranged near the bar. "It's too much," said Audrey, but Tom showed no sign of stopping.

"Why, Doctor," he said, but before Tom could continue, Stan barreled into the circle and shoved him back into the bar, rattling the glasses and tipping a bottle of liquor into the thirsty grass.

Audrey finally got hold of her husband's party prop and shook it, and if anybody expected a cocktail-napkin script to fall out from between the pages, Tom's idea of a joke, they were sorely disappointed.

"We're all in it," said Tom, jerking away from Stan and straightening his blazer. "They're selling copies on Main Street, if you don't believe me. Read it for yourselves."

All at once everyone pressed in toward Stan and Tom so that without moving Bob was again standing outside the group. He spotted Betsy Cavett halfway across the lawn, in a huddle with two other women, and he was momentarily grateful that she hadn't sought comfort from him. Bob's mind felt fuzzy, as though he'd consumed several more than his two gin and tonics. He wondered what time it was and if it was too early to go home.

Stan emerged victorious from the fray and waved the book over his head. The thirty or so guests that had also been clamoring for it sighed back into the audience.

"Elaine Dorian," Stan said, reading the author's name off the cover as though he were taking role call. "Elaine Dorian?" He looked around for someone with information, but there were only head-shakes and confused murmurs.

"Tom?" said Stan.

Tom shrugged.

Stan opened the book and scanned a page, then turned to a new page and scanned again. He stopped and read, "'The doctors at the hospital,' Clark Stevens had informed her, 'are all a bunch of horses' asses. When I want a doctor, I'll get my doctors from New York. I just keep that hospital for the peasants.'"

"Are you kidding me?" asked Herb Lindsay, the longtime head of public relations for the hospital.

"Wait," said Tom. "It gets worse."

The ice at the bottom of someone's glass settled, a reminder that their drinks were empty and in need of refilling, but that particular party had ended. The name Clark Stevens was so perilously close to Stephen Clark that, if the author would risk characterizing Mr. Clark—whose family had founded the hospital, the Hall of Fame, and the village library—as a feudalistic lord, there was no telling what else she might say.

Jack Logan grabbed a bottle of whiskey from the bar and tipped it over his glass. Never mind the ice. Never mind the soda. The sun had set, dragging an eraser-pink smudge along the horizon, a last great hope that they might all still forget this day.

As Stan and his friends continued to pore over the book, Bob began to retreat. He was suddenly relieved that Joanie had gone into the house. Whatever was in Tom's book—and from the sound of it, it wasn't good—Joanie didn't need to know about it. His wife had been right: they should've stayed home. Now Bob would go find Joanie in the Cavetts' kitchen or their sitting room and tell her to collect her things, that it was time to go, but just as he started off toward the back porch Joanie came into sharp focus not ten feet away, a borrowed stole draped over her shoulders, her lips turned down in a curious frown.

The next day, Bob spent both the morning and the afternoon catching up on chores. He raked and bagged the first fall leaves, cut and edged the lawn, replaced three broken bricks in the front walk, and was considering tarring the driveway when Joanie returned from running errands. In her hand was a shopping bag from a bookstore in town.

On their way home from the party, Bob had insisted that the book was a hoax, Tom mugging for an audience, but Joanie's willingness to be placated had apparently evaporated: she was meeting this potential mortification head-on. It occurred to Bob that she suspected him of playing a role in the story. Even as the thought nibbled at Bob's mind that such a thing was, in fact, possible, he was already pushing it away.

Bob could barely swallow his throat was so dry but he resisted the urge to follow Joanie. He assumed she'd eventually call him for lunch, then dinner, but when the sun set after seven o'clock, neither Anne nor Joanie had come for him, and Bob realized with a growing sense of dread that he and his wife had not actually spoken that day. He finally went inside, exhausted, hungry, with dirt smudged on his khakis and oil staining his hands. He left his Top-Siders in the mudroom, then padded sockless across the linoleum to the kitchen.

Bob found Joanie and Anne together at the breakfast table, Joanie with her new copy of *The Sex Cure*, Anne nursing a tall glass of milk, each of them nibbling a cookie.

"You already ate," said Bob, noting the dirty dishes in the sink.

"There are leftovers in the fridge," said Joanie. "I figured you would've come in if you were hungry."

Bob turned the bar of soap over in his hands, watching it blacken. He scrubbed his fingers, his wrists, his forearms, then ran his arms under hot water and began the process again.

"Anne," said Bob without looking up. "Go watch TV."

Reluctantly, Anne went to the den, but there was no sound from the television set and Bob knew his daughter was probably eavesdropping.

Bob shut off the water and dried his hands, then looped the towel around his fist as though he were preparing for a fight.

We're all in it, Tom had said, and Bob thought of the stole he'd removed from Joanie's shoulders last night before they'd left the party, red fox and scented with Betsy's perfume.

"You bought it," he said finally, nodding toward *The Sex Cure*.

"One of the last copies," said Joanie.

"Really?" asked Bob, wishing he'd never met Stan and Betsy Cavett. He'd always been happy to go with secretaries in Oneonta or salesgirls he met after work on Water Street. If he worked late, stayed over at Charlie Stanwood's house near the office, kept a change of clothes in his desk drawer, what could Joanie really know?

Since he was a little boy—long before he'd taken Maud Corley up to his father's hayloft—Bob had loved women. His mother, who'd pinched her cheeks in wintertime to bring out a flush in her pale skin; his teacher, Miss Gray, whose skirt had been just that much shorter in front; his cousin Sophie, from Buffalo, who'd pushed him into the tall grass during a walk in the back meadow when Bob was seven: his first kiss. Now, at the age of fifty-five, Bob still marveled at their endless varieties: the ones with the full lips and button noses; the leggy brunettes with no bosoms to speak of; the black-haired beauties whose grandmothers had been part Mexican or full Iroquois; their eager or hesitant kisses; their salty or sharp tastes; the looks in their eyes when it was over, because Bob was always clear on this point: he had a wife.

But Bob and Joanie had never talked openly about his affairs; their marriage was a dance, a measure of closeness and distance, and when Bob sensed that he'd strayed too far, that Joanie was in turn pulling away, he would come bounding back with gifts of handpicked wildflowers or broken arrowheads from a field, visibly repentant if also unreformed. Now he'd let this get too close to home, and it seemed to have ignited a combative instinct in Joanie. She sat with her legs crossed knee over thigh, her forearms resting easily on the table, her right hand thumbing the pages of *The Sex Cure* as though she were testing the tension of a bowstring.

Bob's nerves were starting to fray. He wanted to ask Joanie if he was in the book—just get it over with—but that would suppose there was reason to think he might be. And so he started to assume he wasn't, but then, what if he was? Bob couldn't ask for forgiveness without admitting guilt, and he couldn't presume innocence when he and Betsy Cavett had been going together since July, and with a dawning sense of fear, Bob realized that Joanie had already moved into checkmate.

His attempt to minimize the book last night, his decision to flee the party, his willingness to do his chores today when normally he had to be asked three or four times—these had all been tacit admissions of guilt. Now, whether his name was on the page or not, it was too late.

"Joanie," he said.

"Yes?"

He glanced at the book on the table and Joanie tapped it with her index finger.

"This?" she asked.

Who was this woman, his wife of twenty-two years?

"Yes," he said, and his voice sounded frightened, and he realized that he was.

The author had used a pseudonym, Joanie told him, though Bob wasn't asking about the author. It'd taken Joanie all of three seconds to deduce that "Elaine Dorian" was Isabel Moore, the forty-something writer from New York City who'd recently rented the house at the corner of Lake Street and Hoffman Lane. Bob was positive he'd never laid eyes on any Isabel Moore but Joanie said, "Oh, sure, you'd recognize her." In fact, Mrs. Moore had been spotted that very afternoon at Danny's Market, doing her shopping without a care in the world.

"It's all anyone can talk about," said Joanie. In hushed voices and shocked whispers, at the First National bank and at the A&P, written covertly inside checkbook registers and on the backs of grocery-store receipts: cast lists were quietly being drawn up and filled in with real-life names.

Bob felt light-headed; he needed to sit down, but Joanie hadn't offered him a seat at the table, hadn't offered him lunch or dinner, had instead polished off the last cookie on the plate. Was this what it would be like? Bob thought of twenty-seven-year-old Charlie Stanwood's bachelor pad, the mismatched furniture, the cupboards with only three cups and two plates, the sharp smell of Pine-Sol that Charlie's cleaning lady left behind. Bob didn't want a divorce. He didn't want Betsy Cavett. At that moment, he never wanted another woman in his life besides Joanie.

"It's all spelled out," said Joanie. "Like *Peyton Place*."

Joanie had devoured the Gilmanton, New Hampshire, scandal six years before, while Bob had been appalled that anyone would write such a thing. Now it seemed Cooperstown was having its moment, and Bob realized with a jolt that if he were in the book, he would have to leave town. It would be too much to be talked about incessantly, to be looked at askance; even standing here in his own kitchen guessing at what Joanie was thinking was making him sick.

"Is it that obvious?" asked Bob. "The who's who?"

"You certainly don't need much of a road map," said Joanie. Then, "You should read it." She slid the book across the table and waited for Bob to pick it up. "Just make sure to give it back when you're done."

He considered refusing—if Joanie had found something in the book that she wanted him to see, she could go ahead and tell him— but Anne was lurking only a few feet away on the other side of the wall, listening to every word Bob and Joanie said. He couldn't bear to have his infidelities cataloged aloud for his daughter. So he took the book and, without meeting Joanie's eyes, told her he would read it.

* * *

That night Bob remained downstairs long after Joanie and Anne had gone to bed. At first Anne wouldn't stop pestering him about the novel—was it any good? Did he know anybody in it?—but Bob told her to mind her own business and finally she went upstairs.

The Sex Cure opened with the local rumor mill churning over the news that a young woman had been brought into the hospital, hemorrhaging from a botched abortion and naming Justin Riley, Ridgefield Corners' favorite playboy surgeon, as the father. Stu Everett, OB resident extraordinaire, would have to operate to save the girl's life. The questions remained: Would the young girl live, would the playboy surgeon be run out of town, and would Stu finally marry his longtime mistress, Olivia Riley, giving their biological son his legitimate name?

Bob quickly turned the pages, his heart rate vaulting over every capital R, B, or C, then steadying when these letters turned out not to be the beginning of his own name. Bob had spent the summer with Stan and Betsy Cavett, Preston and Elva Hanson. He'd let them sign for his drinks and tour him around in their cars. He hadn't initially understood when Stan mentioned that Bob would hit it off with his wife, Betsy, but it was Betsy who'd initiated the affair, and it'd quickly become clear that Stan and Elva were going together on the side, as well.

Now here they all were: Olivia Riley and a spouseless Stu Everett and fifteen other people whose names were only slightly tweaked if at all. Bob's neighbors, acquaintances, people who lived right here in town. Marlene Poynter, who ran the Community Chest raffle with Joanie every Thanksgiving, had been cast as a gossip, a floozy, and a drunk. Bob's own name never graced the pages, thank God, and although he was weak with gratitude that publicly, at least, he had dodged the bullet, privately he knew Joanie was nowhere near finished with him.

A white-hot knot of anger formed in his stomach and spread through his chest to his hands: it wasn't right—Isabel Moore had no right. A book like this could ruin people's lives, their marriages. Botched abortions, rapes, scandalous affairs—if the author had begun her story with grains of truth, she'd ended up with such a gross misrepresentation of life in Cooperstown that Bob couldn't see Cooperstown in it.

When he finally went up to bed at a quarter after three he was only mildly surprised to discover Joanie awake and ready to chat, and Bob quickly found himself on the losing side of a moral debate.

"It's not like they didn't know what they were doing," said Joanie. Her position seemed to be that if the storied affairs were true to life, then the heels had gotten their just deserts.

"Maybe," Bob hedged, "but what gives the author the right to splash people's private affairs all over town?"

"It's a cautionary tale," said Joanie pointedly. "If this is happening in some houses, you can bet it's happening all over."

"It's not happening anywhere," said Bob desperately.

"I'm sure that's not true," said Joanie. Then, "You should hear the gossip."

Gossip hardly began to describe the furor that erupted over *The Sex Cure* as Anne began her eighth-grade school year, and Bob and Joanie were completely at odds as to how to handle the matter when it came to their daughter. Bob forbade Anne to read the book, but Joanie left her copy unattended throughout the house. He assured his daughter that the author would soon be brought up on charges, while Joanie took to scrapbooking—clipping and saving every *Sex Cure*-related article that the local press put out. No matter how irritated Bob grew with Joanie's campaign to promote the book, there seemed to be nothing he could do to stop her. If he denounced Isabel

Moore for writing it, Joanie accused him of defending the characters'
behavior; if he denounced the characters' behavior, Bob was effec-
tively condemning himself. In Joanie's hands, the novel had become
an instrument of torture that left Bob never wanting to have another
affair in his life.

It wasn't until the last week in September that Bob finally heard
from Stan Cavett. They hadn't spoken since the lawn party—Bob had
thought of calling Stan, but the talk on Main Street had been so
damning he'd decided to keep to himself. Bob told his secretary to
put the call through, then closed his office door.

"Stan," said Bob.

Stan sighed irritably. "Did you hear Preston's taking a sabbatical
from the hospital? Not entirely his idea, of course, but with everything going on it can't be helped. He and Elva and the kids are already
making plans to spend the year with her family in Baltimore."

"That's terrible," said Bob.

"Meanwhile, I'm paying our housekeeper a king's ransom to stay
on seven days a week and overnight. She does the shopping, takes the
kids to and from school—Betsy won't leave the house."

Bob wondered if Stan expected him to ask after Betsy. The last
time they'd been together was at a country-club dance in late August,
when Bob abandoned Joanie during the twist to lead Betsy to the
seventeenth hole on the golf course overlooking Blackbird Bay. Now
Bob couldn't believe he'd gotten caught up with all that. Never in
his life would Bob share Joanie with another man, although he wondered if in some way his hypocrisy made him an even worse husband
than Stan.

"It'll blow over," said Bob.

"I guess," said Stan. "No one in New York seems to know about
it yet. Maybe Betsy and the kids can go there for a while. You can't
imagine it," said Stan, "opening a book and seeing your own name
written there. You know the author is John Moffat's mother-in-law?
What was he thinking?"

"I'm sure he didn't know," said Bob, who had never exchanged a word with the man, owner of Cooperstown Stables, the thoroughbred-horse farm on Beaver Meadow Road. Bob didn't jump horses or play bridge at the country club or keep an apartment in Manhattan or any of the other highfalutin things Stan and his friends did, which was no doubt why Bob had been spared. He wasn't rich enough; he wasn't an interesting character. No one in town cared what Bob got up to—except his wife.

"Well, he should've known," said Stan, and Bob agreed that a man in his own house ought to have a measure of control. Stan sounded defeated and Bob wanted to offer him some comfort, so he asked if there was anything he could do.

"Actually," said Stan, and it seemed to Bob that, with that one word, what Stan had really said was *I've done a lot for you.* "Tom and I can barely show our faces in town without starting the talk all over again, but no one's watching you," said Stan.

Bob thought of Maud Corley's father, who had sabotaged his father's livelihood in retribution for Bob's imprudent night with Maud—his father hadn't done a thing to fight the cooperative's decision; he'd simply accepted that he was out and tried to make do with what he had left, which was next to nothing in a few years' time. Bob fundamentally believed that Stan and Tom had a right to avenge themselves, and, frankly, Bob, who felt as if he were on probation himself, was also eager to get even.

So when Stan asked him to buy a few cans of spray paint and a small can of kerosene, Bob agreed and didn't ask what else this plan might entail. He went to a hardware store in Oneonta, where he wouldn't be recognized, and took his time selecting the paint, finally settling on the brightest, the most stigmatic, the most enduring color and type he could find: three cans of Kerpro automobile paint in cherry red.

At home, Bob ducked into his shed and was hastily arranging the paint cans on a low shelf above his worktable when Anne suddenly walked in.

"What's that for?" she asked, a stack of library books in her arms.

"Nothing," said Bob. Thankfully, the kerosene was still hidden in its paper bag.

"Are you painting the Buick?"

"No." But his cheeks were beginning to roast.

"That's automobile paint," Anne pointed out, reading the label. They regarded each other for a moment and finally Anne shrugged and said, "Maybe you can return it."

For her part, Joanie continued to report on every new tidbit of the unfolding scandal: the thrice-divorced author had gone to Barnard, or maybe Columbia; had an apartment in Yorkville, or was it Holly-wood; and counted as her friends Cary Grant and even the late Marilyn Monroe. After church one morning, Bob lost his temper and slammed her scrapbook into the garbage can, but Joanie just waited until he'd stormed upstairs to retrieve the volume and brushed it off.

Then one Saturday in the car on the way to a high school football game, Joanie announced right in front of Anne that Isabel Moore was working on a sequel about how a small town persecutes an author.

"That's enough," said Bob, anger pressing vertiginously behind his eyes so that all he could see were his hands clutching the steering wheel.

"I agree," said Joanie. "It's just that she has so much material in town to work with, I guess she feels there's enough for another book."

"Another?" asked Anne from the backseat. "I read it, and I don't think she should've been allowed to write the first one."

Bob braked in the middle of Walnut Street and turned around to face his daughter. "What do you mean, you read it?" he asked.

Anne shrank toward Joanie's side of the car. "Mom said I could."

"Joanie," said Bob, turning his gaze on his wife. "We talked about this."

"You talked about it," said Joanie evenly, and suddenly Bob felt as if he had two teenage daughters. Without hesitation, he grabbed Joanie's upper arm and when Joanie tried to twist away, Bob held on.

"You're hurting me," said Joanie, but Bob wouldn't let go.

When another car pulled up behind them, Bob reached through the open window with his free hand to wave the driver by. He let go of Joanie's arm only as the car passed, but he could still feel the strain of the grip in his fingers, his digits ghosting the shape of his wife's arm.

"This can't go on," said Bob.

"It can," said Joanie, meaning, Bob supposed, that she had found a weapon, a tool to curtail his behavior, and if Bob thought she would easily relinquish it, he was wrong.

Joanie pressed herself against her window, cradling her left arm in her right hand, tears starting to fall, and Bob considered opening his car door and simply walking away. There seemed to be nothing he could say now except that he was sorry, and he was sorry, but he didn't say it.

Bob looked in the rearview mirror and caught Anne's eye. "You're not to read that book again," he said. "Do you understand?"

"Yes."

"And there's not going to be another book," said Bob. "People have had enough. Pretty soon, someone's going to take care of her."

Anne's face appeared at his elbow. "Take care of her how?" she asked.

"Good grief," said Bob. He hadn't heard from Stan in nearly three weeks; for all he knew there was no plan. "Run her out of here!" he said.

"Can you just run someone out of town?" asked Anne.

Bob shrugged. Right now he felt capable of anything.

* * *

On October 21, Bob was finally summoned to Tom Halloway's hunting cabin, twelve miles outside town. As the only one of the three men

to have served during wartime, Tom appointed himself general and
doled out orders, first to Bob, whose job it would be to phone the
village police department and warn them that "something" was going
to happen to Isabel Moore.

"Why would I do that?" asked Bob incredulously.

"Maybe she'll take a hint and leave on her own," said Tom.
"Think of this as the diplomacy phase."

So the next evening at his office, as soon as Charlie had gone,
Bob pulled the phone under his desk and wrapped his handkerchief
over the mouthpiece. He felt like a patsy for accepting an assignment
Tom could easily have done himself, but when the time came for
phase two—which would apparently involve kerosene—it might be
useful to have already taken a turn.

Bob dialed the number that Tom had copied down and asked to
speak to the officer on duty, then nearly hung up twice while waiting
to be put through.

"Go ahead, sir," said the operator.

"Something is going to happen to Mrs. Isabel Moore," Bob read
from Tom's index card.

"What's that?" said the officer.

"Something is going to happen at Twenty-one Lake Street," Bob
continued.

He could almost hear the officer shaking his head. "Do you
know what's going on tonight, buddy? Forget Lake Street," he said.
"Turn on the TV."

* * *

And there it was: from the island of Cuba, Soviet missiles had been
trained on the United States of America, and the nation's attention
shifted utterly to the possibility of full-scale nuclear war. Cast lists
and who's whos on Main Street were abandoned for the terrifying
new vocabulary of Strategic Air Command, B-47s, and DEFCON 2.
As President Kennedy prepared to defend the security of the entire

western hemisphere, Joanie prepared to defend her family with cyanide salts, if it should come to that—better to go quickly than to wait for radioactive fallout—but Bob told her to get rid of them before Anne saw. The two of them hunkered down in front of their television set and tried to keep Anne close, inviting her to sit on the couch or even on Bob's lap if she was scared, but she skittered away, catlike, watching her parents as much as they watched the news. She was almost fourteen; it was only natural for her to withdraw, perhaps, and Bob was too busy contemplating the lunacy of mutual assured destruction to truly worry about Anne's teenage mood swings.

From the night of the president's address to the morning of Khrushchev's promise to remove all Soviet missiles from Cuba, less than six days would pass, but to Bob it would feel like a lifetime. After his ridiculous phone call to the police, he stayed home from work; then he and Joanie pulled Anne out of school, too, where she was being drilled hourly in the futile exercise of ducking under her wooden desk and covering her head with her bony arms. At night Bob tucked in his daughter, then watched his wife sleep with his hands folded in constant prayer: that Khrushchev would come to his senses; that the man with the jug ears and balding head of a doddering grandfather would be reasonable; that when Bob awoke from this nightmare he would be forgiven, and he would do better next time.

At the end of October Khrushchev blinked, and Bob's relief was palpable. He breathed easier, slept better, woke early to do squat thrusts and lunges in the backyard. He greeted neighbors with hugs instead of handshakes, and he was extremely affectionate with his wife. They were alive, and life in America would indeed return to normal, just in time for Halloween.

Anne had never been one for costumes or trick-or-treating and predictably planned to hole up in her room, but this year especially Bob felt like celebrating. He went all out with scarecrows on the front lawn and jack-o'-lanterns on the porch. He bought a witch's hat for Joanie and a pair of plastic fangs for himself. To punctuate the end of the Soviet Union's threat of world domination, Bob and Joanie would hand out homemade popcorn balls to an endless stream of cowboys and hoboes in their tidy front yard.

Bob hadn't thought about Stan Cavett or Tom Halloway in nearly ten days when he opened the newspaper the next morning and noticed a short wire item at the bottom of page three:

Local Author's Home Vandalized

State and local authorities are searching for clues in a vandalism attack at 21 Lake Street, on the home of Mrs. Isabel Moore. Village police discovered the offense after midnight. The culprits used red paint to spray obscenities on all four sides of the large white frame house.

Mrs. Moore is the author of *The Sex Cure*, which deals with Cooperstown. She told reporters she had been warned something might occur and was staying with relatives overnight.

Joanie sat at the kitchen table directly across from Bob, with only a bowl of strawberry preserves and the salt and pepper shakers between them. He glanced up and she glanced up, then smiled.

"Anything interesting?" she asked.

In the last two weeks they'd held each other through the night, whispered kindnesses to each other in the dark, and neither of them had mentioned what Bob had done to Joanie in the car.

"Nothing interesting," said Bob. He returned his eyes to the newspaper. In the next few hours he would memorize this item, but right now the words swam away on the page. He couldn't imagine eating another bite of scrambled eggs. "I should get going," he said. He folded the paper and slipped it into his briefcase, then kissed the cheek that Joanie offered him, first pushing back a curl of his wife's silky hair.

In the driveway, Bob set his briefcase and overcoat in the passenger's seat of his Buick, then crossed the backyard to the shed. It was locked. No broken windows, no apparent tampering. He glanced back at the house, then stood on his tiptoes and peered through the window closest to his worktable—there was the spray paint he'd bought on Market Street in Oneonta, right on the shelf where he'd left it, and Bob swayed with relief to know that the vandalism attack wouldn't be tied to him.

But by the time Bob got to work he'd already missed a call from Stan Cavett, and he was debating whether to return it when Stan phoned again. Bob felt he had no choice but to take it.

"Jesus Christ," Stan whispered into the receiver.

"Where are you?" asked Bob.

"Where do you think? Home with Betsy and the kids. We've got the entire Channel 4 News team on our lawn. The AP, the goddamn *New York Times*. Are you out of your mind?"

"I didn't do it!" said Bob. "Tom never even told me the next step in the goddamn plan."

"Fuck the plan," said Stan. "You bought the paint, you made the threat. Whether you did it or not, they're going to be looking for you."

"Stan," said Bob, "I had nothing to do with this. There are half a dozen places to buy red paint in town, and I checked my supply this morning—it's all there."

"Good luck with that story," said Stan. "I heard from one of the reporters that they found a paint can in the bushes and they're sending it to Albany for fingerprints. This was completely dead in the water before you pulled this stunt," said Stan. "So fuck you." And he hung up the phone.

Bob held the receiver in his hand, the sound of the dial tone washed out by the deafening noise in his own head. His mind was reeling—had his entire paint supply been there? Because Stan was right: no adult in his right mind would risk reigniting the scandal now that it was basically forgotten.

No adult.

Bob felt feverish and he didn't object when his secretary sent him home. Joanie put him straight to bed, and he waited until he heard her car pulling out of the driveway—to Church & Scott for aspirin and ginger ale—before he bolted to the utility room for the keys to his shed. Now Bob wished to God he had returned the spray paint, but dozens of kids would have been out roaming the town on Halloween, and any one of them might've done this to the author's house—there was no reason to suppose it had been his daughter—and just as Bob had convinced himself that he was being paranoid, he let himself into his shed and there, between the Turtle Wax and an old thermos bottle, were exactly two cans of Kerpro enamel paint in cherry red.

When Anne came home from school that afternoon, Bob met her at the kitchen door.

"Are you sick?" she asked.

"No," said Bob.

Anne kicked off her saddle shoes and set her schoolbooks on the bench in the mudroom. "Why are you in your robe?"

"Do you have something you want to tell me?" asked Bob.

Anne wide-eyed him, the portrait of innocence, her black bangs cut ruler-straight across her forehead, her kilt neatly safety-pinned at her knee. Bob raised his hand to her, thinking a slap across the face was the least she deserved, then froze when he noticed her socks: one standing at attention, the other slouching wearily around her calf, completely worn out. Suddenly, whatever the truth was, Bob didn't want to know it. If his daughter had done this, Bob alone was responsible. He told her he wasn't feeling well after all, then went straight to bed, sick with the knowledge that he'd dragged his family into such an abyss.

By the next morning, the vandalism story was in every newspaper in Otsego County and the Mohawk Valley. By Monday, the *New York Times* and the *New York Mirror* had published their own versions of events. A Utica paper ran a four-part series introducing the world to the woman behind the author and the *sick town* that *loved to hate.* As for the investigation, the chief of police announced that they were looking for three or possibly four adults who had spray-painted obscenities on the author's house: letters twelve to fifteen inches in height and ranging from two to six feet above the ground. The police chief dismissed the idea that the vandals could've been kids acting out on Halloween. "The job was too perfect for teenagers to do," he was quoted as saying, and Bob thought, You don't know Anne.

Just as Stan had said, the investigation hinged on the paint: the police had recovered one can of red automobile paint from the bushes next to the author's house, and they'd sent it to the state-police crime lab for fingerprint analysis. Apparently the brand Kerpro wasn't sold in local stores. Bob's prints were all over that can—as, he suspected, were his daughter's—and his only comfort as he waited to hear if he'd be caught was the knowledge that he could protect Anne if it came to that. All signs pointed to Bob, anyway, and he would never let her take the fall.

Isabel Moore told reporters that her novel sounded like Cooperstown and it was supposed to, "a Glimmerglass version of *Peyton Place*." Beacon Signal rushed *The Sex Cure* into a second printing, and a sign went up in one bookstore on Main Street saying, WE HAVE NOT SOLD NOR DO WE INTEND TO SELL *THE SEX CURE*, while another store, just down the block, continued to peddle it with a wait list 350 readers deep. When a construction crew appeared at the author's house on Lake Street—whitewashing over messages like GO HOME BITCH and the stranger, more childish GET OUT SEX URGE—Joanie asked if anyone wanted to drive over and see the crime scene, and both Bob and Anne shook their heads.

Preston and Elva Hanson left town. Betsy Cavett took the kids out of school, and Joanie told Bob she'd heard they were staying with Tom and Audrey Halloway down in the city. Bob recommenced his late nights at the office, more to avoid Joanie's *Sex Cure*–related updates than to meet a particular person for a drink—but really he was waiting, waiting for the phone call from the Bureau of Criminal

Investigations in Albany, waiting to hear that they had traced the
threat against Isabel Moore to his insurance agency, waiting for the
police to discover the two remaining cans of Kerpro that Bob had
thrown in a dumpster behind the diner in Milford, halfway between
Oneonta and Cooperstown.

When word filtered through the rumor mill that the police
department was discontinuing its search, that there were too many
fingerprints on the paint can—including several from the police
themselves—Bob finally slept through the night. It was over; they
could go back to the way things had been before Bob had even heard
of Stan Cavett. But they didn't go back, they couldn't, because the
balance of power in Bob's home had shifted absolutely. Anne kept to
herself now, and no amount of courting could bring her back. If Bob
offered to treat her to dinner at Sportsman's Tavern or the Tunnicliff
Inn, the way he used to, she suddenly had homework to finish or TV
programs she couldn't miss; if he suggested an afternoon at the rink
behind Cooper Inn, she said she was too old for ice-skating, then Bob
would find her white skates hanging by their laces in the mudroom,
slushy water dripping from their blades.

One Saturday afternoon soon after Anne turned fourteen, Bob
walked down to Main Street for lunch at Withey's and discovered her
alone at the counter, a vanilla Coke in front of her. He paused outside
the drugstore, watching his daughter through the plate-glass window: she wore a white button-down shirt tucked into a pleated plaid
skirt, and he wondered if she was waiting for someone—a friend, a
boyfriend—but she'd already ordered, and the kids horsing around
on nearby stools didn't seem to notice her. They'd barely spoken in
the last few months, and Bob had missed her deeply. He pulled open
the door and called out her name, and Anne glanced up, looked
straight at him, and ever so faintly shook her head.

His dynamic with Joanie, too, had changed. From time to time,
when Joanie noticed he was staying late at work or had made Saturday
plans with Charlie, she would pull the novel off her bookshelf and

read a chapter or two before bed, and Bob would break off whatever insignificant dalliance he'd been involved in and return to his wife. Nearly a year after the vandalism attack, Bob had taken Joanie to Philadelphia for their anniversary and she spotted a tabloid at the newsstand with the headline THE SCANDALOUS NEW SEX NOVEL THAT SHOOK UP COOPERSTOWN, NEW YORK!! She bought a copy for her scrapbook but didn't read it, at least not in front of Bob.

At some point, though, Joanie had finally gotten rid of *The Sex Cure*—Bob hadn't seen it for twenty years at least—and, truthfully, he'd always wondered if Anne had taken it. Certainly his daughter had never forgiven him for that time in her life, and it would be just like Anne to harbor the one concrete piece of evidence of her parents' marital turmoil.

Bob scooted his chair back from the dinner table and stood, holding the squared edge for support, then made his way over to his daughter's wall of books. He leaned against the corduroy couch and, in the dim moonlight, started with the first volume, running his hand over spine after spine, trying to remember what had happened to all those people, all those years ago. Stan and Betsy Cavett had moved to Chicago before eventually retiring to Florida; Tom Halloway had been killed in a car accident in the early seventies, driving too fast near Cobleskill on his way up to Cooperstown from the city. Bob had lost track of the Hansons, but then, he'd never really known them to begin with, never known any of them, and there had to be a thousand or more books in Anne's library—if *The Sex Cure* was here, it was as good as buried, and Bob had no intention of digging up the past.

5

Tuesday afternoon, I handed Miss Paddy my library detention slip and watched her pore over it like it was a tele-
gram from the front.

"*Misbehavior in the cafeteria,*" she read, winging her
paperback across her generous knee. "Sounds exciting."

Miss Paddy was triangular in shape, with hips the width of a
sedan, teeny narrow shoulders, and hair that peaked in a knotted bun.
We'd given her the slitter *Conehead the Librarian*, but Sam had since
decided she needed a promotional slitter, something she could be
proud of and also talk about on dates. Currently in R&D: *Dewey,
Dewey Dess, Mack Paddy, Miss System,* and *Overdue.*

"It is exciting," I said, leaning in.

Yesterday at lunch, while Carl had been interrogating me about
my grandparents' house—were we selling it? Could we get a lot of
money for it? Was it weird to think of someone else living there?—
Sam had noticed the shelf of tears collecting on my lower lids. "Here,"
he'd said, handing me his gnawed Granny Smith. "If you make it, I'll
muzzle Carl."

So I'd launched Sam's apple over six cafeteria tables to the garbage bins by the exit, missing my mark by fifteen feet. In an instant our lunch monitor was on me, hauling me by the elbow to retrieve the fallen core. After a brief lecture I was allowed to show her how well I could place it in its proper receptacle, and I did such a fine job that she permitted me to do it for every piece of garbage in the cafeteria's busing station.

"What is it with you, Miss Obermeyer?" she'd asked, depositing me back at our table along with a yellow slip for library detention. "Watch her, please," she'd said, and Sam had nodded deeply, his aqua eyes dancing over mine.

"How Edenic," said Miss Paddy. "And I thought I was in the clear today. Guess this means we both have to stay."

"Or we could both leave," I suggested.

She smiled, striping her front teeth with tangerine lipstick. "At least you won't be bored." She gestured toward the shelves and told me to pick a book.

"Actually," I said, unzipping my backpack and producing *The Sex Cure*, which had been in the front pocket since my final trip to Nonz and Poppy's. Sam had spied its faded cover during homeroom—a woman in high heels and a short skirt looking lustily skyward while a young doctor pawed her lacy bra from behind—and said, "Flag the good stuff for me." It was only then that I'd decided to read it.

Miss Paddy whistled appreciatively. "This is rare," she said. "Where'd you get it?"

"It was my grandparents'."

"They were smart to keep it. I read it at the historical society in one sitting."

"Is it any good?" I asked.

Miss Paddy shrugged. "It's historic."

I found a table around the corner from her desk, next to a set of World Book encyclopedias. Every September in the first week of school our English teachers administered aptitude tests on our library skills—dittoed packets requiring numerous trips to the card catalog. We'd grab entire drawers until the cabinet looked like a gap-toothed first-grader, the only recourse being to hunt for the books themselves or, when a teacher wasn't looking, to ask Miss Paddy, who might take pity. I felt sorry for her being stuck in here all day. There were no nooks or beanbag chairs. No windows for daydreaming. Just a theater of laminated posters, fluorescent lights, outdated magazines, and a wall clock that seemed to be frozen at 3:05.

I thought of Sam and Carl driving around in the Badass Scirocco Scirocco without me. I pictured them stopping at Stewart's for snacks, then smoking our OPs on Dead Man's Run, the sledding-hill nunnery behind the courts.

"What're you guys doing after practice?" I'd asked before turning myself in.

"Not sure," said Sam. His car keys clicked against each other in his hand.

"We'll figure it out," said Carl, taking the OPs and leaving me with only a single Camel to smoke on my walk home.

I traced the fresh ballpoint tattoo on my wrist, which was already fading. "Draw something new," I'd told Sam during study hall today, and here it was—a bench: slatted, wooden, like the ones at the tennis courts, or maybe like the ones on the boardwalk at Myrtle Beach; vacant, bare, like someone had just left or maybe like someone was about to arrive.

I opened to the first chapter of *The Sex Cure* and read: *Marge's nakedness was a sliver of earthbound moonlight*. I skipped ahead. I wasn't sure this was what Sam had had in mind. Style-wise, the author had seen too many soaps or something and was high on the art of the recap. Like, okay, we get it: a married doctor financing his girlfriend's illegal abortion is not going to fly with his wife. Porn-wise, the sex scenes were tame enough to be featured on the six o'clock news, and plot-wise, I pretty much had no idea who anyone was.

Still, I was impressed it had been written. An all-out unmasking of everyone in town in 1962, and supposedly the author had lived here. It would've shifted the way people thought about one another, absolutely. To discover that your neighbors weren't really happily married or that your friends were secretly in love with you? I pictured the ground tilting, separating some people while sliding others closer together.

A lot of people had the idea that Sam and I were going out, but we'd never held hands, never kissed. Somehow Megan of Myrtle Beach had, in a single week, bridged a gulf whose existence Sam and I had never even acknowledged. I almost wished I'd been there to see it, not because it wouldn't have killed me—it would've killed me— but because Sam and I were only friends, best friends. We needed to be tilted, and I paged through *The Sex Cure* again, wondering how it could be done.

At four o'clock, Miss Paddy sprang me and I walked home slowly, an OP in hand but without a light. If I'd hurried, I could've caught Sam at the tail end of practice, but if he wanted to see me, he could come to 59 Susquehanna: in *The Sex Cure*, the always-available town drunk was not nearly as appealing as the senator's daughter who waited for everyone to come to her, and I'd decided to channel a little of that in my quest for Sam.

After calling hello to Poppy, I took an apple from the near-empty fruit basket and checked the answering machine. Just my dad saying how crazy it was to be away from school for a week and how he might be home late. Nothing from Sam.

I found Poppy in his recliner with an afghan covering his skinny legs. Already his face was pinker than it'd been two days before, his breathing less raspy. The glass on his end table was empty and I returned to the kitchen to fill it.

"What are you watching?" I asked, handing him his water.

"I don't know," he said.

I used the remote to flip through the channels.

"You go too fast," Poppy complained. "I can't see the programs."

I powered off the TV. "There's nothing on, anyway," I said.

Kneeling at Poppy's feet, I dug into my backpack and produced *The Sex Cure*.

Poppy stared at the cover, his jaw set. "Did your mother give you that?" he asked.

"It's yours," I said. "Mom found it in your bedroom on Chestnut Street."

I watched my grandfather's face drain bone white. "We didn't have it," he said.

I nodded. "Under the mattress." Poppy shook his head slowly, and only then did it occur to me that he might not have known about the book. "Maybe it was Nonz's," I ventured.

"Throw it out," said Poppy now.

"It's rare."

"Get rid of it!"

"What's the big deal?" I asked. And then I had a thought. "Did you and Nonz know people in the book?"

He waved his hand near my face, fanning the book. "We didn't know anybody," he said. Then, quietly, "We knew some people."

"Friends?"

"Yes, friends! That woman had no business writing it."

"Why not?" I asked. "Was any of it true?"

"Absolutely not. There were lawsuits."

"Why, if it was supposed to be fiction?"

"Because you can't go around making up lies about people!" Poppy goggle-eyed me to drive home his point. Which was what? That the book would've been okay if the author had stuck to the truth?

"Did everyone sue?" I asked.

"Not everyone."

"So some of it was right, then? In the book?"

Poppy stared at me. "Why do you ask so many questions? You ask so many questions."

"Sorry," I said. "I'm just curious."

I thought about Sam's two houses, his mom's and his dad's. There was always a moment right before I went inside one of them when it felt like the whole world would disappear behind me—school, my parents, 59 Susquehanna, Teddy—and the only thing left would be Sam.

"Did the book change the way people felt about each other?" I asked.

"Enough," Poppy warned.

"Like when they found out some of the couples weren't really that happy—"

"Julia, stop!"

"And it was possible that they could have whoever they wanted—"

Suddenly Poppy rapped my ear with his knuckles and I froze, eyes closed, focusing on things that also hurt but didn't make me cry. Sam accidentally serving a ball into the back of my head during Canadian doubles. Carl red-bagging me at lunch.

"I asked you to stop," said Poppy. "You don't listen!"

I opened my eyes and saw my grandfather's quivering lips, his eyes fixed somewhere far behind me.

"I'm okay," I said quickly.

He sniffed, waved me away, but I didn't go.

"I'm fine," I told him. I stood. "See?"

Poppy nodded.

I picked up the remote and handed it to him.

"I'm sorry," I said.

Poppy shook his head. He wanted me to go, so I got my backpack and my book and I went.

Upstairs, I crawled into bed and curled on my side. I could feel my pulse behind my ear where Poppy had knocked me, which never would've happened if Nonz were alive. I couldn't understand why he'd done it, and I paged through the book again, wondering if maybe Nonz and Poppy were characters in the story, that I'd somehow missed them, but the novel was about doctors and nurses and senators, not insurance agents and housewives.

After a moment, I fished under my mattress for my journal with the fancy pen clipped to its cover. My entries fell into one of two categories: (1) Panegyrics: n. pl.: lofty orations or writings in praise of a person or thing: e.g., She wrote beautiful, hilarious panegyrics about herself and Sam. (2) Obloquies: n. pl.: censure, blame, or abusive language aimed at people or things: e.g., She delivered beautiful, damning obloquies about her abusive grandfather and her horn-dog brother.

Now I opened to a fresh page and in neat block print wrote, SAM. Then, over the top of it, JULIA. I went back to the beginning and layered on a third sentence: I WANT SAM. The last word stuck out, plain, clear, and I was about to add more when the front doorbell rang. I paused, journal censored with my left hand.

"Poppy?" I called. "Are you getting that?"

Nothing—lazy bastard.

I shoved my journal under the covers and walked to the landing by my parents' bedroom. Through the glass door at the foot of the stairs, I could see a man with his hands stuffed in his pockets, his back turned to the house. He wore jeans, an untucked white polo shirt, and camel work boots—an exterminator, maybe, for the fly outbreak in the basement. It was nearly five thirty; Mom would be home any minute and would off me if I didn't let him in.

I skipped downstairs and opened the door and it was only then that I realized it was Claw in his hardware clothes. His white pickup truck was parked at the curb with a ladder roped to the roof and KLAWSON's HARDWARE painted in black on the passenger's side door.

"Julia," he said. "Hey."

I looked over his shoulder for Sam or Carl but it was just Claw.

"Hey," I said.

"I was on my way to the store and thought I'd stop by for a minute." He paused, shifted, uncomfortable, which, ditto. I reclined against the door, bouncing the knob into the wall. "Can I come in?" he asked.

I figured he was here to bar me from hanging out with the team. I hadn't tried out, and yesterday I'd been caught smoking behind the school bus—it was no big surprise he wanted me gone, but I didn't see why he needed to come to my house to do it.

"I guess," I said.

I stepped aside and Claw squeezed past me, took three steps into the entry hall, and knocked his head against our lantern-shaped light fixture. "Whoops," he said, steadying it.

"Don't worry," I said. "Everyone does that."

Suddenly Poppy called out from the kitchen that he was on his way, just a minute, he'd be right there. "My grandfather," I said, rolling my eyes. Then, "Poppy, I've got it!"

But he didn't stop.

"Poppy!" I yelled again. Last week he'd been living in his own house with his own doorbell, his own visitors at his own front door. Now he was living with us, and even though nothing at 59 Susquehanna was really his, he was acting like it was. "Stop!" I said.

Startled, Poppy paused in the hallway outside Mom's office, blinking. His breathing was labored, his lungs punching out air shallow and fast. I could see in his eyes that he didn't know where he was, and it was only when he lit on me that he seemed to come back to himself.

"Julia," he said.

Claw took a step forward and said gently, "I'm Barry Klawson, the school tennis coach."

"Klawson," Poppy repeated. "Any relation to Harvey Klawson?"

"My grandfather," said Claw.

Poppy nodded, Inspector effing Gadget.

Just then I saw my mother turn into the driveway, and I watched as she hauled her briefcase from the backseat, then folded her jacket over one arm and stepped carefully along the brick walkway to the porch steps. Claw turned to greet her as she opened the front door. He seemed young, nervous, which made me feel younger still.

"Would you like something to drink?" asked Mom, ushering Claw into the living room. Poppy sighed into the puffy couch while Claw perched in one of the wing chairs. I took the ottoman, eye level with Mom's Chinese tray-thing that was always flipping itself on its head.

"No, thanks," said Claw. He checked his Casio. "I'm actually on my way over to the store to meet with Mr. Obermeyer."

"Really?" asked Mom. Then, "Do you know my husband?"

"My nephew goes to Seedlings," said Claw. We waited for him to continue but he only nodded, shifting under Mom's gaze. She glanced at me with raised eyebrows and I shrugged, like what the eff did I know about Dad's hardware needs?

"Anyway," said Claw, "I was about to tell Julia that I have an opportunity for her."

"An opportunity," Poppy parroted.

Claw posted his elbows on his knees and faced me. "I'm arranging an exhibition match for you."

I looked up. "What?"

"On Thursday," he continued.

I shook my head, lost.

"I'm asking Sauquoit to bring an alternate. I want to put you in at singles."

"I don't get it," I said. "Why me?"

"Take it," said Mom before Claw could answer.

I stared at Claw and he stared back. His green eyes were wide, his lips pressed together, his knuckles white, as though he were wringing his hands to death.

"Julia," said Mom, but I didn't take my eyes off Claw.

"What about Carl?" I asked, but Claw just stared at me.

"What about—"

"Julia," said Mom again. I shifted my eyes to my mother and found her mid-grin.

"What?"

She nodded her head toward Claw. "You should play."

"Yes or no," said Claw. "Your choice."

Maybe there was a catch, an equal and opposite drawback to this so-called opportunity, but I didn't look too hard for it. With or without Sam, I could have this match, and tomorrow at practice I would run drills alongside Sam and Carl, teammates but on our own, too.

I nodded. "Okay," I said. "Yes."

Claw stood and said, "I should get going." He shook Poppy's hand, and Mom showed him to the front door.

I didn't move.

"Bye now," I heard my mother say. "Thanks so much," followed by the sound of the door shutting, the bell pinging softly.

Mom returned, filling the doorjamb like a sunbeam.

"What?" I said.

"Julia," she said happily.

I needed her to stop smiling. I felt a Pavlovian response coming on, a smile tugging at the corners of my own mouth.

"Julia," she said again. "Your dad's going to be so proud."

And then, into the safety of my hands, I smiled, too.

* * *

When Claw was gone, Mom rejected the possibility of cooking dinner. "I still haven't been to the grocery store," she said, opening the refrigerator and removing a bottle of white wine. "Besides, we're celebrating. One glass, then we're going to Gabriella's."

Gabriella's was the new fancy restaurant in town, which meant that the waiters and waitresses wore white collared shirts and black pants, and our favorite of these was Jess: Teddy's pretend future wife and my fantasy older sister, who'd be getting custody of me when my parents bit the Titan Big'un.

"I'd better put on a jacket," said Poppy, grabbing the back banister and starting his ascent.

"Fifteen minutes," said Mom. "When Hugh gets home, we'll go."

I remembered then that he'd left a message.

Mom crossed the kitchen to the answering machine and pressed play with her wineglass cradled in her left hand.

"Hi, it's me," said Dad. "Just wanted to let you know it's a week's worth of crazy over here. Mrs. Baxter and I are playing catch-up. Looks like I might be home a little late." The time stamp was broken, so we had no idea when he'd called, but late for Dad was six o'clock.

I looked at the clock on the microwave—6:03. "Maybe he went to Teddy's game," I offered.

"No," said Mom. "Remember? Apparently he's meeting your coach."

We waited half an hour, then Mom called Seedlings—no Mrs. Baxter. After four rings, her call rolled to voice mail. The phone at Klawson's Hardware rang and rang.

It was the second time in as many weeks that Dad had skipped dinner, in spite of the household rule. Even Mom, who worked half an hour away, managed to carve out an hour for our family dinner, while Dad, who worked six blocks from here, was the one who'd made the rule.

"I guess we'll leave a note," said Mom. "He's probably on his way."

In the car, Mom crept along, pausing at intersections and scanning the sidewalks for Dad. Wispy clouds had gathered at the horizon, and the late-day sun cast an orange glow over the streets, pushing the shadows east. I watched the silhouette of our car rolling over the road, Mom's head darkening the neighbors' lawns on Susquehanna.

"Here's Elm Street," said Poppy. He'd pomaded his hair and run an electric razor over his white bristles. Nonz would've said how handsome he looked, but since she wasn't here to see him, I didn't think he looked handsome at all. "Here's a mailbox," he reported.

I cracked my window to drown him out but right away Poppy said he was cold and Mom told me to roll it up. I pressed my forehead against the cool glass and wondered how I could use news of my exhibition match to see Sam.

At Gabriella's, Mom dropped Poppy and me at the curb and told us to wait while she parked. Poppy hadn't brought his walker, and he clung to my arm. It was like he'd completely forgotten he'd whacked me in the head two hours ago, and I tried to sidle away but he held on.

Jess greeted us warmly at the hostess station. "Obermeyers!" she said, draping her arm across my shoulder. "Welcome." She brushed a corkscrew curl back from her face. "I see you ditched your brother tonight."

"He's at an away game," I said. She smiled, displaying two rows of straight white teeth.

"Jess," said Mom, "do you know my father, Bob Cole?"

"Pleasure to meet you," said Jess. Poppy bowed slightly, the skin next to his eyes crinkling as his white eyebrows rose on his forehead.

Jess took three menus from the hostess stand and Poppy held out an arm to let her pass, then stepped behind her as if they were off to do the dip.

I didn't move.

"What's wrong?" asked Mom.

The way Poppy had insisted on combing his hair and putting on a jacket, like he had someone to impress; the way he'd refused to bring his walker, saying it would make him look bad; the way he hadn't once mentioned Nonz since he'd moved in with us; and he hadn't apologized for hitting me—I wanted to tell Mom what'd happened, but I thought maybe it was my fault, so I said nothing, only fell into line behind her, keeping a body between Poppy and me.

We filed past Mr. and Mrs. Henderson—my school nurse—sharing a bottle of red wine. Sometimes Mrs. Henderson let me lay on the cot for an hour or two without asking any questions. I waved and Mrs. Henderson waved back. Then Mom spotted someone she knew—an older couple I didn't recognize, who wanted to tell her how sorry they were about Nonz and how beautiful the service had been.

"This is my daughter, Julia," said Mom. I slouched into her, the closest we'd come to a hug in ages. I could feel her collarbone pressing into my shoulder blade, her skirt button on my hip. She held my shoulders tightly with both hands.

At our table, I took my seat by the window with Mom opposite and Poppy in Teddy's chair to my right. Jess started to clear Dad's silverware but Mom said, "You can leave that—Mr. Obermeyer's meeting us here."

Jess nodded. "Chardonnay?" she asked.

"Please," said Mom.

I ordered a Shirley Temple and Jess winked. Around Christmastime, she'd started making my Shirley Temples with champagne instead of ginger ale, a private present to me, since I was pretty sure Teddy's Cokes were still virgin.

"Mr. Cole, can I bring you something?"

"Dewar's," said Poppy. "With a splash of water."

"Dad," Mom asked, "do you want me to read you the menu?"

"I think I have my glasses in here somewhere . . ." He burrowed for his reading glasses, first in his khakis, then in his cotton zipper jacket, plunging his hand into each of his pockets until he produced a pince-nez.

I looked out the window at a dusky, quiet Main Street. In two months there wouldn't be a single free parking spot down here. Families of tourists wearing baseball caps and MLB jerseys would make the hajj in fleets of minivans, their windows soaped with the words *Cooperstown or bust*. Sometimes I'd get caught in one of their photographs—me trying to get an ice cream at the Red Nugget, them trying to get a shot of the Hall of Fame—and I'd imagine going off to the developer's in whatever town, whatever state. In two years, Sam and I would be leaving for college, and it wasn't nearly long enough. I closed my eyes and pictured his champagne mouth on mine, his liquid hands under my shirt.

"Hey," said Mom.

I sat up, startled.

"I asked you how school was."

I confessed right then to library detention—I needed her to sign the form for homeroom tomorrow, and with two glasses of wine under her belt, now was a good time.

Mom leaned forward and I slid down in my chair. "Why?" she asked.

"I threw an apple across the cafeteria."

"Julia." All disappointment and shock.

"I won't do it again," I promised, slurping through the straw.

Poppy read, "Mushroom and peco—"

"Pecorino," I interrupted. "It's cheese."

"Rizzz . . ."

"Otto," I finished. "It's a rice thing."

Poppy shook his head, moved his finger down the page. "Roasted half chicken," he read. That was mine. With *pommes frites*. "Not for me, I don't think."

Mom rolled her eyes but didn't engage. Instead, she lifted her empty glass to Jess; Jess pointed to me, and I nodded, too.

"Do you want to go ahead and order?" Jess asked when she returned with our drinks.

Mom checked her watch and handed her menu to Jess. "Filet mignon," she said. "Medium rare."

Jess turned to me; I nodded: chicken.

"Mr. Cole?" she asked.

"Let's see," said Poppy. "Where was I? Ah, here." He removed his glasses and looked up. "How's the lamb?" he asked.

"It's great," said Jess. "You won't be disappointed."

"Are you guaranteeing that?"

I looked at Mom, but she was staring off across the room.

"Yes," said Jess. "Guaranteed."

"And what's behind this guarantee?" asked Poppy, holding the menu to his bony chest. "Money back? Free dessert? I was in insurance for forty years, *mademoiselle*, and a guarantee is a guarantee."

"Poppy," I said. "How about if it's not good, you can tell us about it all the way home?" Then the Shirley Temple got hold of me and I shot my hands in the air, shaking and waving my arms, and shouted,

"I GUARANTEE it!" Like the guy on the Forever Leather commercial? Only no one recognized it.

"Julia," said Mom sharply, but I didn't care—Jess was mine, and I was tired of sharing.

She left to put in our orders and no one spoke. I tried to make my second drink last by sipping through the straw and counting to ten between sips. The room was starting to spin and I couldn't feel my shoulders. To steady my vision, I shut one eye and rotated my head, telescoping the room.

"Maybe we should call home," said Mom.

"We haven't eaten," said Poppy.

"Call," I said, "Not *go.*"

"Relax," said Mom.

I tossed my napkin on the table. "I'll call," I said.

I threaded through the dining hall to the hostess station, telling myself Dad would answer. Or better yet he'd walk in the door. But the light over Main Street had turned from orange to gray, and I knew he wasn't coming. Dad was a note-leaver, a phone-homer, a check-inner, always modeling the behavior he expected from us, he liked to remind us. He was not careless, not forgetful. He just wasn't here.

I dialed our number and held the receiver to my ear. After six tolls, the machine clicked on and I heard my voice telling me to leave a message. I pressed the flash button and dialed again, this time Sam's mom's number. Sam picked up on the second ring.

"Hey," I said. I could hear him chewing, potato chips or something. "What are you eating?"

"Cornflake catfish."

"Perkins," I said.

"Mayhi," Sam agreed. "What's up?"

"Can you pick me up in an hour?"

"Where are we going?"

I shrugged, but Sam couldn't see it.

"Hello?"

"To play tennis."

Sam gulped, liquid jogging in his throat. "We just played," he said. "I didn't."

"Fine," said Sam. "The BASS's ass will be there. Wait on the porch."

*　*　*

When we came in from dinner 59 Susquehanna was all lit up, but Poppy announced he was exhausted, going to bed, and we let him go. I followed Mom back to the kitchen, where we found Teddy bent over the island, nursing a Stewart's milk shake. The hips and knees of his gray baseball pants were dusted red, and his dirty stirrups were perched on the rungs of my stool.

I shoved Teddy to one side and sat. "Can I have a sip?" I asked.

"Don't use my straw." I forked off the top and took two gulps. "That's enough," said Teddy. I took one more gulp before he snatched it back.

"Have you seen your father?" asked Mom.

Teddy jerked his head toward the ceiling.

"He's home?" I asked.

"Showering," said Teddy with a mouthful of ice cream.

Mom kissed the top of Teddy's head at the place where his part whipped into a cowlick. "Did you win?" she asked.

"Perfect game," said Teddy.

"Fun," said Mom, but Teddy was like, *No, Mom, a perfect game is a blah blah blah.* No one was listening, except, apparently, Dad, who came down the stairs just then, newly showered, and said, "What's this about a perfect game?"

His hair was damp, his feet bare.

"What happened to you?" asked Mom.

"Nothing," said Dad, frowning. "I was at work."

"You didn't pick up when I called."

"When did you call?"

"Six thirty," said Mom. "It went to voice mail."

"I guess I didn't hear it." Then, "I left you a message." Dad pointed to the machine. "I told you I'd be late."

"Hugh," said Mom, "it's almost nine o'clock."

Sam would be here any second. "I have to go," I said, moving toward the staircase.

"I guess you heard Julia's good news," said Mom.

"No, what?" Dad turned to face me, lacing his hands behind his back: the undivided-attention pose.

"Tell him," said Mom, and the desperation in her voice startled me, stopped me cold.

"I have an exhibition match," I said.

Dad's eyes flashed wide, then quickly narrowed into something like panic. "That's fantastic, Jules," he said, but his voice came out high and thin.

"That's great," said Teddy, missing everything. "You should treat it as a legitimate competition. Maybe if you win, your coach will put you on the team."

"I'm surprised her coach didn't tell you," said Mom evenly. "At your meeting at the hardware store."

Dad moved around behind me, pinning me between my parents. "I forgot about that, actually. Did he call here?"

"He came by," said Mom. "To tell Julia about the match."

Seconds passed, and the only sound in the room was the last of Teddy's milk shake bubbling through his red straw. After a final slurp, he stood and placed one hand on the bottom of the cup and with the other cradled its side. "He pulls up," Teddy announced. "He fakes." It was like he was in a different kitchen with a different family. He launched the cup toward the open trash compactor and we heard it bang the side of the garbage, then bounce twice on the floor. Teddy thundered after it. "It's a put-back," he cried. "And the crowd goes wild!" He cupped his hands over his mouth and *ahhhhed*, cheering himself on. "The effort," said Teddy, "the relentless effort," heading now for the stairs. "He never gives up," Teddy reminded us. "His focus is unparallel."

I changed quickly, then went outside to wait for Sam. The moon was a pancake in the sky. I stood at the curb and looked back at our house, where the white porch rail was offset by the tidy green lawn. I closed one eye, trying to focus against the pull of champagne still bubbling around in my head. Upstairs, my parents' bedroom was lit up, bright yellow, and I thought it was true that you couldn't tell much about a family from the outside.

I heard the Badass Scirocco Scirocco before I saw its headlights and was standing in the street when Sam pulled up.

"You're walking," said Carl from the passenger's seat. "Otherwise one of us has to get out."

I knew right then the night wasn't going to end well. My ticker-tape tally of Sam—a running log of his gestures and responses, glances and touches, where he sat, how he walked, who he talked to, where he looked, when he laughed; his whole self, his every move; his very Sam-ness in relation to me—took a hit for a loss, plummeting on the news that when I'd tried to put us in the same place at the same time, he'd brought Carl.

Sam opened his door and stepped out, pressing the lever to release the seat back. "I'll get in back. You can practice your driving," he said, taking my racket with him.

I settled in front, warm where Sam's body had been. Behind me, his knees punched knots in my back and his breath puffed lightly on my neck.

"No Leaping Stall-Outs," he cautioned. "You almost ended the BASS last time."

I toyed with the gearshift. "Will someone put it in first for me?"

"Can't," said Carl. "You have to learn."

So I stepped on the clutch and pushed the gearshift into what I hoped was first while Carl covered his mouth, trying not to laugh.

As we stuttered forward at about two miles per hour—a classic Shake and Bake—I caught sight of my brother stationed on our porch, standing sentry in his baseball uniform. What must we have looked like, goofing around in Sam's car? Children, I figured. Carl snorting with laughter, in danger of drooling; Sam saying, "You're in third, tardmore," the deepness of his voice belying the puerility of his words. Even if Teddy had been listening, we were coming in on our own frequency, Radio Slitter.

I repositioned the gearshift, jammed the gas pedal, then jerked my foot off the clutch. We lurched forward, the smell of rubber burning the air.

"Profit!" said Carl.

I shifted into second and sped up, ignoring the stop sign and whipping left onto Beaver.

"Third gear," Sam called.

But I wasn't shifting. The car groaned and roared in my ears as I navigated between the stone pillars at the entrance to Bassett Hall, then gunned it around the office buildings to the courts. I drove onto the grass at the top of the hill, narrowly missing a pine tree.

"Clutch," said Carl.

I clutched and he yanked up on the emergency brake and we came to a stop with pine needles brushing the windshield, a branch gently sweeping the roof.

Sam reached between the seats and turned off the ignition. "Very nice," he said. "Now get me out of this bitch."

Carl set off across the dark lawn, disappearing onto the path, then emerging by the metal switch box next to the gate. Seconds later, the giant purple bulbs of the court lights began to hum and glow.

I sprang my seat forward to free Sam, who reached for my hand, and I helped haul him out. Breached, his legs came first, long and tan, with the hem of his shorts rising.

We walked in darkness down the hill to the courts. I could just make out Carl on the opposite side of the net, draped in a gauzy glow of light. He bounced a ball on his racket, knocking it higher and higher, the *thunk* of his strings a drumbeat, the buzzing lights his chorus, and the night was alive; I felt it in the fine hair on the back of my neck.

"You brought Carl," I observed.

Sam said, "He called right after you did. I had to invite him." I felt Sam's hand on my waist and I glanced up. "He likes you, you know—Carl. He told me in Myrtle Beach."

But the name was so far from the one I wanted to hear that I couldn't register it. I shook my head as Carl called out, "Watch this," then I felt Sam's hand pulling me along the shrouded path to the courts. We arrived in time to see Carl drop-serving a moon shot into the air, high up above the lights, which were starting to shine now. It arced easily, weightlessly, before plunging back to earth, bouncing once, dead, then dribbling into the corner, where it came to rest in a crusty patch of snow.

"Sam," I whispered, but he was already busy cracking a new can of balls. He held the can to his nose and inhaled deeply from the fizz of compressed air, then peeled back the metal lid. He tossed one ball to Carl and handed another to me, nodding toward Carl's side of the court.

It made no sense for me to play with Sam. Of the three of us, Sam was by far the best player, capable of feeding alternate shots to Carl and me and keeping the ball in play no matter how poor our returns. But I didn't want to go with Carl.

"Come on," said Carl. "Let's see your tennis spirit."

My stomach knotted around the sound of his voice, balling his words into a fist that I coiled back and held. I couldn't quite see the shape of the blow, but its potential energy swelled in my chest, sending tingles down my arms and flushing my neck and face. The night air couldn't cool me. My vision tunneled on Carl, my roadblock, the wedge keeping me from Sam.

Sam started the rally from the service line and Carl returned his first feed into the net. "Big surprise," he said, fetching it while Sam fed me a slice, which I dinked back.

"How was detention?" Carl asked.

"Swelfare," I heard myself say.

"You didn't miss anything at practice," said Carl. "Except an extra set of wind sprints for sucking at overheads."

He hadn't been given an exhibition match—he would've said something by now, and I began to see where I'd throw my jab. It wouldn't take much. Carl would never see it coming.

Sam started the rally again, but we were arrhythmic—Sam, Carl, net. Sam, me, wide. Carl, Sam, Carl, Sam—and soon the dissonance spread to our conversation. Questions went unanswered, words like feeds knocked straight down into the net. My racket felt heavy in my hand. We backed up to the baseline, trying to redeem the rally, but the game only got bigger, messier, with more ways to mishit and farther to travel to correct our mistakes. Carl hit a ball into Court 2 and trekked after it; the tape at the top of the net caught my slice and I left it where it fell. Sam fed me another, our final ball, and I watched it go by without moving.

"Nice look," said Carl, reappearing at my side. "Next time you should swing."

I stared at him. He had a ball. I held out my hand for it.

"What's wrong?" asked Carl.

"Just hit," said Sam, ignoring me.

Carl bounced the ball twice at his feet, then caught it in his hand and started to rock back for a serve. His racket went up as his left arm lofted and I pictured him gilded, frozen at the baseline, his hand a pink-petaled flower at the toss.

"Claw gave me an exhibition match," I said, and watched as Carl's arms dropped to his sides. The ball landed behind him with a soft bounce.

"Are you serious?" he asked. I shrugged. "When did you even see him?"

"After practice. He came to my house."

"To give you an exhibition match?"

"Right," I said.

"And you just took it," said Carl.

"He offered," I said.

"Did you even ask about me?"

I felt my anger ebb even as Carl's started to flow, the tide of our feelings shifting, and I could see that in a different world we might still have avoided a fight altogether. But our battleground was a bathtub; we'd grown up together and outgrown our vessel, and there was nowhere else for our waves to go.

Carl stepped toward me, saliva on his lips, blood storming his cheeks and ears. He was three inches shorter than I was but he seemed to rise to meet me. "That should've been my match," he said, his breath a visible vapor in the air. "You're not even on the team."

"Claw offered," I said.

"Why?" Carl demanded. "You ditched. I had to file over here by myself and line up for all these fucking drills while you were home watching TV."

"I wasn't watching TV," I said.

"Really?" asked Carl. "Then what were you doing? Watching Sam? Because that's far worse. That's pathetic."

We both looked at Sam, who seemed a mile away on the other side of the net.

"Fuck you," said Carl. Then to Sam: "Let's go."

Sam shrugged, sweeping the air with his racket, and the arcs and curves seemed to mean something, but I couldn't read them. Finally Sam crossed the court to the gate and slipped into the darkness, and I heard the doors open and close on the BASS. The engine roared to life and Sam and Carl motored off, brake lights shining, then dimming as the car disappeared down the hill.

At home, I hooked my racket next to my mother's coat in the entryway, then I pried off my tennis shoes and dropped them next to Teddy's cleats. Quietly, I padded up the front stairs and past my parents' room to Teddy's bedroom, where the light glowed under his door.

"Teddy," I said. "Can I come in?"

I peeked around the doorjamb. Teddy was sitting on the floor, flipping through one of his baseball-card binders, a collection he'd spent ages amassing.

"What are you doing?" I asked. I stood with my hand on the door in case he told me to get out.

"Seeing how much my cards are worth."

I started to sit but Teddy told me to shut the door, so I went back and shut it, then knelt on the rug with my hands folded in my lap.

Teddy looked at me. "I'm thinking of selling them."

"Could you get a lot?"

He shrugged. "That's what I'm seeing."

Teddy had open the *Beckett Price Guide* next to his left knee, which was newly skinned, pink at the edges and deep red in the middle. He'd showered since I'd seen him on the porch and now wore a pair of mesh shorts and an old Cooperstown Redskins T-shirt, ripped beneath one armpit. Deep in thought, he'd pushed his hand into his hair, and I noticed a line of tiny pimples on his forehead.

I thought of all the girls who would've killed to be sitting across from Teddy in his room and I looked around, trying to see what they'd see, but it was just my brother's room: Michael Jordan posters on the walls; a bed with a bare comforter; a bureau covered with trophies that were strung with ribbons and medals.

"How much is my Oddibe McDowell worth?" I asked.

Teddy smiled. "Look it up." I reached over his leg for the book and lugged it back to my lap. "1985 Donruss Highlights," he reminded me. "Mint."

I checked the table of contents and moved off to the Donruss section. Teddy kept my rookie Oddibe for me in the back of one of these binders. "Fifteen cents?" I read. "I thought it was my best card."

"He hasn't done a whole lot in the last ten years."

"Would you really get rid of all these?"

"Maybe. No point in just keeping them."

"I guess," I said. I'd sort of thought that was the whole point. "Why do you need the money?"

Teddy studied me and I sat up straighter, trying to appear worthy.

"Can you keep a secret?"

"Sure," I said.

"I'm buying a Jeep."

"Did Mom and Dad say you could?"

"It's my money," said Teddy.

"Right," I quickly agreed, although I wasn't sure if that mattered.

Teddy said, "I'd let you drive it, except I saw you outside tonight."

I watched him for a moment, then said, "Can I ask you something? If you'd had a friend who liked Kim before you did, would you still have gone out with her?"

"I have like eight friends who like Kim," said Teddy.

There was no point in asking Teddy for his advice about Sam and Carl. He'd tell me to do whatever I wanted: take the exhibition match, play, win—maybe Sam would want me more in the end. Or maybe he wouldn't.

"I'm going to bed," I said.

"Don't tell Mom and Dad about the Jeep."

"I won't," I promised, and pulled the door shut behind me.

In my room, I peeled off my clothes and yanked on a T-shirt, then turned off the light and climbed into bed, feeling for my journal under the covers with my toes.

It was true that I'd taken an exhibition match that rightfully should've been Carl's, but Carl had taken something from me, too. By laying claim to me, he'd drawn a line in the sand that Sam couldn't cross. Now both of my friends were aligned against me, and I needed Carl out of the way if I had any hope of getting Sam.

Thinking about *The Sex Cure*, I opened my journal and flipped to a clean page. All the narrow lines—between truth and fiction, want and need, friendship and love—seemed suddenly traversable: Elaine Dorian had done it. By the stroke of her pen, she had roiled and rippled the town with one story, a story everyone believed, so much so that she may have made it true. Roman à clef. A novel with a key. I uncapped my pen and wrote:

CARL'S MOM TRIED TO KILL HERSELF.

Like Misty Powers in *The Sex Cure*, divorced, lonely, raising three kids on her own—in the middle of the night, she'd dialed the drugstore's emergency number to renew her prescription for something called Nembutal, planning to take a few too many because her boyfriend wouldn't marry her.

CARL'S MOM TRIED TO KILL HERSELF.

At Cooperstown High School there was only one Carl, and even though his mom was nothing like Misty Powers, it was still true, so I tore out the page and folded it into eight equal pieces until I had a white cube like a Chiclet, which I slid deep into the back right pocket of my favorite jeans, where the fabric was worn thin.

LAST WILL AND TESTAMENT

OF

ANNE COLE OBERMEYER
59 SUSQUEHANNA AVENUE
COOPERSTOWN, NY 13326
WEDNESDAY, APRIL 6, 1994
1:57 A.M.

1 Declaration

1.1 I hereby declare that this is my last will and testament and I hereby revoke, cancel, and annul the will and codicil previously made by me jointly with my spouse, Hugh Obermeyer. I declare that I am of sound mind to make this will, though admittedly a bit tipsy [see: one (1) bottle of 1988 Pétrus, a present from Dale for the Trevor-Moreland settlement, totally insufficient as a bonus but more than adequate as a nightcap].

1.2 This last will and testament expresses my wishes without undue influence (under the influence!) or duress, though I'd take a little duress, frankly, an out and out screaming match with my husband. In lieu of information, my imagination is running wild. I'm up at two in the morning reallocating my assets, for Christ's sake. You have to talk to me, Hugh. You have to tell me what's going on.

1.3 Let's start with tonight: Were you really at work late; if so, why didn't you pick up the phone when I called; and what about this meeting with Barry Klawson; was it really *in re* my parents' stone foundation, damp, according to you, along the west wall, possibly requiring the installation of a French drain; if so, why didn't you mention this alleged leak on Monday, when you supposedly found it; and what about Julia's fortuitous exhibition match, dropped in her lap like manna from heaven just before your French-drain meeting with Julia's coach; was it really Barry's idea; if so, why would her coach extend himself like that? He wouldn't, is the point. It's fishy, Hugh. Your story lacks credibility.

2   Family Details

2.1   My mother, Joan Elizabeth Cole, died last week while my father was asleep in his plaid pajamas next to her. Dr. Brash insisted she went quickly, which was more than Dad could offer, being hard of hearing and under the influence of no fewer than twelve medications. In fact, Dad didn't notice she was dead until he woke around 6:30 a.m. to ask for a glass of water. In death as in life, I suppose I should be grateful she didn't die while getting him the water.

2.2   My father, Robert Murray Cole, wears prescription-strength rose-colored glasses that actually sharpen his myopia so that he'll never be at risk for seeing anything he doesn't want to see. Like Mom's mortification at the beauty parlor in 1958 when she overheard the new stylist telling Regina Fratelli about the Cooperstown man she'd been going with in Oneonta? It was me who found Mom crying in her bedroom with her rollers in, and I helped her the only way I knew how.

2.3   From the time I was a little girl, I knew my marriage would be different. There would be no children as foot soldiers, for example, and my husband and I would be faithful to each other. All I'd ever wanted was someone to grow old with, a partner in this life, a husband who desired only me, but from the beginning there has been a third person in our marriage, and her name is Cooperstown.

2.4   I was pregnant with Teddy when Mom called to announce that Dad was about to retire. "You don't know what a grandchild would mean to him," she said, and it was late but I knew by the volume of her voice that she was alone. "He'd want to be with that baby day and night," she said, "right here at home." I was well versed in my mother's way of asking for things. First it sounds as if she's confiding in you, then you realize her need is so great you will ford oceans to save her, and it will sink you again and again.

2.5   No doubt Hugh was confused—why had I moved us here if I didn't want to be here?—but I was confused, too: Why did it seem my husband loved Cooperstown more than he loved me? As soon as we arrived, the familiar feelings from my childhood—the stomach-lurching discomfort of being stared at in the A&P, the ear-burning embarrassment of being gossiped about at Withey's—came racing back. Hugh thought I was being paranoid, but he hadn't lived through the sixties here.

2.6   At some point between the time I graduated from high school and the time Hugh and I moved back, Mom forgave Dad, and I think there's a lesson here: *The Sex Cure*, my mother's silent vessel for confrontation, was now buried under the bed and out of sight, and if Mom can forgive Dad for all that, Hugh and I can get through anything.

2.7   But we are up against a very big "anything."

2.8   There is literally no way Hugh could know about Dale. There's nothing to know. Dale tried to kiss me and I turned away. This was four months ago, just before the Trevor-Moreland settlement, when Dale and I both knew it was in the bag. We'd been celebrating, a bottle of Dom for each of us. Dale called me his "work wife," and I said I don't need another husband, like, ha! one is already too many, ha-ha! What I'd meant was, sometimes it's hard being married. What Dale heard was Hugh-Schmu, and then his lips were on mine, and I was sorry it had come to that, sorry to see Dale in that position. I like Dale, but when he pulled back, flustered, blushing a deep shade of Bordeaux, and I looked away to spare him further embarrassment, and he said, "Are you fucking kidding me, Anne?" I no longer felt sorry for him. I felt like I'd picked up a script for *General Hospital*. It was too ridiculous, too silly—as if I would *ever* sleep with this guy when my husband was so sweet and cute, when Hugh had a full head of hair and Dale looked like a *bearded pear*. No, no, it was absurd, it was something Hugh and I would laugh about later, but later I didn't know where to begin.

2.9   After the settlement, I did not immediately renew my caseload. I'd been billing 100+ hours a week, and I'd missed my family. Also, I thought Dale and I could use some time apart. It was the week before Hugh's forty-seventh birthday, and I decided to do something special—February in Cooperstown can be long and dark and cold, and a surprise party sounded like the right antidote to our respective hibernations, a good excuse to come together over a few bottles of wine.

2.10   I spun through my Rolodex, skimmed the country-club directory, even paged the phone book—then I remembered I have no real friends. As a child, I had my parents' undivided attention, making playmates inessential, and by the time I was in junior high and could've really used a confidante, I was too apprehensive to reach out. Every one of my eighth-grade classmates read *The Sex Cure*, whether their parents knew it or not, and even though I could never find my father on the page, I was terrified someone else would.

2.11   So Hugh's birthday surprise was me. Mortifyingly, I bought a *Cosmopolitan* in Oneonta and skimmed it for ideas. I'm not a prude. In twenty years together, Hugh and I have tried everything at least once, but I was looking for something new. All the suggestions, however, were silly, involving chocolate syrup, crushed mints, or equipment we didn't happen to own. I skimmed a sidebar on threesomes—why and why not to have them—then made a dinner reservation for two at the Horned Dorset, the nicest place I could think of near home.

2.12   And that was where I saw it, our "anything": the vast span between us, Hugh's terrifying remoteness at his birthday dinner with his wife. What should've been romantic—white tablecloths, full wineglasses, duck confit on the way—was instead extremely awkward. I felt as if we were on a first date that wasn't going well. This Hugh was nothing like the Hugh I'd met at a law school party twenty years ago. He barely seemed to notice me, laughing instead with our waitress about a water spill that coated one sleeve of his shirt, then spending the entire appetizer course studying a partially visible man on the other side of the dining room to determine if he was indeed Burt Schlessinger from Hugh's fast-break basketball league. With my wineglass empty and Hugh neglecting to refill it, I realized suddenly that in tiny increments, over hours and days and weeks and years, while we were busy shuttling Teddy and Julia to their millions of activities and tending to our own overstuffed work schedules, that old Hugh had gotten away from me, and I wasn't sure what to do with the man he'd left behind.

2.13   By nine o'clock we were home, in bed, drunk, and I forgot everything I'd read in *Cosmo*. I wanted only to reconnect with my husband, but while I was watching Hugh, he was somewhere far away, with his eyes closed and his cheek turned toward me, and I thought, wasn't it enough that I had to watch out the window for my father's car hours after he should've been home from work? Now am I going to have to watch out for my husband's, too?

2.14   It was over in ten minutes. I never even had time to put in my diaphragm. I'm forty-five years old and if you ask me the best thing Hugh and I ever did together was make children. But a third wasn't meant to be.

2.15   I have the following children:

2.15.1 Theodore George Obermeyer. Teddy is eighteen (18), of legal age to buy cigarettes and to act as his younger sister's guardian but constitutionally incapable of both. Teddy is fiercely protective of his health: He stretches after running, ices after throwing, rests after starting, decompresses after winning. He wants everyone around him to share his passion for baseball and he is a dedicated teacher, placing fingertips on phantom seams to elucidate curveballs and miming batting stances at mock home plates to demonstrate swinging through the ball. Just last week, Teddy put his hands on my hips and turned me left to right, rotating me through a make-believe pitch, powering my bat—a baguette— with my legs, and I felt the thrill of knowing what it is to be at the center of Teddy's world. Many girls will feel it, but few will have the staying power of Mom. Which is one thing Teddy is most definitely not ready to be—if Hugh and I were to die, I'd have to find a suitable guardian for Julia. Last week, this guardian was my mother. Today, I have no idea.

2.15.2 Julia Anne Obermeyer. Julia is fifteen (15) going on seventy going on eight. She is braver, smarter, stranger, and sillier than her brother, which is both delightful and annoying, provoking, and comforting. People either get her or they don't. She has a discerning eye for friends, and when she finds them, she keeps them. Right now she has a crush on her friend Sam (which he'd have to be blind not to see), but that darling little Carl is forever in the way. It's sweet to watch, but I do worry someone will be hurt. Three is not a good number. It certainly didn't work for my parents and it won't work for Julia and her friends. I wish I could talk to her about it, but it's hard for me to open up in that way. I never so much as had a date in high school, much less a boyfriend. Really, what do I know about anything? Less and less every day.

3   Beneficiary

3.1   I bequeath the whole of my estate, property, and effects, whether movable or immovable, wheresoever situated and of whatsoever nature, to 1974 Hugh. That's the Hugh I want back. Who else would have followed me home after that party, held my briefcase while I fumbled with the keys, and not said a word about the kind of girl who brings a briefcase to a party; not said a word about the tidy one-bedroom apartment with a stuffed rabbit on the bed; not said a word when I pointed to the rabbit and intoned, "My roommate's," rolling my eyes? Who else would have stayed the whole night, then the weekend, then the week, going out to the corner store for toilet paper and milk when he noticed we were low on both; never mentioning the phantom roommate again; instead becoming the roommate, moving in with me not slowly—a shirt here, a toothbrush there—but all at once, with a duffel bag full of socks and underwear, a garbage sack stuffed with wool sweaters, and a single baseball card that said more about Hugh's childhood than he ever did?

3.2   And then I was pregnant, and even though we were unmarried he said okay: okay to moving home to Cooperstown with me; okay to Teddy, okay to Julia; okay to my job, okay to my career; okay to my plans while eventually making his own plans— Seedlings—until he began to belong in this town more than I ever felt I did, until he fit here with our children in a way I never will; and I began to begrudge him the ease with which he makes himself happy. He watched his brother drown and it should explain him, but it doesn't even inform him, except perhaps to remind him to strive to appreciate the good things and to let the bad things go.

3.3   Is that what's happening to us, Hugh? Are you letting me go? I admit that I've been distant. Maybe I work too much. Maybe I believed that this marriage would take care of itself, but we haven't done anything we can't undo. Nearly nineteen years. We can figure this out.

4   Alternate Beneficiaries

4.1   Should my 1974 spouse not survive me by thirty (30) days, I direct the whole of my estate, property, and effects, whether movable or immovable, wheresoever situated and of whatsoever nature, be divided between my children named above in equal shares. Don't fight, kids. Don't tease each other. You're on the same team. Teddy, look out for Julia. Ask her questions. Get to the bottom of her. She needs more than she'll ever let on. She doesn't have the whole world figured out, and she still requires her mom and dad. Julia, look out for Teddy. Make sure he does his homework. Life's not all about baseball, and it's not all about girls. Try to keep them at bay, if you can. Teddy needs to learn to believe in himself without a thousand hands clapping him along the way. Both of you: Speak up for yourselves; ask for what you need; call each other at least once a week, even if you're busy, even if you have nothing to say; and be brave, leave this town. Teddy, I'm talking to you now: The world is big, so go, try everything, and don't listen to me if I try to call you back; I love you, but go.

Anne looked up, her eyes blurry after staring at the computer screen for so long. She could hear the sound of her father's television from the guest room upstairs and wondered if they were the only two people still awake.

Did you know Hugh wanted to put you in the Thanksgiving Home?

She paused, the cursor blinking patiently.

Instead, you're watching TV in our guest room, and if we had a different sort of relationship I could talk to you about Hugh, but you are the last person on earth who should be allowed to weigh in with marital advice. I will eschew your counsel herein.
Did you know for years now, Mom and I had been planning for her to live with us after you died? I was going to learn to cook her favorite foods, beef stroganoff and chicken tetrazzini; take her for drives in the country to visit Natty Bumppo's Cave and the Forest of a Dozen Dads; wash and comb her hair as she washed and combed mine when I was a little girl. Instead, your pajamas are wadded in front of my washing machine, urine-stained and mephitic, but they remind me so much of Mom I can't bring myself to touch them. I want to keep everything I can of her. Even you, it turns out.

Anne started to chew a hangnail, then heard her mother's voice telling her not to bite her nails.

Remember last year when I took Mom to see *Swan Lake* at the Palace for her birthday? We never made it to Albany. Instead, Mom asked me to drive her out to the farm where you grew up, though now it's nothing but a field. I threw a fit, of course. Why were we standing on the side of the road when we could've been seated behind the pit orchestra, watching Prince Siegfried fall in love with the maiden swan? But Mom had this whole speech planned, how what she really wanted for her birthday was for me to forgive you, how everything had changed between the two of you, how you were happy together now. Imagine: a cloudless sky in June, tiny purple and orange wildflowers blossoming at the edge of the grassland, and in the far back field near the foothills, a sea of gold, a cluster of a million dandelions. Mom's hair was thinning on top and I could see straight through to her scalp. I tried to remember when her hair had turned white, but when I closed my eyes it was still brown and I was still a child and nothing had changed at all.

Anne tipped the wine bottle over her glass, and a thin purple stream trickled out, then dried up. She ran her index finger over her front teeth, rubbing at the tannins.

Did you know no one in town even really remembers *The Sex Cure*? Hugh dragged me to a cocktail party in December and the host had a copy on her bookshelf, and of all people it was me who got it down. I asked the host if she'd read it and she said, no, she hadn't grown up here, but her aunt had been a nurse at Bassett Hospital when the author checked in after having a nervous breakdown. Figures. Soon other guests had crowded around to discuss the book and among them they recalled little things: the babysitter who sued for libel, the cast lists scribbled on inside covers, and where their parents had hidden it—in attics, nightstands, and bureau drawers. I said, "My mother let me read *The Sex Cure* at the breakfast table," and everyone laughed, thinking I was kidding.

Anne pictured Hugh reading through this document, all her deepest feelings made bare. She had never written anything like it in her life, but she'd consumed an entire bottle of wine, and now even her inhibitions were inhibited.

Hugh, I can't go through this again.

But Anne had barely breathed a word to her husband about her parents' rocky marriage, and she didn't think she should have to trot out her poisonous past to sell Hugh on marital fidelity. They'd made a vow to each other, and, unlike her mother, Anne wouldn't turn herself inside out to coax her husband back.

Or maybe she would. Maybe she would print this and leave it under his pillow, or seal it in an envelope and slip it into his briefcase before he left for work. Hugh used to solicit her feelings all the time, though not so much anymore. If he knew her, if he really knew . . . but it was three thirty in the morning, and Anne was drunk, and common sense dictated that she save the document, power down, then reread it with fresh eyes tomorrow. It was an auspicious beginning just to have gotten her thoughts on the page, in the privacy of her own office, on a computer that was password-protected with the date of her wedding, MaY21ONE975.

6

Wednesday morning Teddy arrived in homeroom as his classmates were wrapping up the Pledge of Allegiance and falling back into their chairs. He nodded conspiratorially to his sister, then let the door close behind him, sealing himself in. For the third day in a row, the chemistry lab was sticky, tropical, worse than an overheated school bus. Teddy's sweat glands sent salt trails down his sideburns and ignited his Right Guard's sporty scent. All around him, his classmates fanned themselves with notebooks or wilted over their desks. Only chubby Ben Fulton, his neck rings slicked with sweat, was showing any fight. He'd twisted around in his chair and was begging Mr. H. to crack a window.

Not a chance, said Mr. H., whose hay fever was acting up. Before spring break they'd all witnessed the fits of sneezing, the folding and refolding of a wet hanky, the honking nose blows, but it was nothing compared to the hell they were in now. Mr. H. had consulted with his allergist over the break, and it turned out that spring's breeze off the freshly mowed soccer field was the culprit. It's wreaking havoc on my sinuses, he'd announced, then administered the ban on open windows.

Seriously? asked Ben Fulton. Seriously.

Because Mr. H. had also returned from spring break with a personal fan for his desk, the kind that clipped to the table and rubbernecked in any direction you chose. Mr. H. had chosen his own face, and through the fan's rotating blades he now replied that his three-year-old grandson didn't whine half as much as Ben.

I think I have to go to the nurse, said Ben.

Mr. H. wrote out a hall pass, and Teddy took this opportunity to slip past Mr. H.'s desk and into his seat across the aisle from Kim.

Teddy, said Mr. H. without looking up. To what do we owe the honor?

Teddy said nothing, only slung his backpack onto his desk and smiled politely.

You're late, Mr. H. clarified. He licked the tip of his pen and marked Teddy down in his attendance book. I guess today isn't a game day?

Nope, said Teddy. Not today.

Right, said Mr. H. Of course not.

Every couple of months Teddy liked to take a breather from school, and the key to cutting was to act normal. Don't change up the routine; don't attract attention. By being late, he had fulfilled every expectation Mr. H. had for him, and in five minutes, *boom*, he would disappear without a trace. If Teddy had been right on time, Mr. H. might've taken special notice, might've looked him up and down and noted Teddy's dress shoes, might have thought, Today's not a game day, so why does he have on his dress shoes? Not only that, but Teddy's hair was wet—he had showered before school, parted and combed the locks—which he hardly ever did because he had gym first period. No point in showering prematurely. But he didn't intend to be in first period.

What's with the shoes? asked Kim, leaning in close. She sat directly to Teddy's left and with the wall of lockers to their right it was sort of like having a private hotel suite. Teddy reached across the aisle and squeezed Kim's leg above her knee. She was wearing the jeans with the small hole near the pocket, and Teddy went to trace the hole but Kim pushed his hand away.

You didn't call last night, she said.

Teddy shrugged. My mom was talking to her friend in California.

Not true, said Kim. I called and hung up.

Teddy remembered one of those. His father had answered, said, Hello? Hello?, then offered the dead receiver to Teddy. This has to stop, he'd said, but Teddy kind of liked it: contact without the trouble of actual communication. It was exactly the level of commitment he was up for. Teddy reached for Kim's leg again.

You're an asshole, she said, but she let him trace her skin through the golf-ball-size hole, and Teddy felt his dick stir. He wondered if he should invite Kim to go to Albany with them. Dave would refuse to drive.

What are you doing fourth period? asked Kim.

Sometimes they snuck out—Teddy from typing, Kim from study hall—and found an empty classroom where they could commit acts of PDA. Teddy was too afraid to have actual sex in school, but they'd done pretty much everything else.

Now Teddy's knee jumped under his desk as he *tap-tap-tapped* his heel, toying with the idea of telling Kim that by fourth period he'd be in possession of enough money to buy a Wrangler. Teddy was terrible with secrets. If he had good news, he liked to share it. If he had bad news, he liked to get rid of it. He felt the secret tickling the back of his throat.

Want to meet up? asked Kim. She slid down in her seat so that the hand that had been touching her thigh was now touching her zipper.

Teddy quickly pulled his backpack onto his lap to hide his erection, then leaned across the aisle and let his lips brush Kim's ear. I can't, he whispered. I'm cutting.

Fuck you, said Kim. Take me with you. He told her he couldn't and she said, You can. You just don't want to.

We can meet after school, said Teddy. He'd gone down on her. Not as often as she'd gone down on him, but still. At your house. Before practice.

Kim pouted. That's only like ten minutes, she said.

Yeah, so? How long did they need? Now Teddy took her hand and tried to guide it under his own desk, but Kim yelled, Get off me! and suddenly their suite was not so private after all.

Mr. H. *ding-ding-dinged* his silver bell, while Kim's coterie (which the girls had taken to calling themselves and Teddy never said aloud, in case it related to a woman's period) trained their evil eyes on Teddy. Teddy could almost hear his father telling him to grow up, but what his dad didn't get was that Teddy and Kim were like the paragon of maturity, as far as their friends were concerned. In the classrooms, in the halls, in the cafeteria and the gym and the courtyard by the flag-pole, Teddy and Kim talked, fought, made up, made out, exchanged gifts on birthdays, on Valentine's Day, waited for each other after home-room, after lunch, before practice, after games, on the nature trail, on the walking path, in the backseat of their friends' parked cars. They didn't have the luxury of a house, the privacy of a bedroom, the free-dom of a fenced-in backyard, but they did have high school, and as the most popular couple, they were the stars of their own soap opera, the student body their devoted viewership. Kim really likes you but doesn't think you're going to stay together next year; everyone is say-ing that you're only going out with Kim because you couldn't get Ava; Steve wants Kim back; and on and on and on. Most of his guy friends were as bad as the girls, except for Dave, who was kind of above it or below it, depending on how you looked at it.

As soon as the bell rang, Teddy slipped out of homeroom with his sweatshirt in his hand and his backpack secure over his shoulder. He'd apologize to Kim later. He'd make it up to her by nailing her in his very own backseat. Teddy slammed through the cafeteria doors and slid into shotgun in Dave's running vehicle, releasing the lever on his seat back and quickly reclining out of view.

They'd be caught later—maybe not till second or third period, but someone would finally take attendance and there'd be a call to his house. Fortunately for Teddy, his parents worked, and answering-machine messages could be erased. As for Dave, he'd been offered early admission to Yale and now seemed to have a permission slip to come and go as he pleased.

Kim's fucking annoying, Teddy announced.

Dump her, said Dave.

I should, said Teddy, bracing himself as Dave revved his Saab around the circle, whipping them onto Linden Avenue.

You should, Dave agreed.

Dave thought Kim was a moron. He thought Teddy was a moron, too, but they'd been friends since preschool and were still sort of close all these years later. They didn't have any classes together, but Teddy liked to listen to the Affect Effectors rehearse during study hall, Dave on bass. Teddy wondered what would become of Dave at Yale when he joined the crowds of people as weird as he was—would Dave ever come home again?

Teddy had no intention of leaving home, really. He was going to college only forty-five minutes away, and now that he was buying a car, he'd be able to pop back whenever he felt like it. But who else would still be here? Teddy had developed a phobia of life after June 26, graduation day, when one by one his friends would pack up their rooms and leave for foreign lands: Ithaca; Binghamton; Springfield, Mass. Why did this have to happen? It seemed unnatural, and Teddy was refusing to participate.

Eyes closed, he spun the radio dial. In three tries—his best was a lucky single—Teddy hit Lite 98.7. He had just started to sing along when Dave's long fingers appeared out of nowhere and retuned the radio to NPR.

No, said Teddy.

Find a tape, said Dave.

Teddy rooted through the glove compartment, silently vetoing Luscious Jackson and the Cocteau Twins. Dave was so fucking gay.

Prince, said Teddy, feeding the tape into the deck. Dave nodded his approval.

Without signaling, Dave turned right onto Susquehanna and tore over the bridge toward the gym. In their dusty wake, Teddy charted the disappearance of his house until it was only a tiny square in his side-view mirror.

Christ, said Teddy. Slow down. There are always cops here.

Dave said, I divine the police.

Teddy monitored Dave's speedometer as they went 40 through a 20, past the gym.

So, which cards are you selling? asked Dave.

I haven't decided.

Dave glanced at him, then nodded at the backpack by Teddy's feet. What's in there?

All of them, Teddy admitted.

You're selling all of them?

Teddy started to squirm. As boys, Dave—not a collector himself but happy to do whatever Teddy suggested—had taken charge of Teddy's collection. He'd engaged the shopkeepers on type, condition, and rarity, while Teddy stood directly behind his shorter friend and pinned his eyes to the floor. Teddy hadn't been able to understand where scrawny, bespectacled Dave, with a severe allergy to peanuts, had gotten his confidence. Teddy was average height for a ten-year-old and still he'd preferred slinking in with his head down, sliding a five-dollar bill across the counter, then silently choosing his wax packs from the bins near the registers before retreating to the comfort of the sidewalk to shuffle through his decks, admire the one or two keepers, and work his jaw over the brittle sticks of gum. It wasn't until Teddy began to shoot up—presaged by excruciating pains in his long bones—that he'd taken ownership of his collection. By age fourteen, Teddy was marching straight up to the counters at places like Third Base and Diamonds, and he didn't have to explain his decision now to sell that collection—not to Dave and not to his dad, on whom Teddy had two inches.

I might, said Teddy.

He went to crack his window and was for a moment completely baffled, then remembered that his window control was on the center console. Saabs were so weak.

The wind washed through the car and drowned out Prince and also Dave, who was now telling him that it would be insane to give up his entire collection when individual cards were the locus of a collector's *blah blah blah.*

Teddy closed his eyes. He'd sensed the same disapproval from his sister last night and was sick of all the negativity. Maybe he'd outgrown baseball cards, okay? Teddy still had in his closet three shoe boxes full of GI Joes, Transformers, He-Men, and Garbage Pail Kids; a stack of *Mad* magazines nearly as tall as he was; and a library of *Sports Illustrated Kids* dating from the first issue, in 1989. What business was it of theirs if he wanted to cash in? It wasn't like he was giving his cards away. He knew what they were worth and he had a so-so idea of his walk-away price. If the manager of Major League Collectibles lowballed him, *boom,* Teddy would be out of there.

Teddy felt his window going up and opened his eyes to see Dave's finger on the center console.

You can't hear me, said Dave.

That was the point, said Teddy.

So, what's the deal with Kim? asked Dave.

Teddy shrugged.

Do you think you'll stay together next year?

Teddy began to sweat. All morning his temperature had been off. It was the button-down shirt, the dress shoes that Teddy hadn't worn since Nonz's funeral, the gray sky draped like a blanket over the day. The trip to Albany had been Teddy's idea, but when they crossed into

Middlefield, leaving the WELCOME TO COOPERSTOWN sign behind, Teddy wanted to grab the wheel from Dave and spin them back toward home.

I heard she got into Gettysburg, said Dave. Not that close to Oneida, but I guess that's what the Jeep's for.

I guess, said Teddy.

Is it serious? asked Dave.

It was deadly serious, but not in the way that Dave meant. Teddy had a problem, and he couldn't talk about it with anyone, and he couldn't even really explain it to himself. He was definitely still Teddy—MVP and captain of the baseball team; homecoming king and winner of the Senior Superlatives most popular, most athletic, best eyes, and best legs—but recently he'd discovered he was also a second Teddy, a smaller Teddy, and this Teddy was a loser, and this Teddy was getting left behind.

While the Oneida College athletic director had toured Teddy around their facilities last month—including a brand-new weight room, where Coach Peterson expected him to gain twenty-five pounds by the first captain's practice—Teddy had been trying to hide his sweating palms and hear over the roar in his ears. All the guys here were benching 200, 210, while Teddy couldn't even manage his own weight. A kid in an Oakland A's cap, who looked to be less than Teddy's 170, had given Teddy a quick once-over, then gone back to adding twenty-five-pound disks to his bar.

All around him, people were buzzing about college, and not only Teddy's parents and teachers but his friends. Opening envelopes, celebrating acceptances, sending in deposits, making plans to go. Take Kim, for example, who was deciding between Gettysburg College, in Pennsylvania, and Syracuse University, forty-five minutes west of Oneida. Syracuse, right? Except, to Teddy, it made no difference: if he made it as far as Oneida, he knew he couldn't go an inch farther. The idea of getting in his Jeep after the last baseball practice on Friday and turning west instead of east, doubling the distance between himself and home, made Teddy's head spin. He had everything he wanted right here in Cooperstown, and he was having trouble understanding why he should leave.

Are we—Teddy braced himself against the dashboard—are you, like, pumping the gas?

Dave glanced at his feet.

Can you open a window? said Teddy. Now.

Dave fumbled for the controls. Are you going to be sick?

It was true that Teddy had been a barfer as a kid, and now he trotted out his old tricks: breathe in through the nose, out through the mouth; keep your eyes on the horizon; let the blustery air in.

Should I pull over? asked Dave.

Teddy shook his head. How to tell him that it wasn't the way he was driving, it was that he was driving, carrying Teddy to the far reaches of his comfort zone.

Can you slow down or something? asked Teddy. You're shaking the wheel.

Dave rolled his eyes but eased up on the gas. Edgy and cool in his horn-rimmed glasses, black jeans, and Charlie Brown T-shirt, Dave didn't care what people thought of him. Teddy cared deeply. He cared what they thought of his girlfriend, his friends, his parents, his sister. Teddy would've loved to have had a normal sister or brother, the way so many of his classmates had siblings and cousins—even aunts and uncles—scattered throughout the grades, clansmen disguised by different last names, ready to fight when called to arms.

Dave was like family. He'd been Teddy's only friend at Nonz's funeral, the rest having scattered for spring break. While Teddy had shaken one adult's hand after another, he'd thought about how Nonz used to scrub his feet with a scratchy washcloth at bath time, between each toe, behind his ears, in the creases of his neck, going after dirt like it was a playground bully, polishing and shining him like a first-place trophy, her best prize. She'd never missed a home baseball game, never forgotten his birthday, never failed to give him ten dollars on

Valentine's Day, and as these thoughts had inched closer to Teddy's consciousness, he'd felt tears brimming, getting ready to fall.

Then suddenly Dave had pushed through the greeting line, wearing a three-piece suit and bow tie. Hey, he'd said with his hands in his pockets, no need to shake. You know who'd get a huge kick out of this whole thing? Dave had looked left, then right, then said, Nonz.

I'm okay, said Teddy now. It's just—his mind shuffled a stack of words, pulled one out, tentatively played it—college, he said, blowing out the candle, breathing in the flower.

College? Dave repeated.

Yeah, said Teddy. I don't know. Everyone keeps talking about it.

Right, said Dave. Well, we're going. Then, Are you worried about Kim?

Teddy shrugged, started to speak, stopped. He was not very excellent with words.

Dave said, You know there's going to be like a million new girls there, right?

Suddenly Teddy flashed to a memory of a five-year-old Dave pulling the beautiful Laurie Youngblood onto the swing with him and hooking her legs to either side of his body so that they could pump together, a four-legged, four-armed insect in a brilliant new game. A softness washed over Teddy, a lightness. Maybe they weren't lost. Maybe they weren't disappearing. Maybe they weren't too young for it all.

Teddy felt his nausea give way to hunger pangs, his second-most familiar feeling. I'm kind of starving, he said, and Dave agreed that he could eat.

In Sharon Springs, they turned into the Stewart's parking lot and Dave killed the engine. What do you want? he asked.

Teddy placed his order, forked over a five, then asked if he could drive.

If it'll keep you from getting sick, said Dave. He blessed Teddy with the keys.

Teddy jogged around the front fender and slipped into the driver's seat, locking the door behind him. Eyes closed, he shifted through the gears one at a time, gently fondling the smooth gear knob, paying special attention to where first and third needed a little finesse, a lover's touch. Was it wrong that this turned him on? He checked to make sure there was no one near the car, then put his left hand down his pants. There wasn't enough time to do anything, but for thirty seconds he was happier than he'd been all day.

Dave beat on the store's plate-glass window and waved.

What? asked Teddy, returning his hands to the wheel. Dave held up a sixteen-ounce Coke; check, said Teddy. Then a giant bag of Cheetos; Teddy nodded. Had Dave forgotten his Sno Balls? But no, Dave had a mind like a fly strip; he would've skipped a grade after Seedlings if he'd been able to hold a pencil, and Dave would not let him down.

When Teddy saw Dave crossing the parking lot, he reached across the console to open the door from the inside.

Don't spill, said Dave, handing him his Coke. I just had the car detailed.

Teddy ate while Dave filled the tank, then Dave gave him the green light and they pulled back onto Route 20, heading east.

Go easy, said Dave as Teddy shifted into third. Push the clutch all the way in. Don't shift too early! See the RPMs? Then, Shift, shift, shift! until Teddy told him to calm the fuck down.

Let's play a game, said Teddy.

Twenty questions?

No. Teddy shook his head violently. No, like Hump Island.

Oh, God. Fine. Jean Seberg in *Breathless*, Patti Smith on the *Easter* cover, Dagny Taggart over her desk.

Nice, said Teddy about the desk.

Dave shrugged. Hump Island's only fun when it's plausible, he said.

Right, said Teddy, feeding the word back to him. So make it plausible.

Dave cocked his head. Okay. Ava Streeter. Louise Hart.

Teddy nodded. Good choices. He'd had sex with both of them sophomore year.

There is one girl, said Dave. He folded his hands in his lap and Teddy could tell that it was no longer a game.

Okay, said Teddy, settling into the conversation. He was an expert at talking about girls. He knew all the right questions. Is she hot? he began.

She is, said Dave. In a coltish way.

And? Teddy prompted.

And in a not-coltish way.

Dude, said Teddy. What does she look like?

Pretty, said Dave. Smart.

A senior? asked Teddy.

Sophomore.

Hannah Quigley? She was in Teddy's Spanish class and always seemed to be getting a drink when Teddy was coming out of the bathroom. Chocolate-brown eyes, round muscular calves. Teddy could definitely see wanting to date her.

No, said Dave.

Who?

Dave looked at him.

I don't know any other sophomores, said Teddy.

Right, said Dave. You only live with one.

Teddy felt his mind circling Dave's words, trying to get purchase. There was no way Dave was talking about his sister. Was he?

Do you even know Julia? asked Teddy.

She's your fucking sister, said Dave.

Right, said Teddy. They were probably in rocket science together. Well, she's kind of annoying.

What's the deal with her and Sam? asked Dave.

No clue, said Teddy. He stole a glance at Dave and pictured him visiting Julia from New Haven while Teddy was home from Oneida, his house filled to capacity. It wasn't the worst idea.

Dave pushed the eject button on the stereo and began rooting through his glove compartment for a new tape. Before Teddy could suggest the radio, Dave selected a yellow cassette and pressed it into the tape deck, then cranked the volume.

Automatic for the People—the suicide song.

No, said Teddy.

Yes, said Dave. Or get out of my seat.

Teddy drove on, through Carlisle, Sloansville, Esperance. Past empty storefronts, empty fields. In front of a double-wide trailer, a plywood 4-SALE sign leaned against a John Deere tractor, and Dave said, You could buy that and save five hundred bucks, then laughed with his mouth open.

Teddy consulted the dashboard clock and was stunned to find that it was only nine thirty. Gym would just be ending; next stop, math, which suddenly sounded better than Michael Stipe. He could feel his mood starting to slip and tried to soothe himself with images of his Jeep: white with a soft black cover, stereo with a CD player that Rick Delaney had installed himself. Not only that, but Rick had put in two subwoofers behind the backseat that absolutely throbbed when Rick trailed up and down Main Street. Teddy needed that Jeep. He needed a space in the world where he could play Phil Collins as loudly as he wanted, go when and where he wanted, bring with him whoever he wanted. The Jeep would be Teddy's safety net between life as he knew it and the dining halls, dorms, and roommates waiting below. Worst-case scenario, Teddy couldn't hack college and the car would catch him, carry him home.

They made it to Albany as Major League Collectibles was opening, but Teddy still didn't have a game plan for selling his cards, so he steered them toward a diner he'd spotted on Western Avenue.

Again? asked Dave.

I need to think for a minute, said Teddy. Over eggs.

It wasn't until they were inside the restaurant that Teddy remembered he and Dave were cutting school. They were the youngest patrons by fifty years, the only diners with color still in their hair.

Men reading newspapers, couples eating in silence, a woman with a smoker's cough who picked at a plate of pancakes: the tables were mostly occupied, but the booths were completely empty. Arthritis, knee replacements, broken hips. It took effort to scoot in.

Jeez, said Dave. It's like visiting my grandmother in Florida. Then he seemed to remember where he'd last seen Teddy's grandmother and quickly apologized.

Whatever, said Teddy, nabbing a choice booth by the front window. He passed Dave a laminated menu, then took one for himself.

Dave held up his utensils and said, There's crap on my fork.

Teddy squeaked, This dirty old fork is too dirty, while continuing to scan his menu.

Seriously, said Dave, there's no way this place passed mustard with the department of health.

Teddy shook his head. Whatever the fuck.

When their waitress appeared, Teddy sat up straighter, older, the word *truant* echoing around in his head. But it wasn't Teddy who was the problem. Across from him, Dave absently combed his sideburns with the tines of his fork.

Are you ready to order? she asked. Teddy read her name tag: Michelle. Heavy blush, aqua eye shadow, foundation that Kim, an aspiring makeup artist, would've called streaky. But there was a softness around her mouth that Teddy found alluring. He tried to catch her eye, do the Teddy thing.

Could I have a new fork? asked Dave.

Michelle turned and lifted a set of silverware from the empty booth behind them, then carefully laid it in front of Dave, paper napkin and all. Good? she asked.

Good, said Dave.

Teddy ordered an egg sandwich and a large Coke, while Dave went for the dry toast and a chamomile tea.

Teddy smiled—chamomile tea!—but Michelle wasn't looking at him, at either of them.

Anything else? she asked.

No, said Dave. That will be all.

When Michelle was gone, Dave announced he was getting the paper, then scooted out of the booth and headed to the box by the entrance.

Teddy watched Michelle make the rounds with a pot of coffee. A million new girls in college. It was an enticing prospect, and it buoyed Teddy's mood. He liked Kim—maybe he loved Kim—but he didn't want to marry her. If Teddy ever got married, it'd be to someone as smart and pretty as his mom.

Dave returned and sprawled sideways in the booth with his sneakers hanging over the edge, his shoulder to Teddy. With fanfare, he flapped open the paper, shook it, then began to read.

Behind the counter, Michelle filled a plastic cup from the soda machine, then located a mug for Dave's tea. She reminded Teddy of Jess at Gabriella's, and not because they were both waitresses. Teddy had never been with an older woman. It was definitely on his list.

She crossed the dining room with an oval tray hoisted over her shoulder, her blond ponytail swishing in time with her step.

Egg sandwich, said Michelle, setting a plate in front of Teddy. Toast, she said to Dave.

Could I get some lemon? asked Dave.

Teddy rolled his eyes, but Michelle said, Sure, then smiled conspiratorially at Teddy, the corners of her mouth turning up just for him.

So, said Dave, folding his paper. What's the plan?

Teddy applied ketchup and Tabasco to the underside of his bun.

You do know Rick Delaney's an ass, said Dave. There's no way that car is worth seven hundred bucks.

Oh, for fuck's sake, said Teddy. It runs.

Really? asked Dave. Have you taken it to a mechanic?

Teddy snorted and said, No, Dave, I don't own it yet.

Dave stared at him. You do that before you buy the car.

Teddy frowned. Did everyone know that? Right, he said, but I still need to be ready with the money for when the mechanic gives it the okay.

Dave squared himself to Teddy. Okay, he said. So which cards are you selling?

Teddy got serious. If I only go with the big ones, I'll never make it to seven hundred, he said. My '83 Ryne Sandberg is worth sixty bucks, and I have two of them because I also have an '83 complete set. So that's one-twenty. Then I have an '84 Dwight Gooden, which is worth twenty-seven, and an '85 Roger Clemens.

Don't sell that, said Dave. That's going to be worth a shitload one day. What about your doubles?

I tried that, said Teddy. Not enough.

Dave nodded. How much would you get by selling the big ones?

I'd be breaking up complete sets to do it, said Teddy, so it makes more sense to look at the value of the sets as a whole. My Topps '83 through '88 are worth about four-fifty total, but that's only because they include my rookie Wade Boggs, Tony Gwynn, and one Ryne Sandberg. My '85 Fleer set is worth two hundred, but that's with the Clemens. Teddy dropped his hands. There's no way I'm getting to seven hundred without selling the big cards, and once you've done that, you might as well sell the sets.

Or, said Dave.

Or what?

Or you could sell one card.

Teddy shook his head. That's not my card, he said.

Your dad gave it to you, Dave said.

To hold, said Teddy. It's not even his.

Come on, said Dave. You must've looked it up.

Teddy had looked it up.

Well? asked Dave.

Six-fifty, said Teddy. Dave raised an eyebrow.

No, said Teddy.

Sell that card, said Dave, come up with another fifty bucks on your own, and you have a car. If you walk in there with a backpack full of complete sets, you know they're going to rape you.

Teddy shrugged. Maybe, he said. He chewed on a cuticle.

In the car, Teddy called out directions while Dave drove and in less than ten minutes they were idling in the parking lot in front of Major League Collectibles.

Dave cut the engine. Do you want me to come in with you? he asked.

Teddy shrugged. Do you think it'll help?

I don't know, said Dave. I look sort of young.

You look about twelve, Teddy agreed.

Dave smiled and reached for his newspaper. Good luck, he said, and Teddy suddenly felt twelve, too. He socked Dave in the shoulder, then grabbed his backpack off the floor of the car.

Major League Collectibles was a single room dimly lit by fluorescent lights, with dusty blinds blocking out the sunlight along with the view of the parking lot. It took a minute for Teddy's eyes to adjust. Slowly he saw a worn industrial carpet, whirring ceiling fans, and a 1986 Mets World Series poster above the front counter—that'd be it for his father; they'd be out of here. Teddy approached the display case with his backpack clutched to his chest.

The man behind the counter was jacked, veins like ropes under his skin. He wore a muscle T cut halfway down his sides so that Teddy could see his abs flex when he leaned forward over the counter. This guy was no baseball player. Too pumped, too groomed. Something. Teddy could just tell.

Can I help you? he asked.

Is there a manager I could speak to? asked Teddy.

That's me, said the man.

Teddy swallowed. I'm here about selling some cards. He set his backpack on the counter, building a wall between them.

The manager nodded toward Teddy's bag. What do you have?

Complete sets, said Teddy. Mint. He slid out the first binder, including his Topps Traded from 1986, priced by *Beckett* at twenty-four dollars. The manager flipped through Teddy's Topps, bored. He didn't even pause to admire José Canseco or Barry Bonds.

Ten, he offered.

Ten?

Ten dollars.

Teddy looked around the store for someone else he could talk to. It's worth twenty-four, said Teddy.

To who? asked the manager, and Teddy felt his neck and face start to burn.

That's not enough, said Teddy firmly. The manager closed his mouth and opened it again. Teddy shifted, crossed his arms over his chest, tried to steady himself. Twenty, said Teddy.

Twelve.

Fifteen.

Twelve, said the man again. Teddy swallowed, nodded. The manager turned to the next set in the binder.

On a black solar-powered calculator, the numbers were added up. Twelve. Sixteen. Thirty-nine. They were never going to make it to seven hundred. Once, Teddy tried to bargain harder, but the manager shook his head, said, Keep it, and Teddy backed down, sold his 1985 Fleer set for a third of what it was worth. There went the Roger Clemens. Now the manager pulled binders from Teddy's backpack without asking, turning pages, calling out figures, and Teddy's palms began to sweat and there was a familiar ringing in his ears.

Sixty, said the manager.

Teddy nodded.

Twenty-two.

Please, said Teddy. The manager glanced at him and Teddy nodded and the manager added the binder to his growing stack.

Teddy closed his eyes, breathed, breathed again. Head bowed, he no longer saw the manager or the worn carpet or the dark windows and faded posters of Major League Collectibles. Instead, he saw the top shelf at Third Base in Cooperstown, where he'd built his collection: a 1952 Topps Mickey Mantle, rookie card; a mint 1916 Babe Ruth, issued when the Babe was still with the Red Sox; a shoeless Joe Jackson and a rookie Joe DiMaggio; an autographed Jackie Robinson and a limited-edition Roberto Clemente.

On the second shelf were the living Hall of Famers, former players who returned to Cooperstown every year for Hall of Fame Weekend, with its free meals, cocktail hours at the Otesaga hotel, golf and tennis matches at the country club, and shooting the shit with one another about old times. Some of these guys looked good, strong and tall, and you knew they could still hit the wall, could still throw an eighty-mile-an-hour fastball if they wanted to. And some were getting old.

When Teddy was ten, he'd gone with his father to the country-club tennis courts to watch Ted Williams—one of Teddy's namesakes, the other his dead uncle George—rally with his son, John Henry. It wasn't a competition, but Ted Williams kept slicing it and lobbing it until John Henry was throwing his racket and kicking up the Har-Tru. It was a cloudy day and when the thunder started the other players packed it in, but the Splendid Splinter wouldn't call it. Then the rain came and John Henry took off for the parking lot and didn't look back.

For a few seconds, Ted Williams was alone on Court 4 in the rain, a white towel around his neck, and he looked lost, an old man, but then Teddy's dad had struck like lightning and the next thing Teddy remembered his father's hero was riding shotgun in their station wagon, Teddy in the backseat behind him. No one spoke during the short drive along West Lake Road—his father had been too awed and Teddy had known better than to break the silence. At the gate to the Otesaga hotel, Ted Williams spoke to the guard and they drove on to the hotel's covered entrance.

I have a card, said his dad when they stopped. You signed it for my brother when we were boys.

The signature had faded in the thirty years since, but Teddy's dad had brought along a black ballpoint pen and now he handed the pen and the card to Ted Williams and said, Would you sign this for me again?

Teddy could not swallow the knot in his throat. It was pushing up from his chest and into his mouth and nose and eyes.

The manager was down to the last binder.

What's this? he asked.

Wait, said Teddy.

The manager looked up.

Not that one.

The manager studied him, then studied the card through the plastic without touching the sleeve. It was a 1957 Topps—the year they'd cut their cards to the new industry-standard size—and they'd taken the top off Ted's hat. Ted at bat, Ted on the follow-through, Ted with his arms crossed wrist over wrist, his bat breaking behind his right shoulder, his hips twisted to the side. *Character* was the word Teddy's dad used. The Splendid Splinter had fought in two wars. He had flown a plane over Korea. He had left and come back, left and come back. He hadn't been afraid of anything. But Teddy was afraid.

I'll give you eight hundred for it, the manager said. You can keep the others.

Teddy paused as the figure scaled his eyes and played a quick game of what-if on his mind.

Nine hundred, said the manager.

But it was like his dad was in the store with him.

Nine-fifty.

No, said Teddy. He moved his hand to the plastic sheet and silently slipped his father's card from its sleeve, stowing it in his shirt pocket.

The manager shrugged, showed him a figure on the calculator, then opened the cash register and paid Teddy in twenties and tens.

In the car, Teddy tossed his empty backpack behind his seat and slammed the door. Let's go, he said.

Dave started the Saab. What happened? You were in there forever.

Nothing, said Teddy. Go.

Dave reversed out of the parking lot and shifted into first, joining the traffic on the road. So? How much did you get?

Seven hundred, Teddy lied.

Really? Dave glanced over his shoulder at Teddy's empty backpack. Even?

Yeah, said Teddy. He felt sick and wanted to be home but they still had an hour and a half to go.

Where do I turn? asked Dave. Teddy opened the map and tried to read it, but the picture was a jumble of blues and reds.

Teddy said, Where the fuck is Route 20 on this thing?

Dave had to pull over and read it himself. He made a U-turn and they sped back past Major League Collectibles, but Teddy kept his eyes straight ahead.

They listened to the rest of R.E.M., then to Morrissey, sides A and B. The tape flipped again but Teddy heard nothing. He stilled his mind. It was after one o'clock when Dave sailed past the shortcut by the Tepee souvenir shop on Route 20: they'd have to take the long way. Five miles later, Dave exited onto 166 in Cherry Valley.

Dave said, When will you get the Jeep?

But Teddy didn't answer. He wanted wind sprints and group stretches, batting practice and red dirt on his hands. He was tottering at the edge of something and he was desperate not to tip over. Teddy lowered his window and stuck his head out like a dog. It was something he'd done as a kid. Ears battered by the wind, eyes dry and bulging, he watched the houses slip by: long driveways cutting muddy paths up to painted two-stories, sunlight starting to burn through the gray overhead and winking off the cars parked beside front lawns. The wind was warm on his face and it smelled like spring—grass and dirt and wet pavement and manure from the dairy farms. Green hills rolled beside them and yellow fields behind them. What was done was done. Colors and shapes blurred before his eyes. His cards were sold. He couldn't go back.

Hey, said Dave.

Teddy felt the car slow and lifted his head.

Check it out, said Dave. How debonair.

Teddy followed Dave's gaze to where a woman stood at the wide mouth of a driveway, her right arm extended through the open window of a silver station wagon.

You never see shit like that anymore, said Dave.

But what Teddy saw was not the woman, or even the man's face bending to kiss the woman's hand, but the bumper of the station wagon dented in the same place where his mother's car had nicked his father's in their driveway the year before.

His first thought: That is not my dad.

His second: That's my dad.

Dave pressed the gas pedal and Teddy glanced at him nervously—did he know?—but there were at least three silver Tauruses in Cooperstown, and they were not even in Cooperstown, and suddenly Teddy was back to thinking that that could not have been his dad.

He craned his neck, pinning his 20/10 vision on the station wagon in the driveway; on the ski rack that Teddy had installed himself for a trip to Deer Run; on the woman's hand, moving now to the side of his dad's face; and on his dad, releasing her hand to touch her face. *Caress*, Teddy thought, just before closing his eyes.

Stop the car, said Teddy, as a wave of nausea hit him. Dave started to pull over but Teddy said, Not here. He pointed up the road to a bend out of sight of the driveway.

Are you going to throw up? asked Dave.

Teddy shook his head. He felt gutted, his stomach punching up inside him, but he was not going to be sick. What had he really seen? He plugged in to the side-view mirror, to the road spooling out behind them. Teddy watched and waited, but there was no sign of his dad's car.

Here, said Teddy, and Dave pulled onto the shoulder just beyond a mailbox hammered to a wooden post in the dirt at the side of the road.

Teddy opened the door and unbuckled his seat belt, then reached for his sweatshirt and backpack.

What are you doing? asked Dave.

Teddy got out and closed the door, then said through the open window, I think I'm going to walk. I'll see you back in town.

It's like fifteen miles, said Dave, but Teddy was already gone.

Maybe Dave called his name. Teddy didn't hear it. Anyway, there was no stopping him. He ducked off the road and ran alongside the woods, his dress shoes mashing his toes and slapping at his soles, the ground below him sticks and mud and patches of snow, the sky above him bright gray. Teddy knotted his sweatshirt around his waist and ran. He tried not to think, but he couldn't stop his mind: the woman's skirt had been long and purplish, a hippie skirt. His mom wore ironed skirts in gray and black and dark green, not skirts from fucking Woodstock. And sleeveless—the woman hadn't been wearing a jacket in this early-spring air. She'd been hugging herself with one arm, maybe trying to keep warm while her other arm was extended for his dad's kiss. And then his dad's hand was on the woman's cheek, his fingers curling around behind her neck, his thumb stroking her skin, and what was Teddy supposed to think?

All the questions his dad was always lobbing him: Did he work hard enough in school, was he 100 percent respectful to his girlfriend, was he kind and generous to his sister? Clearly no, but now Teddy was wondering just exactly what his dad knew about character. Teddy had been ripped off to the tune of seven hundred dollars—his life's work sold for pennies on the dollar, his dream of buying a car shot to shit—because you don't sell your dead uncle's baseball card to a douche in a muscle T, and you don't cheat on your wife with a hippie chick from Cherry Valley.

That's what he'd seen, hadn't he? Teddy slowed to a jog, then a walk, as the weight of the knowledge hit him; he closed his eyes to smother the image of his moon-eyed father, another kiss coming, his dad already tugging her down.

Off to his right, Teddy heard the faint sound of cars whipping by and climbed a hill to a get a look, panting at the view. The sky had cleared, sun flooding the valley. Below him was Route 20 and, to his right, 166, which put him somewhere between Cherry Valley and the lake. All along he'd been running toward home.

For the next three hours—a guess: in the first week of January, Teddy had lost the watch Kim had given him for Christmas—Teddy walked along the shoulder of the road with his sweatshirt on, the hood pulled up to camouflage his face. Jim Lowry at the *Cooperstown Crier* and Leo Greer of the *Freeman's Journal* had each photographed him for their sports sections so many times that the old guys in the bleachers called him "the mayor." Height: 6 feet 2¾. Weight: an aspirational 175. Favorite movie: *Caddyshack*. Favorite book: *Friday Night Lights*. Favorite food: Sal's pepperoni pizza. Last month they'd added "Plans after CHS," which had initially freaked Teddy out. To pitch for Oneida College, he'd finally answered, but, come on, he'd be a freshman at a D-I school: he'd be socked away in the dugout, chewing sunflower seeds or watching the game through a crack in the bullpen wall.

Teddy made for Glimmerglass State Park, at the north end of the lake. It wasn't open yet for the season and he walked right in through the front gate, past the empty security booth and over a concrete bridge to the recreation hall, with its windows boarded up for winter. Behind the recreation hall was a small, sandy beach and, from there, nine miles of open water to the shores of Cooperstown.

The lifeguard stands stood like storks at the water's edge. Eventually they'd be moved out into the water, but the ice had only just melted. You couldn't swim in Otsego Lake before May. Sometimes people drowned. Not in April, but in January, February. It was one of his father's rules: no swimming before May, because of his uncle George.

But fuck his father, and fuck his father's rules. It wasn't even all that cold out—Teddy was still sweaty from his run. He dropped his sweatshirt on the sand and pulled off his dress shoes, then held them in his pitching hand while he examined his socks: wet and sandy and also bloody at the heels. He'd be shit at stealing bases all week. Teddy cocked his arm and torpedoed his shoes into the grass near the beach, where a picnic table was turtled on its head. Then he bent and carefully rolled his argyle socks down over his blistered heels and threw them, too. They unraveled midair, floating like deflated balloons back to the beach.

His dad's baseball card, secure in his breast pocket, was burning a hole in Teddy's heart. It was an angry pulse that needed cooling. Still wearing his shirt and pants, Teddy waded straight into the lake, but he didn't get far, because the cold needled through to his lungs.

Jesus Christ, he said. Fuck fuck fuck. Fuck fuck fucking cold, until his feet started to go numb.

Teddy watched the cuffs of his khakis floating underwater. The mud wasn't coming out. Maybe in the wash. His mom was excellent with wash. His mom was smart and pretty and tall and thin and earned a lot of money, more than his dad did, but she was also a good mom. She did the grocery shopping and always bought at least two gallons of OJ for him and she remembered that John Rolston had basically fucked Teddy's ERA last season due to lazy throws to first, even if she didn't know what an ERA was. And now this: his mom didn't know, or maybe she did, and Teddy either had to tell her or not, he didn't know which.

He took another step into the water and his legs went electric, his skin seizing up, his nerves sending charges to his heart. If he'd stopped to think, he couldn't have done it, but he needed to do it, so he dove straight into the next wave that rolled up against his knees, like diving into a wall of bricks. The water was so fucking cold it hammered him down to the weedy lake bottom. He kicked but he couldn't put his feet down, and when he touched the ground with his fingers he realized his whole body was numb. It was like when he woke in the middle of the night with a dead arm and threw it against the wall and felt nothing. Teddy was dead, but not. Anyway, his dad was going to kill him.

He slogged on his hands and knees back up the beach, his clothes weighing a thousand wet pounds. Teddy peeled his shirt over his head, then dropped his khakis on the sand and wrung out the legs of his boxers. Shivering, he crossed the beach to his argyle socks and used them to towel off his frozen skin. The sun painted a stripe over the lake, brightening the sand at Teddy's feet and warming him. Sometimes the water was black and sometimes it was blue and sometimes it was green, and sometimes it was ice-still, which was why it was called Glimmerglass, and other times the wind whipped and chopped across the water until whitecaps rose and crashed.

Soon the sun would settle on the hills over West Lake Road, threatening to set. Teddy knew the time of day by heart. Practice was under way, but—strangely—he did not feel pulled to the red-dirt kingdom of Doubleday Field, to the pitcher's-mound seat of his throne. Instead, Teddy homed in on the sandy lakeshore. He lifted his white oxford shirt by the collar, a yellowish ring where his sweaty neck had been, then reached into the breast pocket and closed his frozen fingers over his father's Ted Williams card and pulled gently so he didn't rip the corners, gently so he didn't hurt the card more than he already had.

Teddy felt untethered, as if he had let go—or been let go of. Somewhere in the distance, the pine-covered hills bled into the baseball town at their feet. It wouldn't be long now: headlights, then house lights, the church steeples ringed by the sun's last light. Teddy couldn't make out any of this from where he stood, but he could see it in his mind. Back at home on Susquehanna Avenue, they would be worried, and it was strange to think that Teddy had the power to fix it but also the power to make it worse. Maybe he didn't have to tell. But he was crap with secrets, and he'd been schooled for eighteen years in his father's preschool curriculum: be honest, take responsibility for your actions, be brave.

7

That night, after writing the note about Carl's mom, I dreamed that Sam and Carl were super-pops with Teddy, his new pals, best friends. Images of the three of them—in Rick Delaney's Jeep, in Mr. Hershey's homeroom, in the dugout at Doubleday Field—minced through my filmic nightmare, and in every scene I was behind them, close enough to hear, but I couldn't call out, because the words I knew belonged to a dead language, a code with no key, and I alone spoke it, and I was already forgetting what the words could mean.

Wednesday morning Teddy and I left late for school, dragging our feet on the cracked sidewalks to slow ourselves down. I was nervous about seeing Sam and Carl, worried that my dream would prove a kind of premonition. Teddy was nervous about selling his baseball cards. He kept rehearsing how he'd explain it to Dad, cocurator and patron of his collection, which basically meant Dad owned the cards. I said nothing—Teddy was going to do whatever he was going to do, and Dad definitely wasn't going to understand.

"See you later," said Teddy at the door to his homeroom. "Remember." He held a finger to his lips—we were in on this Jeep-buying business together. I promised not to say a word.

As soon as I entered Mrs. Boulanger's homeroom, I saw I'd been right about Sam and Carl. Instead of welcoming me into the fold of my empty desk, Carl commenced eye-effing his chemistry textbook, while Sam drew pyramids on an old history handout. I stood behind them for a count of ten, waiting, waiting, but they wouldn't look at me and they wouldn't look at each other. Finally I crossed the room to my locker and spun the combo right-left-right through blurry eyes.

"Julia," said Mrs. Boulanger. "Find your seat, please," but I stayed at my locker, my classmates' voices echoing in my ears.

Kneeling in front of my backpack, I glanced at Carl. He wore a Myrtle Beach T-shirt and jeans with a blue ink stain on the pocket, and I could tell that he wasn't really reading by the way his eyes kept darting to the clock on the wall. In the same way I tried not to know too much about my parents' disagreements, I guess I'd avoided knowing this about Carl: he liked me, and the evidence was in the way he waited for me after class, looking for reasons to let his arm brush against mine, and in the way he called me at night with homework questions, the answers to which it was clear he already knew. It occurred to me that I was Carl's Sam, and I pictured a paper chain of broken hearts, each of us hooked on to the one person whose arms were out of our reach.

Just then I caught Sam stealing a look at me, his blond head bobbing up, his eyes—green-blue like the shallows of the lake—sweeping my face and pausing, locking on my eyes. My sinuses started to ache and I pushed my fingers into my tear ducts until I saw white. The day stretched out before me in light-years as I thought of all the places I'd have to see him—gym, lunch, tennis. I felt for the folded-up note about Carl's mom in my back pocket. In *The Sex Cure*, the characters were forever sabotaging their relationships because they loved each other too much, and I thought I could understand that. The only people who could really hurt us were the people we loved. I pictured someone unwrapping the note, discovering the nugget about Carl that couldn't help but be true, and there was a kind of power in the truth—by breaking the social bonds of friendship, I could send Carl running back to me; when the whole school was feeling sorry for him, who else would he want around him but his best friend?

When the bell rang for first period, I muscle-memoried to math class, eyes on my feet, sensing Carl in the hallway up ahead.

Mr. Robin was already stationed at the chalkboard, pumping his arms and marching in place as though he were going to lift off.

"Quiz day," he said, setting a kitchen timer for ten minutes. "Eyes on your own papers. Good luck." With a flick of his wrist, the projector screen sailed up, revealing five quadratic equations all requiring Carl's formula.

It felt like a month had passed since Monday night, when Carl had tried to get me to study with him. I could feel his finger poking my ribs, picture his mom's translucent orange pill bottle in the cabinet—but the pulse of the memory was still.

"Julia," Mr. Robin called, beckoning me to his desk. Arms out, palms up, he appeared genuinely baffled. "You've already wasted one-tenth of your time."

"I forgot my notebook," I said. "I don't have any paper."

Mr. Robin tapped his number-2 against his forehead, then pointed the eraser at me. "Who could help Miss Obermeyer with a sheet of paper?" he called.

No one responded—bungholes—then Carl opened his notebook and ripped out a piece without removing the fringies. Mr. Robin nodded in his direction.

Inside Carl's halo of desks, he reached up from his chair and handed me the white sheet without looking at me. There was a word, maybe. An open sesame or an abracadabra; a Perkins tardmore or a super big H. I closed my eyes and tried to see it. Ten times a day, through spontaneous acts of our imaginations, we pioneered new slitters for our lexicon: Sam whippoorwilled a forehand into the net; I went Cecil, letting a drop shot bounce twice; Carl's plan to get the goods was the key to salvation. Words burst out, broke in, and we played them, played with them, tasting them on our tongues. File, file out, you're filed out, that was the all out, I'm going all out, I'm going professional, profesh, provides, profit, please, oh please, take an order please, tardmore, two by two, file in, file. Let me have Sam. Dunghi, mayhi, bihi, sky high. Let me have Sam. My lights, my stars, for my sake.

"Carl," I said.

Carl glanced up, his jaw set, his gray eyes like stone, and I saw that this wasn't the Carl I knew, and there was no word for this.

Back in my seat, I wrote my name at the top of the page and copied down the first problem, but I couldn't concentrate. Suddenly I stood to lose both of my friends—Carl, when he found out I liked Sam; Sam, who had already taken Carl's side. The note about Carl's mom wouldn't fix anything—I wanted my friends back.

If I could reschedule the exhibition match, or somehow give it to Carl, maybe I might buy back their collective affections. This time I'd do everything out in the open and there'd be no ditching, no silent treatments. I practiced explaining it to Claw:

It's not that I don't want to play—

No.

I'm into—

No.

I want to play—I do want to play, but I can't on Thursday.

I exhaled and repeated it. The English language. Not so hard.

When Mr. Robin's timer went off, I passed my blank paper forward and asked permission to go to the bathroom, then headed off to the main office.

The secretaries' phones were reserved for emergencies, and it took a song and dance to convince Mrs. Bryant that I was having a tennis emergency.

"Honey," she said, "are you even on the team?"

I told her I was, but she had an official roster and my name wasn't on it.

"I'm co—team manager," I lied. "It's probably in the addenda."

Mrs. Bryant blinked. "Shouldn't you be in class right now?"

"Please, Mrs. Bryant. This is really important."

She glanced around the office and saw that Mrs. Hoeke wasn't listening, then bent low over the phone to dial. Her frosted hair fanned her face, hiding her mouth, and she spoke softly into the receiver before passing Claw to me.

I heard a saw buzzing in the background and then the sound of Claw's voice, pitched up a note.

"This is Barry," he said.

"Coach Klawson, it's Julia Obermeyer." For a second there was only the sound of the saw.

"Yes," he said. "What is it?"

"It's about the exhibition match tomorrow. I do want to play, but I can't on Thursday."

For a second I thought the line had been disconnected, then I heard him clearly, sharply. He seemed to have stepped into a private office and closed the door. "I went out of my way to arrange this for you," he said.

"I know," I said. "But Sam and Carl aren't speaking to me. I can't just go behind Carl's back and take a match without telling him."

"You didn't seem to have a problem with that yesterday," Claw pointed out.

"Right," I agreed. "But I've changed my mind."

"I see," said Claw. "Well, I guess that runs in the family—changing your mind."

My heart started to thump, sweat clamming my hands. He was talking about my father, I gathered, but just then it seemed incidental that I should be related to my parents—Sam and Carl were my family—and I didn't care what my father had done.

I turned my back to Mrs. Bryant and cradled the receiver with both hands. "Look—" I began.

"No, you look," said Claw. "I'm the coach. I run the team. If we're being honest here, you're not even on the team."

I said nothing.

"If you want to play, you do it my way. If not, don't bother coming back."

"Okay," I said, and okay that Poppy had backhanded me, and Teddy could buy a Jeep, okay. I pictured my brother halfway to Albany; Nonz was already gone. 59 Susquehanna, which had once felt enormous, had lately shrunk to the size of my parents' marriage. Okay was wishful thinking. Okay was willing it to be true.

"I'll think about it," Claw conceded. Then, "See you at practice."

I handed the phone to Mrs. Bryant. "All done?" she asked, but I was already backing away.

I went to the nurse's office. Mrs. Henderson took one look at me and forked over the Kleenex. "Are you sick?" she asked. I shook my head. "Do you want to lie down?" I nodded and she pointed to the back of her office.

On a cot in the dark, I hugged the Kleenex to my chest and pictured 122 Chestnut Street, where I'd had a room down the hall from the one that'd been Mom's when she was a little girl. Maybe Poppy missed Nonz, and maybe that was why he'd drummed my ear. He didn't hate me; he just didn't want to live with me. But he couldn't go home, because home wasn't a place, really; it was a set of people acting a certain way—alive, married, happy-ish—and when that was gone, you were sunk. I pictured Sam traveling between his parents' houses with two sets of everything. Two of everything, and still it wasn't enough.

* * *

Second period, for the first time in months, I made my way to the girls' locker room for gym class, spinning my combo 17-27-37, the same as homeroom, the same as Sam and Carl's—we'd shared everything back when we were friends.

"Is that Julia Obermeyer?" called Miss Horchow, following me to my locker bay near the showers. She stood with her legs apart, her arms crossed over her chest, her wraparound sunglasses perched on her head. "Glad your injuries have finally healed."

Two girls from my French class—Carrie Bosworth and Trisha Pashner—exchanged looks and I felt something pass between them, unspoken and knowing, and I thought of all the billions of words and signs coursing through the air at that very moment, electric pulses, signals picked up, signals ignored.

"Girls," said Miss Horchow, tapping her Timex.

"We're going as fast as we can," said Trisha.

I removed a pair of stiff gray sweatpants from my locker and pinched the plug of fabric jutting out where the hook had pressed through.

"Help yourself to the lost-and-found," said Miss Horchow. "The janitors cleaned over spring break. The clothes are mostly clean."

Carrie giggled and I turned in time to see her rounding the corner toward the field exit. Trisha followed, hopping on one foot, her left sneaker still in her hand. The smell of bubble gum—gym-class contraband—hung sweetly in the air.

I suited up in a long-sleeve T-shirt and a pair of cardinal mesh shorts with ONEONTA COLLEGE ATHLETICS printed on the leg. My socks were ossified at the bottom of my locker, so I went barefoot in my old Nikes, doubly sorry that I hadn't thought to shave my legs the night before.

Pausing at the full-length mirror, I thought of Sam in the boys' locker room on the other side of the painted cinder-block wall. Would he look for me on the bleachers? Would he be surprised not to see me? Did he even care? In the past, when Carl and I had fought, Sam had gone Switzerland; this time he'd taken Carl's side.

He likes you, you know.

In all the years we'd been friends, I had never taken Sam's hand, never taken his warm cheek in my hand, never touched his wheat-colored stubble with my fingertips, more golden than the hair on his head. And Sam had never pressed his callused palm to my cheek or run his hands along the ripples of my ribs. I had wished for it a thousand times. Eyes open, eyes closed. Clothes on, clothes off. Not just Sam but all of Sam.

He likes you, you know, he'd said, and now I saw Sam's words as a coin in the air. Maybe in telling me Carl liked me, Sam had really been asking if I liked Carl.

At the field exit, I pushed open the metal door and a blast of cold air penetrated my thin T-shirt. It was just past nine in the morning, the sky overcast, the grass thick with dew. I crouched and hugged my knees, rubbing the goose bumps on my shins.

"Bring it in," called Miss Horchow. She dropped a stack of Frisbees in the grass and started to hand out orange cones.

I saw my friends Katie and Em huddled with an orange cone at their feet. It'd been a couple of months since we'd last hung out, but I'd known them forever. In elementary school we played Cabbage Patch Kids and jumped Chinese jump rope and pierced our ears on the same day. In the fifth grade, we'd used Em's older brother's razor to nick our fingerprints, pressing our index fingers into the shape of a tepee, blood trailing our fingers to our wrists and staining our shirt cuffs red. It wasn't only me who'd drifted away this year. Katie had been farming Luke Fletcher since September, and Em had gotten mayhi into a group of juniors who did theater stuff. Somehow we'd remained friends, though, which gave me some hope for Sam and Carl and me.

I crossed the field toward them, waving once. "Hey," I said. "It's freezing."

Em twisted in place with her arms tucked inside her sweatshirt, her sleeves beating her like a drum.

"What are you doing out here?" said Em. "I thought you were too cool for gym."

"She's not too cool for gym," said Katie. "She's too cool for us."

Katie smiled—*kidding!*—her button nose wrinkling at the bridge. When we were little, Nonz had called her peppy, by which she'd meant that Katie was small and blond and pretty. Sam and Carl called her Teen Spirit.

"I heard Sam hooked up with someone in Myrtle," said Katie, frowning sympathetically.

I shrugged. "It was a dare."

"It didn't look like a dare," said Em.

Had she seen it? I kind of wanted to ask her what it had looked like. The way I kept picturing it was broad daylight, Sam and Megan holding hands on the boardwalk and stopping every few steps to make out. Sam would've been wearing a T-shirt and his baseball cap—he burned easily—but this girl? Short-shorts, bikini top, SPF 4. In that outfit, it might not have mattered how Perkins she was.

"Okay, ladies," said Miss Horchow. "Teams of three. You know the drill. Miss Vincent, Miss Chatham—Miss Obermeyer is on your team."

"Go, team," said Em, stooping to pick up our cone. She set it on her head and walked heel-toe, with her chin in the air, her pigtails bobbing.

"Are you and Sam going out?" asked Katie. She tossed me our Frisbee and I caught it in my stomach.

"No," I said.

"Everyone thinks you are," said Katie.

"What does everyone think Carl's doing with us?"

"Carl's so cute," said Em, nodding the cone into her hands. "I think my sister should go for him."

Em's sister, Maggie, was in the eighth grade and had enormous boobs. I earmarked the idea.

"We're just friends," I said finally.

"Do you like him?" asked Katie.

"Do you guys hook up?" asked Em.

I held the Frisbee in front of me like it was a plate I was afraid to break. In the last few months, Sam had found at least as many reasons to brush up against me as Carl had, and he'd called at night without even the pretense of homework, and in the dark on the path down to the tennis courts the night before, I had to believe that he'd been trying to tell me that he liked me, too, Sam did, it had to be.

"Do you?" asked Em again.

"No," I said.

"Then you're not going out," she said.

Miss Horchow blew her whistle and Em staked our cone near a rickety goalpost still used for youth soccer games. It was the same field we'd played on when we were little, Em and Katie and me in the backfield, goals scoring one after another while Katie's dad screamed his head off from the sideline and we made daisy-chain crowns for our heads. The field had stayed the same size but we'd grown up, gone coed.

Back in the locker room, Em did an impression of our elementary school gym teacher pulling us up by our ponytails to correct our postures. I laughed, wondering if maybe I'd missed them after all, and then the bell rang for third period and I asked if I could eat lunch with them later that day.

"I have rehearsal," said Em apologetically. "We eat in Mr. Drury's room. And Kaaaay-teeeee—"

"Shut! Up!" said Katie.

"Katie has lunch in Luke's big, huge—"

Katie clamped a hand over Em's mouth and then their hands and arms were intertwined, their long hair masking each other's faces, their voices lashing at each other's unfinished sentences. I tried to follow, I wanted to get the joke, but I couldn't understand what they were saying, and after a while I got bored and wandered away.

The rest of the day passed quickly—no one spoke to me, and I spoke to no one. At lunch I sat by myself in the corner of the cafeteria and worked on the *Daily Star* crossword puzzle. Halfway through the period, our lunch monitor asked me where my friends were, and I looked over my shoulder and saw that they weren't at our table. "Did something happen?" she asked. I stared at her blankly, then shook my head no.

After school I went to the gym to wait for Claw to bring the Womb around—without a ride to Bassett Hall, I'd have to take the team bus. It was strange to be spending so much time by myself. I tested my voice on Claw, told him I hadn't brought my tennis clothes, and when we got to the courts, he sent me home to change.

Back at Bassett, I joined the drill line behind Alan, who was six foot four, our center forward, and an excellent barrier to Sam and Carl.

"What are you doing?" asked Alan.

"Practicing," I said.

Doug snorted. "This should be interesting," he said.

At three thirty, Claw dragged the hopper of tennis balls to the middle of Court 1 and called for everyone's attention. "Evan," he said, pointing to the baseline. "Ground stroke, approach shot, volley." Nothing about my unexpected participation. "Ready?"

He fed Evan three balls and we watched our captain pound three straight into the back fence.

"Evan," Claw groaned.

"Sorry," he said, scuffing his toes on the dark-green surface.

"End of the line," said Claw, and practice was under way.

Next up was Sam, who advanced on the ball, kissed the sideline with a topspin forehand, then picked up Claw's short ball at the T and hooked it into the deep ad court. At net, he finished with a slice volley to Claw's feet, impossible to return, and jogged away, satisfied.

This was what practice would've been like if I'd tried out, if I'd made the team—someone behind me said, "Your turn," and I stepped to the baseline and crouched low. Claw fed me a forehand and I looped the ball down the line, sailing it just long. Eventually I would've gotten better, started making my shots, reducing my unforced errors. I approached the net and punched a volley crosscourt.

"Back of the line," said Claw.

I went to the back of the line. Sam and Carl were right in front of me but it was also like we'd never met and I didn't watch to see how they played; I didn't want to know.

"Points," said Claw, when he introduced the next drill. "Play them out. We've got our first match tomorrow. Settle in, think about your footwork, think about your placement. Hit high-percentage shots and control the play."

I listened to the sounds of the points, and as the rallies went on I found that I could identify the shots by the pitch they made coming off the strings. I'd hear a solid *thunk* and feel my feet backing me up to the baseline. An uncertain *thwink* brought me up to the T. But when my turn came, I fluffed the first feed into the net.

"Concentrate," said Claw.

I stepped in and took the second feed on the rise, moving it deep into the forehand court nearly beyond Claw's reach. He scrambled over in carioca step and uncoiled a one-handed backhand lob, a bit of a desperation shot that fell short of the T. The point was mine to win, and I moved in to crush it, plowing it instead into the net.

"Dammit!" I yelled.

"Language," said Claw. He pointed to the gate and I trolled out for five penalty laps. It was the kind of thing Sam and Carl and I would've laughed about, but we didn't even look at one another.

At five fifteen, Claw called for suicides. Sideline to center line and back, sideline to opposite sideline and back. Repeat five times.

I ran as if I were being chased. My lungs heaved and my legs were jelly, but I willed myself in—third after Phillip and Evan—collapsing at the baseline on Court 1.

"Nice," said Claw, clapping. He stood with his fingers laced through the chain-link fence. His cheeks and nose were sunburned, his millions of freckles colored in. "Get a water break if you need one."

No one moved. The sun danced on the court, breaking through the pine trees in wobbly yellow lines. I looked up, cupping my hands around my eyes like blinders until all I could see was sky.

"Okay," said Claw, "listen up."

We spun to face him. Sam sat cross-legged at the front of the group, his arms locked at his sides, his shoulder blades jutting out like wings under his T-shirt. Far to the right, Carl hunched with his elbows on his knees.

"We have our first match tomorrow," said Claw. "For those of you who don't remember or weren't here, Sauquoit beat us last year, and all their players are back."

"Great," said Evan. "I get the paddy-baller again."

"What do you do with junk balls?" asked Claw. "You attack. Hit the ball out in front of you; use heavy topspin. And come to net."

"Except I can't volley," said Evan.

"You were swinging up there today. Punch it. Shorten your back-swing on your approach shot."

Evan nodded.

"Sam," said Claw. He scanned the group until he found him. "What's the plan?"

"Hit a massive serve."

"Right," said Claw. "Then concentrate on holding."

Sam nodded, and Claw pointed to Danke Schoen.

"Friedrich," he said. "You feel good?"

"Yes," said Danke Schoen, nodding.

"Doubles," said Claw. "Phillip and T.J.?"

"Locked up," they said in unison.

Alan and Doug high-fived and agreed they were ready to go.

"Okay. Announcement," said Claw. "There's going to be an exhibition match tomorrow, so everyone plan to stay. Julia and Carl." My stomach dropped, then rose, as I calculated, computed. Sam turned to face me, asking me with his eyes if I'd known about this, and I shook my head no.

"Carl," Claw continued, "you're trying out Julia for the team. If she wins, she's on."

"What if she loses?" asked Carl.

"If she loses, she's off."

It was a fair deal. I tried to catch Claw's eye but he was already collecting the equipment, his hand on the hopper. "Anyone coming with me," he said, "get on the bus. The rest of you, see you tomorrow at three o'clock." Soon the Womb was motoring off toward Beaver Street and Sam and Carl and I were alone.

Carl said, "I'm not going to let you win."

"I know."

He walked over to the bench to collect his sweatshirt while Sam scooted closer to me.

"Hey," he said.

"You're speaking to me again?"

"That was more Carl," said Sam.

"It was you, too."

Sam ran a hand over his buzzed hair. "An exhibition match between you and Carl," he said, considering it. "You could win, you know? You played really well today." I felt a thaw pass into my stomach and legs. Sam stood and dusted off his shorts. "Want a ride?" he asked, and I started to say yes but then I remembered that he'd have to drop me off first.

"I'll walk," I said. Sam took a ball from his pocket and threw it at me, and I caught it and kept it, bouncing it on the sidewalk on the way home.

*　*　*

At 59 Susquehanna, both my parents' cars were in the driveway and I steeled myself for their iciness but instead found Mom and Dad huddled with Poppy around the kitchen island, Mom gripping the cordless phone, her face ash gray.

"What's wrong?" I asked.

"Have you seen your brother?" she asked.

"No."

"He cut school," said Dad. "He didn't show up for practice."

I studied Dad's face. He looked tired, dark shadows circling his eyes. His cowlick was sticking up like he hadn't combed his hair in days.

"How do you know he cut school?" I crossed the kitchen to the cabinet and got out a glass.

Mom nodded toward Poppy. "Your grandfather told us."

"The school called this afternoon," said Poppy officiously. "I said, 'Mrs. Hoeke, I'm going to hang up this phone right now and I'm going to call his mother.'"

Mom turned to me. "Did you know anything about this?"

I shook my head, filling my glass at the tap. If Poppy was answering the phone, our fail-safe plan to erase the answering machine before our parents heard the school's message was shot. Even so, Teddy should've been home by now.

Mom studied my face. "What?" she said.

"Nothing."

Dad stood, scraping the legs of the stool against the polished wood floor, then started toward the back stairs.

"Where are you going?" asked Mom.

"To shower. I can't think straight."

We listened to Dad's footsteps on the stairs, over the kitchen, over the hallway.

Mom said, "Did you see your brother at school?"

"We walked in together."

"And he didn't say anything about cutting?"

I shook my head again, a weight settling in my stomach. Even if I told them where he'd gone, that didn't explain where he was now. Teddy and Dave should've been back hours ago.

Mom scooted past me, pulling a bottle of wine out of the fridge and uncorking it with a pop. I watched the buttery liquid flood her glass, sloshing up the sides and settling near the rim.

Before taking a sip, Mom pushed her hair back with both hands, giving herself a mini face-lift. Suddenly her brow was smooth and the tiny lines at the corners of her eyes disappeared, and she looked young. It was weird to think she'd been my age once, that she'd grown up here, gone to school here, had some friends but not a boyfriend, same as me.

"Are you really worried?" I asked.

"What do you think?"

I shrugged. "He'll come home soon."

"He's never done anything like this," said Mom, and it was true. The very fact that he'd skipped baseball practice was enough to make you think he was pinned under the wheels of a bus somewhere.

I took the long way to my bedroom, pausing in Mom's office to grab the phone book, then hightailed it upstairs. On my bed, I flipped to the Bs and used my Swatch phone to dial Dave's number. When his mother answered, I told her who I was and asked to speak to Dave.

"Is he home?" asked Dave as soon as he came on the line.

"I thought he was with you."

"He was," said Dave. "We went to Albany, and then on the way home he jumped out of the car. I'm not kidding. Outside Cherry Valley. That was, like, one thirty."

I held my breath. It was past six now. In an hour, it would be dark. "Julia?"

"Did you try looking for him?"

"He took off."

"Why would he do that?" I asked.

"I have no idea," said Dave. "I thought maybe he was upset about selling his baseball cards. Or just sick of me."

I said nothing and Dave said nothing. We'd known each other for ages but we'd never spoken on the phone and I was eager for it to be over.

"We could go look for him," Dave suggested.

I pictured Dave's blue Saab and the two of us inside it.

"I don't think I can," I said. "My parents are really worried."

"Do they know he was with me?" asked Dave.

"No."

Dave paused, then said, "You should probably tell them." Before I could hang up, he said, "Julia, would you want to do something this weekend?" He cleared his throat. "Like, go to dinner? Or there's kind of a cool art museum in Utica."

I tried to picture Dave opening the car door for me, buying my museum ticket, then kissing me on my front porch at the end of the night, but I couldn't see it, not the way I could see Sam. "I have a boyfriend," I said, willing it to be true.

"Oh," said Dave. "Right. Well, tell Teddy to call me."

"I will." I hung up the phone and counted to ten, then went downstairs to confess.

"Wait," said Mom. She went to get Dad, leaving me in the kitchen with Poppy. He licked his lips with saliva so thick that I could hear it on his tongue, and when he shifted on his stool, his arm skin flaked onto the island.

"Okay," said Mom, returning with Dad in tow. "Let's hear it."

I told them everything: Rick Delaney, the Wrangler, Dave, the baseball cards, the trip to Albany, Teddy running off into the woods, my promise not to tell.

"He just jumped out of the car?" asked Mom.

"I guess."

"Where?" asked Dad.

"Dave said Cherry Valley."

"Cherry Valley?" Dad repeated, alarmed.

Mom looked up.

"Maybe I should go after him," he said, already moving toward the door. "He can't be far."

I couldn't picture Teddy sitting on the pitcher's mound waiting for us to pick him up—if he was missing, he didn't want to be found—but Dad collected his car keys and shut the door behind him without saying goodbye.

Upstairs, I sat at my desk and stared at my backpack. I had fifty pages of *Wuthering Heights* to read for English and a chem lab to write, but I couldn't concentrate. It meant something that Teddy hadn't come home to erase the school's message—he wouldn't have thought of Poppy answering the phone. He wanted to be caught, maybe, or he wanted Mom and Dad to worry, but there was enough to worry about without Teddy's tardmore antics, and I found myself angry at him for making things even worse than they already were.

Forty-five minutes into my homework, I gave up and considered calling Sam. Carl hadn't looked at me when he'd left the courts, but he had said goodbye, which at least meant he was speaking to me. The question was, what now?

It was then that I remembered the note about Carl's mom, and I picked up my jeans off the floor and felt inside the back pockets, but they were empty. I stood and stuffed my hands into the front pockets, turning the liners inside out, milking the fabric: empty. Sweat beaded on my forehead—it was too bright in the room, two thousand degrees. I flapped the jeans. Nothing. I thought of all the desk chairs I'd sat in that day, all the classrooms in which the note might have worked its way up and out of my pocket; I thought of the girls' locker room before gym class, where I'd carelessly dropped my jeans on the floor. I dug into the clothing pile in my bedroom, shaking shirts and pants over the rug, whipping empty sleeves, but it was gone, MIA, out in the world for anyone to read.

Downstairs, the front door opened and I had no choice: I left my room and crept to the seventh step on the back staircase, where I could spy into the kitchen without being seen.

"Where have you been?" asked Mom.

Teddy walked into the kitchen with his shirttails untucked beneath his sweatshirt, his laces untied, his khakis wet and dirty. His lips were nearly blue: it looked like he'd been swimming.

"You have five seconds to start talking," said Mom.

The sound of Poppy's steps from the den echoed in the stairwell, and I hugged my legs to my chest and stayed low.

Poppy sat on Teddy's stool. "Your principal called," he said, as if he were our father.

"Why would the principal call?" asked Teddy. There was something new in his voice, a go-eff-yourself-ness that sounded wrong on Teddy's tongue. He took a granola bar from the bread drawer and began to unwrap it.

"Teddy," said Mom desperately. "We've been worried sick about you."

"We?" Teddy looked left, then right. "Where's Dad?"

"Where do you think?" Mom snapped. She took a step toward Teddy. "What's that?"

Teddy shifted, hiding what looked like a wet piece of paper.

"Nothing," said Teddy, but when Mom took his hand, he allowed her to pry back his fingers, and I leaned over the railing until I could make out Dad's Ted Williams card, signed for his brother, George, just before he drowned at a place called Reacher Falls.

No one spoke. The front door was opening again and soon we heard the sound of Dad dropping his car keys in the silver bowl and then, "It's too dark out there. I could barely see the sidewalks."

"Hugh," said Mom.

Dad walked into the kitchen and stopped. He looked at Mom, who nodded toward Teddy's hand.

"I saw you today," said Teddy.

Dad reached for the card, but this time Teddy stepped back.

"I saw you kiss that woman's hand—"

"Stop," said Dad, and in two quick steps his hands were on Teddy's face, not so much hitting him as trying to push his words back into his mouth.

He grabbed Teddy's arm and Teddy jerked away, and for a second I thought Teddy was going to hit our father, but instead he crushed the baseball card in his hand, then slapped it on the island, the wet cardboard curling at the edges.

I wanted to move but I was Tasered. Teddy thundered past me on the stairs and I told myself to follow him, but I couldn't move my legs.

In the kitchen, Mom picked up a tea towel and threw it at Dad. She was crying but Dad didn't go to her. Instead, he folded the towel and leaned over his card and gently began to blot.

8

Despair tugged at Anne's heart and danced in her peripheral vision. She tried to listen to Hugh's story about an injured boy on the playground at Seedlings, but she was too distracted by images of her own children, just upstairs, who had come into this world when called, dutifully showing up for years now to clean their rooms, finish their dinners, ride in the backseats of cars—all the things that kids did—and now Hugh had brought something horribly adult—complicated, insoluble—into their house, while Anne, who ought to have known better, had instead been steeled by her own childhood wounds, certain it couldn't happen again.

Now her eyes were wide open, trying not to cry, and all she could think was, I want my mother. How would Joanie have managed this? Hints and innuendos would not solve Anne's problems: from what she understood, Hugh had committed adultery with a woman whose son was being treated for an injury whose cause may have been the Seedlings School's negligent supervision on the playground (though if schools must supervise their students only as a parent of "ordinary prudence" would supervise his or her child [*Ramirez v.*

Brookhaven School District], then Caroline Murphy, who fucked the school's principal while her son lay semiconscious seven steps away, ought to think twice about introducing the topic of negligent supervision). God only knew how many people had witnessed this tryst. Ron Metcalf, MD, the boy's surgeon and Anne's cochair on the booster club's annual Not Quite Free Throw committee? Luanne Thompson, RN, who'd kindly squeezed in Teddy for his third MMR shot before the September 1 school deadline? Wally O'Shea, PsyD, pediatric psychologist and Anne's junior high science partner, who'd once pushed her into Mr. Franconi's coat closet for a not-unwelcome French kiss? To date, the only known witness was Graham Pennington, age five, the injured boy at the heart of the case.

But Teddy, too, had seen something, this very afternoon in Cherry Valley, witness to his father kissing a woman's hand. Anne was not nearly guileless enough to believe that Hugh's hospital-room incident was an isolated event, though he maintained he'd been at Caroline Murphy's house today only to discuss the lawsuit, kissing her hand as a way to say thank you. Was Anne supposed to believe this shit? Part of her wanted to stand up right now and toss Hugh out of the house. Instead she remained locked to the seat of her desk chair, arms crossed, and when her body began to shake, right foot hooked around left ankle, anchoring herself to herself.

She pictured an early autumn evening in Boston, a Saturday, when she was seven months pregnant with Teddy. Anne and Hugh had spent the day at garage sales, hunting for a set of dining-room chairs, and now Anne had collapsed on the couch with their plastic shopping bags—six records, an alarm clock, a new paperback, but no chairs—and kicked off her espadrilles, which had carved deep purple lines into her flesh. Hugh, meanwhile, had gone to their bedroom to change and she'd expected him to return in sweatpants and a T-shirt so that they could spend the rest of the evening right there on the couch, but instead he'd emerged in khakis and a pressed shirt, his hair combed and parted, his face newly shaved.

Hugh's coworker was having a birthday party in Beacon Hill, he reminded her, and it was true that he'd told her about it a week ago, but they weren't really going to go, were they? They'd been running around all day, and now that they were home, Anne couldn't think of a reason in the world to go back out again.

"Come on," he said, "we'll only stay for an hour."

But they'd have to take the T, and she'd have to shower, and Anne didn't think she owned a pair of shoes that could contain her swollen feet.

If she had demurred, waffled; if she'd said that the party would be crowded, that the birthday boy wouldn't miss him; if she'd pointed out that Hugh had recently complained about this very coworker for hijacking Hugh's research before Hugh himself could make sense of the data; if she had simply asked him to stay. But Hugh was all dressed up, looking so handsome in the plaid shirt that Anne had bought for him, and so what if he wanted to go to a party and she didn't? Hugh was nothing like her father—his face was an open book, and she would know immediately if something untoward had occurred.

So she told him to go without her. "Have fun," she said. A permission slip, her blessing. "I'll be fine," she said.

But as soon as Hugh was gone, Anne's hands began to tremble, and no amount of reason or logic would still them. She was slipping; she couldn't hold on. She felt thirteen years old again, still playing a part in some other play, and she reached instinctively for the device that had soothed her as a child: Anne envisioned a metal cage descending over her heart. Impenetrable. Inviolable. She could not be hurt. And when Hugh had returned two hours later, just as he'd said he would, when her husband kissed her on the forehead and asked her what she'd been up to while he was out, Anne had said coolly, "Nothing," feeling nothing. "Just catching up on work."

Work, up to eighty hours a week for more than eighteen years now, with children at home who had, when suffering from fever or nightmares, inevitably gone to their father's side of the bed. Work to defray the considerable start-up and subsequent operating costs of the Seedlings School—her husband's dream—for more than fifteen years. Work to keep their children in Levi's and Swatch watches, Nikes and Walkmen, CB jackets and Nintendos and *all the things they had to have*. Work, too, because her own mother hadn't, and because Anne had witnessed firsthand what could happen when fathers were too often away from home. And now work as Seedlings' legal adviser to save her husband's school, to save their marriage, or to at least give them a fighting chance, because that was what they wanted, wasn't it?

Anne rested her pen on her legal pad and regarded Hugh. After an hour and a half holed up in her office, their children and her father in isolation upstairs, Anne-the-lawyer was confident that she had the facts of the negligence case. She understood the issues presented by the facts, she was prepared to outline the applicable rules of law and write a motion, but she was not prepared to address Hugh's infidelity. Because although Anne-the-wife might have wanted to send Hugh packing—straight over to Randolph DeVey, who specialized in wayward spouses—Hugh was unfortunately *her* wayward spouse, her kids' father, and for their sakes alone neither Randolph DeVey nor anyone else in Cooperstown could find out about this.

"At her house today," Anne prompted, "what exactly did you talk about?"

"I told her that I strongly believe the playground is safe, that Graham's accident was just that—an accident—and that if it's a question of money—"

"You discussed money?"

"Not in so many words."

Anne frowned, crossing her legs knee over thigh. Her khaki pants hiked up over her bare left ankle and she quickly yanked down on the hem.

"It's not like that," said Hugh, averting his eyes.

"It's not like what?"

"She's not after money. She's on our side."

Now Anne cocked her chin and raised her eyebrows, daring him to elaborate.

"I only mean that she wants this to go away as much as we do. But I guess her ex-husband has custody or something, so it's his decision."

Ex-husband and *custody* gusted through the room like Arctic breezes. Anne hugged herself while consulting her yellow pad but found nothing useful on the page. At her law firm she was famous for the "aha" moment, when an argument would be made known to her, when she would see clearly, before anyone else, how to string the facts into a cogent tale so that a judge, a jury, heard only what she wanted them to hear. But this case—Hugh's case—was unfathomable. Their interaction felt clinical. Anne tried to recall when was the last time they'd spooned at night or planted foamy kisses on each other's cheeks while brushing their teeth. Years had passed. Years.

"This husband," said Anne. "This ex-husband. Have you talked to him?"

"Not yet."

Hugh ran a hand over his head. Sweat had pooled under his arms, staining his blue button-down a damp navy. His unfastened shirt cuffs yawned at his wrists. The windows along the alcove behind Anne's desk were cracked, a breeze evident in the occasional fluttering of papers across her blotter, but the overhead lights were on and Anne's gooseneck was spotlighting Hugh like an interrogation lamp.

"Sorry," said Anne, adjusting the desk lamp, then crossing the room to the switch plate, where she shut down one set of track lights. "Better?"

"Much," said Hugh. "Thanks."

Anne returned to her swivel chair, marveling at her capacity for civility. If asked earlier today how she'd planned to spend her evening, she would not have forecast the meltdown of her marriage, yet here she was, and in a way it was not so surprising, not so utterly shocking. Just last night, hadn't she drafted a fifteen-page legal document addressing Hugh's suspicious behavior? But there was "suspecting" and there was "knowing," and Anne had not truly believed him capable of this.

Anne could feel Hugh watching her. She hadn't been this aware of his gaze since they'd starting dating, twenty years before.

"What?" she asked, touching her hand to her mouth.

"Nothing."

Hugh leaned back on the leather couch, his feet extended in front of him. He was barefoot, his second toes longer than his first. His arches curved gracefully, the skin delicate and smooth where his feet had never touched the ground.

"She was talking about their divorce proceedings," Hugh offered. "Apparently he made them pretty tough."

Anne clicked her pen, rapid-firing the nib.

"She said he got some million-dollar lawyer and used the AA thing to completely wipe her out."

"The AA thing?"

Hugh stopped, looked up. "I don't know. She's in recovery, she said."

"Did you see any alcohol in the house? Empty bottles? Did you smell anything?"

"In *recovery*. We had peppermint tea."

Now Anne conjured a tin of assorted teas slid across a worn wooden table, the light through the window coating her husband's hand as he picked through his choices—Lemon Zinger, Earl Grey, orange pekoe—before selecting the green wrapper, the stomach settler, the breath freshener: almost as good as brushing his teeth.

Anne looked up at the ceiling, blinking rapidly.

"If she's compelled to testify—"

"She won't say anything," said Hugh.

"Why? Because you asked her not to? What happens when her ex-husband threatens to take back the kid?"

"She doesn't want to be involved," said Hugh.

"Too late," said Anne.

Hugh squeezed his temples, hooding his eyes, and Anne sensed a shade being drawn down between them: Hugh was on the inside and Anne was on the outside, and it was not clear he wanted her back in.

"Hugh," she said, ashamed of the pleading in her voice.

Now Hugh lowered his hand and looked at her. "What happened at the hospital," he said carefully, "is irrelevant. She said so herself."

Anne's heart flip-flopped in her chest. In the left ventricle, joy— maybe it had been only the one time. In the right ventricle, fear— Hugh, it seemed, was disappointed; evidently, he might've been open to more.

"You mean—"

"I mean my only concern is the school."

Anne waited for him to elaborate, to include his wife and children in this realm of concern. When he didn't, she laughed once, a single *ha!* that startled Hugh into asking what was so funny, and she shook her head in disbelief, wondering if she'd ever find anything funny again.

"I don't think you're really hearing me," said Anne, anger finally creeping into her voice. "Before you all but had sex with this woman, there was no problem. Now, if she says something, or if the *child*, who saw it *happen*, tells his *father*? That's the school, Hugh. And almost certainly our marriage."

"Tell me what to do," said Hugh.

"Time travel," said Anne. "Go back. Undo."

Hugh pinched the bridge of his nose between his dark eyes, his brows draining into a V, and the thought occurred to Anne—a revelation, her "aha" moment—that he could leave. He could leave this house, go outside and find Randolph DeVey and tell him everything, go to the Hawkeye or the Pit or the Doubleday and tell the bartender everything, go to school in the morning and tell every mother who pulled up to the curb everything. Picturing the whole town armed with Hugh's story, ready to talk, Anne was angry, hurt, confused; also restless, energized, anxious; she was other things, too, things she never would've expected: forgiving, regretful, placating; lonely, culpable, tired; she was, shamefully, turned on. And she couldn't resolve this tumble of feelings into a single purpose—forgiveness brought on anger; hurt gave way to regret. She needed time, Hugh's patience. But were Hugh and she still on the same team? Did being on Hugh's side against Richard Pennington mean that she forgave him for what he'd done with Caroline Murphy? Worse yet, did Hugh want to be forgiven?

"Do you think they have a case?" asked Hugh. "About the playground?"

"I don't know."

"I should tell you," he said, "there wasn't a head teacher on yard duty at the time." He shrugged helplessly. "Just two assistants."

"Did you send a copy of the accident report to the licensor?"

"Mrs. Baxter did it."

"Did you call Charlie Stanwood?"

"No," said Hugh, shaking his head. "Until yesterday, I didn't think Graham's fall was a problem."

Anne made a note: *Call Charlie.* She checked her watch—9:15; too late now.

"Maybe nothing will come of it," Hugh offered.

"Maybe."

The ticking of the wall clock was a third heartbeat in the room. Anne flipped the pages of her legal pad. In the margin of one page, she found that she'd sketched a picture of a house—their house, she supposed, though it could've been any house with a front walk and a door centered between two windows with three more upstairs: Hugh and Anne's bedroom.

"Hugh," she said, her voice wobbling. "How could you do this?"

He ducked his head. "I don't know," he said. "I don't entirely know."

Anne requested a few minutes alone and Hugh nodded, then crossed the room to the glass-paned doors. He stopped, turned. Anne saw that he was about to speak and she quickly looked away.

When Hugh was gone, Anne stretched across the couch, curling on her side, her back snug against the puffy brown leather, her toes pressed into the dusty tufted buttons. She took a deep breath, then another. On her third breath a sob welled inside her and finally broke.

Cleaning out her parents' house last week had not been nearly as therapeutic as Anne had hoped. Too much time had passed, maybe, and the rooms had acquired new associations since she was a little girl. Standing in her old bedroom at the top of the stairs, Anne had thought not about lying awake under her polka-dotted bedspread, listening for the sound of her father's car in the driveway, but about laying her tiny daughter down for a nap in the corner of the sectional sofa. She couldn't conjure her old bedroom, which had long since been converted into a sitting room, her furniture replaced with a navy velour living-room set. Even the smell was different: her mother had switched laundry detergents, her father had quit smoking, and the carpet on which Anne had spilled her bottle of Jungle Gardenia had been traded in for a sky-blue low-pile that faintly reeked of glue.

While Hugh and the kids were downstairs dismantling the den around her father, Anne had stood in the center of her old bedroom and tried to see herself in it, but the repapered walls wouldn't turn into her daisy border, and the velour furniture was like a boxy policeman blocking the road back to her single bed, her rolltop desk, her vanity, which had been her mother's. Finally she'd had to close her eyes in order to see the room she was already standing in, and even then she was not *in* it but floating above it, looking down from the ceiling on her teenage self, as though it had happened to someone else.

And how many times had it really happened? Twice? Ten times? Twenty? Anne was not prone to exaggeration—she liked certainty, precision, exactness—but she honestly didn't know. The memories had blurred, blended, and rearranged themselves into a temporal impossibility: both that it had and had not happened. Every single night of Anne's life, her father was home by six and they sat down to dinner at six thirty, except for the nights when he wasn't home by six, seven, eight, and inside those memories was his untouched plate of food at the head of the table, she and her mother picking at their dinners, stalling, talking sometimes but mostly not, until they had waited as long as they could and her mother stood and cleared the table and placed her father's plate in the oven, set to one hundred degrees, to be kept warm for whenever he arrived.

Anne could still smell the greasy chicken, dry white rice, buttered carrots slow-cooking through the night; feel her mother's presence ghosting the house like a force field, unapproachable, unavoidable; hear the unmistakable sounds of housework, undertaken before dawn, so that by the time Anne descended for school at seven o'clock the kitchen had been scrubbed, the burners scoured, the linoleum mopped, the Formica bleached, and her father's single gleaming plate propped in the rack to dry, its face wiped clean.

And then there was *The Sex Cure*—pressed between her parents' mattress and box spring—and it was 1962 again, Anne a gangly eighth-grader who'd long substituted books for best friends. In those days, Joanie had left her copy in plain sight, bookmarked on her nightstand or tented over the arm of her reading chair in the tiny library, where Anne had always been welcome to borrow anything, and it was here that Anne began to consume the story. June Dieterle, the babysitter in *The Sex Cure* with a proclivity for administering chloral hydrate to her charges, was one letter removed from Anne's own childhood babysitter, Mrs. Jane Dieterle, whom Anne remembered as a gracious tea-party guest and great cutter of paper dolls. Art Peevers, henchman to the Potter-like Mr. Stevens in the novel, had the exact same name as Mr. Arthur T. Peevers, her father's friendly rival in the insurance business.

Anne had desperately wanted to see her parents in Sandy Miles, who ran the thoroughbred riding stables, and his wife, Marge, a lab

assistant at the hospital, because, unlike the rest of the characters in
The Sex Cure, the Mileses were happily faithful and in love. And half
the story had tracked: Joanie had been a nurse at Bassett Hospital until
Anne was born, but Anne had failed to find her father in Sandy Miles,
who had never loved any woman but Marge. Anne could still recall
one of the book's saddest lines: *Why did children persist in thinking the
years brought wisdom?* Anne had expected to be able to protect herself
from all this when she became an adult—armed with the knowledge
of what was possible, she would know how to avoid it. But how stupid
she had been! While Anne had smugly believed she was in control,
Hugh had been cavorting with a divorcée in the aptly fogged-in
Cherry Valley, and it was all so predictable in a way that Anne wondered if she hadn't invited it. Was there a difference between *being
prepared* and *preparing for*? Because here she was, right where her mother
had been, with the same problems, the same decisions to make, the
same children upstairs.

Anne opened her office doors and found Hugh sitting in the
doorjamb between the kitchen and the center hall, waiting for her. He
stood, balancing a cup of milky coffee in his right hand. "I made you
one, too," he said, nodding toward the kitchen.

He realized then that she'd been crying and took a careful step
toward her, shifting his coffee to his left hand. With the pad of his
right thumb, he wiped under her nose, then cleaned his thumb on his
shirt. He stepped back and asked her if she was okay.

"No," said Anne. "Not exactly."

She ignored the steaming coffee he'd brewed and went instead to
the refrigerator, where she retrieved a bottle of white wine, half depleted,
and upended it into a stem glass. Four gulps later she shuttled the
empty bottle into the recycling bin under the sink, then returned to
the fridge for a second bottle.

"I'm going to talk to Teddy," said Anne, cradling her glass in both
hands.

Hugh leaned against the counter, an island between them. His Roman nose was burned from afternoons passed on the playground at school. Just about any other man in the role of nursery school teacher would've given Anne the creeps, but Hugh was a grown-up version of the sensitive camp counselor, the one all the kids clung to when it was time to go home.

Now he pinched his chapped lips into a line that neither frowned nor smiled. When was the last time she had kissed those lips? It had been nearly two months since they'd had sex. They kept different schedules, went to bed at different times, and, really, he hadn't seemed to miss it.

"Maybe I should go with you," said Hugh.

"No," said Anne.

"If you go up there alone, Teddy's going to think we're not together on this."

"We're *not* together on this," said Anne reasonably.

Hugh pointed to the ceiling: Julia's room and, across from hers, Anne's father's. He held a finger to his lips, then nodded back toward her office. Anne wrung the wine bottle's neck, toting it along.

They sat next to each other on her chesterfield, with only a narrow space between them. She refilled her wineglass and offered Hugh the first sip. He shook his head.

"I was saying, we"—Hugh paddled the air between them to show that this particular *we* excluded the children—"aren't really together on this. But we"—here Hugh made a circle, encompassing the entire room and presumably the entire family—"are always going to be together. Right? Because children want to know what's going to happen to them. Are they safe? Are they secure? Are they loved by both parents?"

Watching her husband pantomime his bullshit child-centered approach, it occurred to Anne that she had married Mister Rogers. Patience, routine, reliability, reassurance. And, of course, the Neighborhood of Make-Believe.

"He saw you kissing a woman," Anne pointed out. "If I don't give him a context for it, he'll make his own."

"What are you going to say?" asked Hugh.

"Nothing about the hospital, if that's your concern."

"Right," said Hugh. "That's good."

She didn't want to think about their lives without Seedlings. Eight years of college to pay for, her father to take care of. Anne was still the primary provider in the family, but Hugh was gaining on her; each year, Seedlings was more profitable than the last. Not that Anne's law firm wasn't doing well, but it was a rural practice and there was only so much money to be made. Seedlings, on the other hand, could grow—unless the entire town found out that the principal had slept with a student's mother. Then see how many fathers signed up to pay the tuition.

Anne leaned forward, elbows to knees, and Hugh reached over to rub her neck, work her tendons, find her pressure points. She had always been a sucker for a massage.

"And there's nothing else to tell," said Anne. "After the hospital."

Hugh nodded imperceptibly, giving her neck a good squeeze.

Anne's eyes darted over to the sabotaged baseball card drying on a tea towel on her coffee table, its corners pinned by back issues of *ABA Journal*. George Obermeyer, twelve years old. Hugh had lost a brother, and this early brokenness was part of what had attracted her in the first place, except that it didn't usually manifest itself in ways Anne considered attractive. First of all, he didn't talk about it. He wasn't hollow or brooding. He didn't cry out in the night. He was sensitive and boyish, kind and affable, and Anne was irritated to discover that now, when she least recognized her husband, he was even more attractive to her, sloe-eyed, smirkish, distant, new.

Hugh's free hand crossed the chasm between them and came to rest on her thigh, just above her knee. She felt a volt of electricity in her stomach but sat perfectly still.

"I don't want the kids to find out," said Anne.

"No," he agreed.

She stood and took the smallest step toward him, ready to retreat if he became Hugh again, but with uncharacteristic confidence he reached for her hips and pulled her in. He rested his forehead on her stomach and she cupped his ears and they rocked, Hugh leaning into her, pushing her away, Hugh leaning back, reeling her in.

For ten seconds they stayed where they were, Hugh hugging her thighs, Anne draped across his back so that she could see the outline of his small love handles through his shirt. The waistband of Hugh's boxers, which Anne had bought for him at Crossgates Mall, peeked over the top of his jeans. Their lives were knit together in ways she could only begin to imagine. Boxers bought by Anne at a mall reached in Hugh's car while Anne's was in an auto-body shop in Fly Creek that Hugh despised because they overcharged but it was Anne's car although Hugh's name was on the title because Anne had points on her license from when she was caught speeding—80 in a 45—on the way to the airport to pick up her parents. Negotiation, your turn my turn, back and forth and up and down. Anne was curled over her husband's back like a single cross-stitch in an impossible pattern, and she took comfort in the fact that they would never completely finish with each other, no matter what decisions they made.

She untangled herself from Hugh's grasp and this time Hugh let her go.

Upstairs, Anne knocked once on Teddy's door. "It's me," she said. "Can I come in?"

Anne stepped into his room and was immediately assaulted by the sickly sweet smell of wet towels and sour milk, deodorant and sweaty socks. She eyed a wastepaper basket full of balled-up tissues next to his bed, then sniffed delicately and left the door open a crack.

Teddy had changed out of his wet clothes and was now reclined in a T-shirt and a pair of shorts on his bare mattress, sheets and comforter crushed into the footboard, a single, uncased pillow stuffed proprietarily under his head.

"Hi," she said, searching for a place to sit. His baseball uniform—clean, dirty?—trailed along the rug like a deflated player, and his desk was lined with empty cereal and ice cream bowls, their spoons hardened to the basins. "Your room's a mess," Anne reported. With a swipe of her hand, she cleared the desk chair.

Teddy crossed his arms, his newly broad shoulders flexing under his Cooperstown Redskins shirt. Not so long ago he had been all birdcage chest, knobby knees, and hands like bear paws. Now the kinesiology of Teddy was beginning to make sense, and Anne felt years too late for "talks" with her son.

"Do you want to tell me what happened today?" asked Anne.

"Not really."

"It might help."

"With what?"

"I don't know," Anne admitted. It wasn't as if she were here to explain his father's behavior; she'd come to put the gag order on him.

Teddy eyed her warily.

Anne took hold of Teddy's socked foot and squeezed his ankle. "Would it make you feel better to know that I know what happened?"

"Do you?" asked Teddy.

Anne paused, considering.

"If you already know what happened," he continued, "sounds like you're cool with it."

"I'm not *cool* with it—"

"Because if Kim saw me kissing a girl on the side of the road, she'd fucking kill me."

Teddy raised his eyebrows pointedly and Anne tried to picture herself running for a carving knife, swinging it wildly at Hugh. Where was her sense of indignation, her moral outrage? A certain kind of woman—Kim, for example—would've gone off her head at the mention of a kiss (never mind sex).

"Teddy," said Anne seriously. "It's only a hand."

"Maybe," said Teddy. "You hope."

Anne rolled her eyes. She'd been on board with explaining that adult things were complicated, but here her son seemed to think he knew more about it than she did. Looking around Teddy's brackish room, it was hard to believe he even had a girlfriend. She'd met Kim only once, in the bleachers at a basketball game. The girl was small-boned, with a moon face and layers of bottle-blond hair cascading to a very large chest; Anne's lasting impression had been that she said "like" too much.

"Listen to me," said Anne. "You may think you know every-thing there is to know, but you don't." Teddy opened his mouth, and Anne told him to shut it. "I'm not happy. I'm not pushing this under a rug or pretending it's no big deal. But this isn't high school—there might be a lawsuit, Teddy. A boy was hurt on the playground at Seed-lings and his parents are thinking about suing the school. The woman you saw Dad with this afternoon was the boy's mother. He was over there trying to talk to her."

"Did you know Dad was going to her house?"

Anne frowned. "I think," she said, "that I haven't really been lis-tening. But I'm listening now. I'm very hopeful that there won't be a lawsuit, but until we know for sure, you can't talk about this with anyone. Not Kim. Not anyone. Do you understand?"

"Yep."

"Do you have any questions?"

"Nope."

"Teddy, this is serious." He nodded and Anne stood and pushed his chair under the desk. "You're grounded, by the way. Terms and conditions TBD."

Teddy looked away from her and Anne felt a fever chasing into her heart. Teddy—her firstborn—had roamed through nine years of life oblivious to the fact that his was not a planned birth—barely looking up from his waffles the morning Julia, age six, did the math—but she would not undo him for all the world.

Downstairs, Anne found Hugh waiting for her in her office.

"Out," she said.

"What happened?" asked Hugh.

"Nothing. I told him he was grounded. I told him to keep his mouth shut. For some reason, I implied everything would be okay."

"Right," said Hugh. "So now—"

"So now I have about a thousand things to do for tomorrow. I wasn't expecting to confront a lawsuit tonight." She stared him into the hallway, then shut the door behind him.

Alone, Anne knelt and opened the cabinet next to the TV, where she shelved her law library. She removed a red-rope file labeled *Seedlings Insurance 9/78* while mentally outlining her case objectives: to arrive at the other side of this moment (1) without the emotional upheaval of an unfounded lawsuit; (2) without the financial pressure of losing the school; (3) without Hugh and Anne's lives becoming public spectacle; and (4) without turning their children into coconspirators, emotional wardens of a dysfunctional home. How naïve she'd been to think Teddy and Julia didn't know about their marital problems—if not by details then by sensorial impressions, broken airwaves and protracted silences, a kind of filial ESP. She owed it to them to dispense with this negligence claim.

When Hugh opened Seedlings nearly sixteen years ago, Anne had boned up on compensation insurance, medical and dental, business liability, and "no-fault" coverage, but the nuances of the policies had long since receded to the back of her mind.

She reached across the table for the wine bottle and brought it back to the carpet along with her stem glass.

Anne did recall that, on Charlie's advice, Seedlings had ponied up for a generous business-liability policy, including $150,000 of "no-fault" coverage for medical expenses, a little palm-greaser of a thing whereby without admitting negligence Seedlings could offer to pick up the bills for the ER and the OR, just to say they cared.

Anne refilled her glass, and when a little chardonnay splashed over the rim, she licked her fingers, not wanting to waste.

So perhaps they could fabricate a few additional medical expenses for the boy, find an out-of-town doctor to sign off on a phantom home health-care aide or cook up a year of biweekly physical-therapy visits— cash in Richard Pennington's hand might entice him to drop the matter altogether. Insurance fraud was widely covered in Anne's law journals, the articles themselves practically blueprints for committing the crime.

But it didn't need to come to that. Graham's fall had been an accident; Hugh's affair had nothing to do with it. If the boy should remember the latter, well, children were notoriously unreliable witnesses. If Caroline Murphy should testify to it, they were in deep shit. Really, how well did Hugh know this woman? Because, in Anne's experience, nothing in Cooperstown stayed hidden for long. Maybe Caroline had already gossiped about it on Main Street or tipped off her ex-husband to Hugh's unsavory side. The school was likely not negligent, but if the whole town found out about Hugh and Caroline's affair, Seedlings was finished, anyway.

Anne touched her cool glass to her forehead and stared through the syrupy liquid to her desk, her couch, her French doors. Then she was staring at the television screen, her own image mirrored back at her. Anne lowered the glass. Ink-black hair cut blunt at her shoulders, falling straight and sensibly from a left-center part, in more or less the same haircut she'd had since she was a girl. She was preserved, with makeup and hair dye and hours on the treadmill before work. She'd stayed exactly the same, while Hugh, evidently, had changed.

Anne had to see her. Had to know.

She slipped out of her office and avoided Hugh in the den by taking the front stairs. From the landing, she stared down the hallway at the three blades of light beneath three closed doors: her children, her father. For a moment it seemed as though she were looking back across her own past, at the many versions of herself locked neatly away. She'd been so vigilant, so watchful, and yet she hadn't seen this coming.

In their bathroom, Anne opened her makeup case and began

again with foundation. Concealer. Blush. She shadowed her eyes and coated on mascara and plucked two wayward hairs from under the arch of her right brow. She combed her hair into a neat ponytail, then let it fall back to her shoulders. Now was not the time to try something new. Anne removed her silk top and slipped into a crisp white button-down, fresh from the dry cleaner, then a pencil skirt and wedge heels. After brushing her teeth, she dropped her toothbrush in the cup and watched it chase Hugh's Oral-B around the toothpaste until her weeping bristles were nuzzled into Hugh's spine. Fuck you, she thought. She turned Hugh's toothbrush 180 degrees, forcing it to kiss her soft head, but his gum-massaging bristles were top-heavy and quickly spun away. She took his toothbrush and dropped it in the trash can, remembering where his mouth had been.

At the front door, her hand on the knob, Anne caught sight of Hugh's reflection in the glass—he'd swapped his coffee for a beer, his button-down for an undershirt. She froze but didn't turn around.

"Anne," he said.

"What?" she asked, facing him. She wondered if this was how he'd felt sneaking around their house, knowing he was going to do something he'd vowed never to do. Now it was her turn, and it was titillating to know he couldn't stop her, that he wouldn't even try. "Actually," she said, her logistical mind *click-clacking* into the plan. "There is something you can do for me. I don't have the address."

Hugh met her eyes, and she silently dared him to deny her.

"I have to talk to her sometime," said Anne.

"You've been drinking," said Hugh. "It's late. Is now really the best time?"

"Maybe not," she said. "But I'm going."

So he told her how to find the white house set back from Route 166, its driveway a pair of tire ruts cut into the lawn. Maybe he wanted to tell her to drive safely. She started to tell him she would never have hurt him this way. On the precipice of their nineteenth wedding anniversary, she noticed that her husband had a nervous habit: cracking his index finger with his thumb. There was no sound but the motion was continuous, deliberate. Also, he wasn't as tall as she'd remembered, or as sensible. There were a thousand ways to carry on an affair—he'd chosen extremely poorly. It occurred to her that nothing was as it seemed. Just last week her mother had been alive and her husband had been her husband, but then that wasn't right either, because by then Hugh had already slept with Caroline Murphy, and the blood vessels in her mother's brain were already narrowing, and Anne, too, was already moving, getting behind the wheel of her car and turning east toward Cherry Valley, refusing to wonder if Hugh was standing at the door watching her go.

9

They had twenty minutes to get their stories straight, fifteen if Anne sped. Sex this afternoon hadn't happened. Kissing Caroline in her driveway had been a gesture of gratitude, a wax seal on her vow of silence. It had not been a tugboat maneuver to lower her face to his car window until her breast was resting softly on the jamb and Hugh had what he wanted: her nipple in his mouth. Then he was back out of the car and hustling her inside for round two.

No.

Anne was a seasoned litigator; she'd get the story out of Caroline in a matter of seconds if Hugh didn't give Caroline a crash course on how to handle the onslaught. His go-to tactic was pretending he was a delinquent child in his own principal's office. Bamboo shoots couldn't drive the truth out of uncooperative five-year-olds. They were like tiny members of the KGB.

Hugh made for the kitchen, zeroing in on the cordless phone with a hazy plan to embed in the garage. Through the foyer, past his wife's office—Hugh averted his eyes. Scene of his inquisition, makeshift

ICU for his brother's ruined baseball card: Hugh felt nothing. A deadened chord had thrummed inside him when he'd seen the card crumpled in Teddy's hand, then, almost immediately, a switch had powered him down: absolute emotional disconnect. *Regret* and *shame* were words like *sweater* and *steps.* Hugh wasn't thinking about what he'd done or what he wanted; he was thinking about the maroon crew neck he'd shed on Caroline's front stairs.

Squaring to the phone mounted on the wall, Hugh's fingers dialed from memory, 2-6-4, and were skipping toward 9 when Teddy said, "Hey," and the receiver was a fish in Hugh's grasp, flipping away from him and skidding across the wood floor.

Hugh tracked the cordless to the base of the refrigerator, where he secured it with shaking hands. "I thought you were grounded," he said.

"I have to eat."

Teddy, who was inexplicably shirtless, had emptied a box of Golden Grahams into a large mixing bowl and was now stirring in milk with a wooden spoon. Dinner. It was close to eleven o'clock and his growing boy hadn't been fed.

"Help yourself," said Hugh.

Teddy palmed the base of the bowl and rafted a whale's portion into his mouth. Pipelike clavicles carved deep pockets on either side of Teddy's gullet—Hugh could've sunk a pool ball in there.

"I was lifting," said Teddy, registering his father's gaze. He leaned back against the counter and cradled the bowl against his countable abs, but all the pectorals and deltoids in the world couldn't offset the fact that the sum total of Teddy still did not add up to an adult.

All Hugh had ever wanted was a family, and yet here he was wrecking his own. Until now he'd been a good father, warm and affectionate, with so many different brands of hugs that Teddy and Julia had named them: the goose hug, which involved hooking chins over shoulders, and the tug hug, where the point was to wrestle free. Both kids had gleefully submitted to Hugh's affections when they were babies, and Julia still occasionally permitted a plain old hug, but here was Teddy trying to grow up, trying to put on twenty-five pounds by next baseball season, and Hugh did understand that he could lose him. Parents lost their children all the time. Some boys drowned, and some grew up and saw their fathers for what they really were.

Hugh put the phone back on the hook. He and Caroline were on their own.

"Teddy," he said.

Teddy moved a spoonful of cereal into his cheek like a squirrel storing a nut. "What?"

"Maybe we should talk about this."

"Okay," said Teddy.

But Hugh faltered. For eighteen years, he had paid attention: he knew when his children were dissembling and when they were sincere. Julia wanted to be on the tennis team, and Teddy was afraid to go to college; Hugh could tell by the way his son refused to even talk about Oneida that it was going to be a problem getting him there. But now, perhaps for the first time, Hugh realized that his kids could read him, too.

"I don't know how much your mother told you," Hugh began. Teddy waited. "There was an accident at the school."

"Was it the school's fault?" asked Teddy.

"No," said Hugh, glad to be able to answer something honestly and emphatically. "There's no foundation for a lawsuit."

"Then why'd you need to go over to the woman's house in the middle of the day?" asked Teddy.

A jab, words meant to stun Hugh, to pin him in place. Hugh had never seen this side of his son. But Teddy was right: Hugh hadn't needed to go to Caroline's house today, and yet he hadn't been able to stay away. He thought back to the night he'd met Anne, to the relief he'd felt, as if he'd been drifting for years and had finally found a buoy. Anne's faith in Hugh had lifted him up, galvanized him, but the mirror of her faith had been distrust—nothing less than all of him would do, which was more than Hugh, and maybe more than anyone, could give. It seemed to Hugh that for twenty years now Anne had been waiting for him to fatally disappoint her, and Hugh wondered if, when she found out what he'd done that day—as she inevitably would—she might not process this final transgression as a kind of relief.

"It's complicated," said Hugh.

"Sounds it," said Teddy. He began to shake more cereal into his bowl and Hugh thought, I'll take you to the mall this weekend and get you some vitamins and powders. We'll get you to college some-how. But Teddy wouldn't even look at him.

Hugh hadn't meant for this to get so out of hand so quickly. He and Anne had a lot to work out before Hugh could talk openly to Teddy. And there was still the matter of the lawsuit to settle—Hugh felt his stomach drop at the prospect of losing Seedlings—complicated by the fact that Teddy had glimpsed him with Caroline. It could have been worse—the nipple, the running inside hand in hand—but that was just it: How had Teddy, normally deaf and blind to anyone's existence but his own, intuited from twenty yards that Hugh was committing an act of indecency? Yale-bound Dave Blunt hadn't discerned anything untoward in Hugh's hand-kiss—though probably Dave hadn't recognized Hugh. Still, hadn't thousands of innings as spectator, father, and number-one fan earned Hugh the benefit of Teddy's doubt?

"About what happened today," said Hugh. "You should've talked to me first."

Teddy stopped chewing. "I know what I saw."

"Tie goes to the runner, Teddy. You should've come to me."

"Why? What would you've said? I saw you kiss a woman."

"Her hand," Hugh corrected.

"You kissed her!" said Teddy.

Wrong. After the hand, before the nipple, she'd rested her chin on Hugh's head for a matter of minutes. He'd been thinking that her front porch needed painting and that he could do it for her this sum-mer. Her skin had felt warm against his.

Hugh tried to put himself in Teddy's place. What did his son need? His father, of course. The best thing that could happen to Teddy right now would be to discover that he'd been wrong.

"Look," said Hugh, "I probably shouldn't have kissed her hand, but I was pretty overwhelmed by the lawsuit. Anyway, your mom's taking care of that now."

"She's over there?"

Hugh's stomach lurched, his throat nearly closing off. He checked his watch and nodded.

Teddy set his cereal bowl in the sink, soggy wheat squares floating in a pond of sugary milk. For a moment he was quiet, then he said:

"I don't believe you. Sorry, but I don't."

Teddy turned his back to Hugh, demonstrably sloughing off childhood, that unrepeatable quality of youth—trust in your parents—gone the way of Teddy's gapped baby teeth, his halting first steps, his *lellow* for *yellow*, his *Dada bye bye*. Hugh felt the sensation not as pain but as loss, a severed umbilicus, a collapse of the continuum linking Hugh to George and their parents, then back to Teddy and Julia—only now Hugh was the father—and of all the breaches it would be this that his son remembered: middle of the workday, Teddy's father in the driveway, a woman who was not his mother, and who really gave a fuck if it was only her hand?

How had Hugh thought he could explain this?

He heard himself say he needed to sit down, then he was sitting down, nestled on the floor between the oven and the island.

"What's going on?"

Julia.

"Maybe he fainted," said Teddy, standing back.

Julia galloped away, made a ruckus, and returned with a glass of water. She handed Hugh a sleeve of Ritz crackers, then opened a jar of peanut butter and dipped in a steak knife.

Soon Hugh was up at the counter on Teddy's bar stool, with Julia stationed at his side.

"I'll stay with you," Julia volunteered.

"No," said Hugh.

" 'Night," said Teddy.

Hugh tried to touch him, reach for his arm, pat him on the back, but his son was already swinging around the newel on the back banister and propelling himself up the stairs.

"Is Teddy in trouble?" asked Julia. "Is he grounded?"

Hugh closed his eyes. He was fragile, sick from the rolling hills of mania. He hadn't eaten since breakfast, hadn't slept in days.

"Is this about the baseball card? Why'd Teddy throw it in the lake?"

"Julia—"

"Forget it," she said. "You never tell me anything."

Hugh opened his eyes. "What don't I tell you?"

"You asked my coach to give me the exhibition match."

That. It was so far down on Hugh's list of problems, it took a Herculean effort to attain the proper level of gravity when he said, "You're *good* at tennis, you *like* tennis, but I know it's not always easy for you to ask for things."

"Well, now I'm playing Carl tomorrow, and if I lose, I'm officially off the team."

"I'm sorry," said Hugh. I'm sorry and I'm sorry. "I'll call Coach Klawson." There was no chance he'd be expanding the school, anyway.

"No, don't. It's better this way. At least Carl's speaking to me." Then, "Did you really kiss that woman?"

Hugh started to say *her hand*, then paused, measuring his next words against all future knowledge, the possibility that Julia would soon know everything. Anne would be home any minute; there was no telling where this night was headed.

"Can you do me a favor?" asked Hugh.

Julia shrugged, nodded. His only comfort: he was her favorite.

"Can you go to bed?"

Julia slid off her stool. "First I have to go to Carl's."

"Now?" Hugh frowned. "It's a little late."

"It can't wait," she said. "You know that book *The Sex Cure?*"

Everyone's favorite cocktail-party scandal, Cooperstown's *Peyton Place*. The recently retired Father French, who had baptized both of Hugh's children, kept an annotated copy in his living room, proudly noting the location of the book's Episcopal church on *French Street*.

"Yes," said Hugh warily.

"I was kind of inspired by it."

Uh-oh, thought Hugh.

From what he understood, the fallout from the novel had been sizable. He seemed to recall that on one Halloween night a drunken mob spray-painted the author's house with threats, running her out of town.

Hugh thought of his own scandal, rippling now from Cooperstown to Cherry Valley at the speed of his wife's car. Recklessness. Not just with his school but his livelihood, not just with his marriage but his kids. Hugh had dropped them off in the carpool lane of family crisis, and it occurred to him that he, too, could be run out of town.

"Some things in the book were true," said Julia.

"I'm pretty sure nothing in the book was true," said Hugh.

Julia seemed to consider this. "Well, the thing I wrote about Carl was."

Hugh braced his head in his hands, pressing his temples. "When you say *wrote* . . ."

Julia gestured expansively to the night, and Hugh thought he knew what she meant. The truth was out there, and nothing would ever again be the same. Anne knew; Mrs. Baxter probably knew. Teddy knew enough, and Bob would guess the rest. Julia was too busy creating her own scandal to bother yet with her father's, but eventually, she, too, would know.

It had only been two weeks since he'd met Caroline, and yet after only two weeks in 1974, Hugh had already decided to move in with Anne—maybe he was the kind of guy who just knew. Hugh pictured Caroline slipping gracefully into his life, their life, tiny enough to be suspended above it until he'd pulled her in and pulled her in again.

She had brought with her a depth of feeling that had eluded Hugh for years. It was a great unkindness he was doing to his family, but Teddy and Julia weren't babies anymore. With a mother like Anne, his children would survive utterly; she would will them into adulthood; she would bend rivers to lift them up from the dead.

Hugh told Julia to forget her trip to Carl's and go to bed, then wiped down the counter, loaded Teddy's cereal bowl into the dishwasher, and returned the peanut butter to the pantry. In the hallway outside his bedroom, he took a sheet and blanket from the linen closet, then went back downstairs to make up his bed.

He sat on the couch in the dark in the den without laying out the sheet and stared at the moonlight through the skylights. The Seedlings School was in his wife's hands now. Hugh was asking her to defend him when she no doubt wanted to crucify him, and as much as Anne disliked gossip, she might easily decide this was his problem, not theirs. Seedlings should've had a head teacher on yard duty, and Graham should not have been standing on the monkey bars; but head teachers took breaks, and kids tested the boundaries of their secure worlds, and Hugh, whose job it was to take care of the children, had not failed: this time when a boy had fallen, Hugh had reached out his hand. Now he seemed to be floating, flying north. Knowing how bad it would look if he was asleep when Anne came home, he did not lie down. Instead, he dove straight into that phantasmagoric pool of memory where the possibility always existed of discovering one more word, a forgotten smile, a blue-sky day, and the sound of his brother's voice saying, *Come on, come on*, his running feet just ahead of Hugh's, flattening the dew-heavy grass with prints that stretched out for all time, a path to follow.

10

Anne was not normally a timid driver, but the magnitude of her mission coupled with the undeniable elevation of her blood alcohol level left her crawling along at the speed limit, tracking the centerline through squinted eyes. A fine mist clung to the windshield, and her wipers swished by at regular intervals until that proved to be too soporific, then on came the radio and down went the windows—she did not want to end up in a ditch.

In order to remain awake, Anne focused on the pending negligence claim. From what Anne understood about the accident, if Mr. Pennington decided to go through with his suit, the court would likely grant judgment for the Seedlings School before trial: New York Civil Practice Law and Rules section 3212. Even if the teachers hadn't been the paragon of supervision—what had Hugh said about assistants on yard duty?—they hadn't *caused* the accident. Kids climbed, kids fell—it didn't matter whether a teacher was watching or not—and no proximate cause meant no case.

As these facts marched logically across Anne's mind, the unlikelihood of Caroline testifying came into stark relief. Anne wasn't the only one who stood to lose something here. Recalling Hugh's reference to Caroline's twelve steps, Anne could assume Caroline's suitability as a caregiver had already been called into question in a courtroom setting. The last thing she'd want would be to revisit that particular locale.

There was a way in which this could be easy, then. Anne had the advantage of anonymity; Caroline didn't know what she looked like. Anne could introduce herself as Seedlings' lawyer, bullet-point the risks of a trial to Caroline's custody agreement, threaten her with deposition under oath, and advise Caroline against participation in any court proceedings. What personal connection to Hugh Obermeyer? Anne could use a pseudonym, perhaps Joanie Cole.

If Anne's mother had ever dreamed of confronting her father's mistresses, she'd made a great secret of it. In a town of only two thousand people, Joanie must have known some of them personally, or at least well enough to say hello. Had she ever been tempted to tip her hand, a little *I know that you know that I know*? Not from what Anne could tell, but in this way Anne was nothing like her mother. She was paid a six-figure salary for her pugilistic spirit and had no qualms about stepping into the ring.

Anne merged onto Route 166 and wound toward the village of Cherry Valley, past the hair salon where she brought Julia every couple of months, easing to a stop at the traffic light. It was after eleven o'clock; hers was the only car at the intersection. Across the street, a gas station beckoned with its dual-access points, an excellent place to make a U-turn, but Anne wasn't tempted. When the light turned green, she drove on, reading mailbox numbers and finally stopping at the long driveway of a white house, where the downstairs lights were still on.

It was the very vantage point Teddy would've had, a clear shot—no curves in the driveway, no obstructing telephone poles or trees. Even in the dark, Anne could see straight to the house. She collapsed her headlights and turned into the driveway, missing the grooved tire tracks by six inches. The car jostled over the muddy earth, rocking left and right until she braked and killed the ignition, just behind a green Subaru.

*　*　*

The last time Anne had gone over to a woman's house in the middle of the night to threaten her, she was thirteen years old. Halloween, 1962, while Anne's parents were downstairs masked in face paint and fake blood, Anne had been curled up in her bedroom with a plate of popcorn balls and her mother's copy of *The Sex Cure*. It certainly wasn't Anne's first read-through (she'd memorized a handful of lascivious scenes), but her father—who had taken her to see *The Blob* at the old movie theater on Main Street and therefore could not be said to be categorically protective—had all but hit her mother when Anne confessed to having read it. In the weeks after that incident, Anne had eavesdropped and spied and snooped on her parents, trying to get to the bottom of their tension over the book, but it had always remained just out of her reach.

Alone in her bedroom, she'd examined the front cover. Elaine Dorian must have written the novel right here in town, at her house on Lake Street, only a few blocks from the Coles'. Anne pictured a desk in a dark study, a ream of paper turned upside down next to a typewriter, the veiled typeface still faintly visible through the onionskin. According to an advertisement on the last page, Mrs. Dorian was also the author of *Love Now—Pay Later*, *Suburbia: Jungle of Sex*, and *Second-Time Woman*. On the back cover: *You will be shocked. You may be angry. But you'll hang on every word.*

Anne, an eighth-grader, had easily picked out many of the town's characters by their fictional names, which meant that she couldn't have been the only kid in town coping with the frightening possibility that the affairs and divorces happening in the book were also happening in her own home.

There had been times when, as a young girl, Anne was ushered into the front seat of her father's Buick for a ride downtown—to breakfast at the Cooperstown Diner or to a picnic at Lakefront Park. Usually they were met by a new friend of her father's. Usually these new friends were women. And, yes, they'd paid attention to Anne only as long as her father was watching, but her dad's fast-paced, convivial domain was so enchantingly different from the quiet, contented life Anne led with her mother that she had been willing to play her part. So what if her father asked her not to mention a Miss Janson or a Miss Pride to her mother? They had all just been sitting on a quilt in the middle of Lakefront Park, and it couldn't be a real secret if everyone already knew.

Downstairs, Anne's father said, "And who do we have here?" Anne pictured an outlaw, a robot, a cowboy holding a cap gun and a pillowcase, a lunch pail, a plastic jack-o'-lantern for whatever treat her parents offered, this happy couple playing along as though all of life were a game. In the last two months, between Nikita Khrushchev and *The Sex Cure*, near nuclear war had played out at Anne's kitchen table, and now that Anne had her parents back—loving, considerate, communicative—she would do anything to keep them. Anne didn't think her family could survive another round from Elaine Dorian. Hadn't her mother said that the author was working on a sequel?

Hopped up on sugar and adrenaline, Anne began to fantasize: on Halloween night, any number of devils and demons would be out tricking up the town with shaving cream and eggs, children on the prowl. Every year, the school janitors had to come in early to wash off soap from the first-story windows and rub out words written with pieces of brick on the cement stoop. How easy it would be to blend in with this madness, to slip into the night and reappear ghostlike with a can of spray paint.

Anne waited until her parents were asleep, then crept to the utility room to get a flashlight and the key to her father's shed. A little rooting around and she found his new supply of automobile paint and slipped one can into the front pocket of her navy sweatshirt, thinking he'd never miss it.

The Halloween antics had already died down by the time Anne set off east on Walnut Street, then north on Delaware, zigzagging her way across town. She saw the village patrol car cruising south on Pioneer, heading away from the lake, which meant she had at least fifteen minutes before the police made another lap.

As she approached the house, Anne was neither nervous nor apprehensive. With her black hair and blue eyes, she looked like a fairy-tale character and was trying to channel one. Her parents needed her help, and Anne could protect them. Superheroes were never caught. They delivered their charges from evil, then woke in their own beds in sole possession of the secret knowledge of their valorous feats.

Anne found the two-story house at the corner of Lake Street and Hoffman Lane completely dark—either the author was out of town or she had already gone to sleep for the night. Anne crouched beside a shrub near the side door and got out her paint; she shook the can, then removed the top, securing it in her sweatshirt pocket, and began duckwalking the circumference of the house.

Once she'd decided, Anne never looked back, printing the neat foot-high letters of whatever phrases came to her mind—GET OUT, GO HOME, LEAVE US ALONE—working quickly, efficiently, and peppering her commands with words she'd never even thought to say aloud: BITCH, SLUT, SEX URGE. Just as she was finishing the last word on the most visible wall, directly on Hoffman Lane, a car turned off Main Street and into the alley, its headlights arcing straight for her, and she tossed the paint and ran, down Lake Street to River and up to Christ Church, where she ducked into the cemetery and slid down between a tombstone and the ivy-covered fence at the edge of the lawn.

Anne decided her parents were lucky to have her—she was back in bed before midnight, with her homework finished and her clarinet already packed for school.

Then came the newsmen and the television cameras, giving voice to Elaine Dorian's every passing thought. Anne's attack, meant to silence the author, had instead turned *The Sex Cure* into a national sensation and single-handedly sent it into a second print run. Out came her mother's scrapbook, out went her father into the world of late nights at the office, and out ran Anne's patience with her parents—she couldn't fix them, she was no superhero after all, so she concentrated instead on her schoolwork and her life after here. Fourteen, fifteen, sixteen, seventeen, then she was gone—Vassar—driven away with no thought of ever coming back.

And yet here she was again, in every sense of the word. But if Anne had learned one lesson from her first foray into intimidation tactics, it was that there could be no new scandal, no newspaper articles, no lawsuits, and when the front-porch light switched on at Caroline Murphy's house, Anne did not even flinch. She sat up, ready. This time she was here to kill the story.

* * *

A slight woman with long brown hair stepped outside and stood barefoot on the doormat, her gray corduroy pants sitting low on her narrow hips, a cardigan hugging her tight. She shielded her eyes against the overhead bulb and peered out at Anne.

Anne removed her key from the ignition, which had the unwelcome effect of illuminating the car's interior. She hadn't yet applied lipstick, hadn't checked her hair. Worse, the taste of wine had worked its way back into her mouth, and Anne quickly hunted in her purse for a tin of mints, then popped in two and chewed.

"Hello?" Caroline called.

Anne opened her car door and stepped onto the front lawn, introducing herself using her real name.

"We need to talk," said Anne.

Caroline laced her fingers across her waist and said, "My son's asleep," but Anne was already mounting the porch steps; she waited for Caroline to open the door for her, then filed through.

Noting the collection of footwear in the front hall, Anne asked if she should remove her shoes.

"You don't have to," said Caroline, but Anne slipped out of her heels, watching Caroline from the corner of her eye. She was petite, with pale skin and full lips, her face scrubbed clean and her eyebrows uneven, as though she'd given up plucking midway through. Anne had expected her to be younger—with a five-year-old, she might easily have been in her twenties—but crow's-feet and a smattering of grays at her hairline put her closer to Anne's age.

Anne lined up her heels alongside a pair of duck boots and two tiny Spider-Man slippers, while Caroline dipped into a wicker basket of woolens and retrieved a blue-and-white-striped scarf, wrapping it over her shoulders and around her neck, then pulling her hair free. Her jaws worked a piece of gum, the smell of spearmint filling the air.

Anne indicated that Caroline should lead the way, then tiptoed behind her in case the child was a light sleeper. The house smelled faintly of mildew, that summer-camp scent of rain-weathered canvas and damp wool. It was sharp but not unpleasant; it heightened Anne's sense of being on a trip.

Caroline led her into the den, which was a cozy mess, all pillows and newspapers and tattered quilts. She invited Anne to sit anywhere, but a cache of knitting supplies had booby-trapped the couch. The only open seat was a child's Adirondack chair pushed right up to the screen of a thirteen-inch television set.

"Shit," said Caroline, registering Anne's hesitation. She started to clear the couch, placing one item at a time in an oversize canvas carryall, but Anne abruptly picked up a jumbo-size papier-mâché frog from the seat of a cane rocking chair and set it on the floor.

"This will be fine," she said.

"Can I get you something to drink?" asked Caroline carefully. "Juice? Tea?"

Anne had had it with the tea; what she really wanted was a cocktail but instead asked for water, no ice.

While Caroline was in the kitchen, Anne swiveled to detail the room: two bookshelves dotted with glazed ceramic vases and lined with titles like *Encounters with the Archdruid* and *Desert Solitaire*, along with a sizable collection of art books; a rattan area rug overlapped with patchy Oriental carpets, one frayed, one with a hole in the middle, one that seemed to be torn in half; a stack of Barney videos on top of a VCR; a Hockneyesque photo collage of a snow-covered fir tree; and an alcove with a large wooden easel pitched over a paint-splattered floor, the back of a stretched canvas barely visible.

Caroline returned from the kitchen with two handmade ceramic mugs and handed one to Anne, then perched at the edge of the couch.

"Are you painting?" asked Anne, pointing to the alcove.

"It's just something I've been playing around with," said Caroline.

"A nude of my husband?" asked Anne, and Caroline didn't speak, did not even move.

"Look," said Anne, "I don't know if Hugh told you, but I'm the lawyer for the Seedlings School in addition to being the principal's wife. As I understand it, your ex-husband is planning to file a negligence claim."

"I—" Caroline's voice quavered, her mug in a death grip. "He said he was looking into the fall but I've already told him I don't want any part in it," she said. "Even if we'd been there, Graham could've fallen."

There went proximate cause. Anne wished to God this were admissible.

"Just to be clear," said Anne, "if he does file a claim, and this does go to trial, you can't testify. It will come out that you had sex with my husband in your son's hospital room."

"We didn't . . . I mean—"

"You mean you *would* have had sex, but then your son woke up. Hugh already told me."

Caroline stared into her mug, and Anne wondered if she were wishing it were wine as much as Anne was.

"Look at me," said Anne.

Caroline looked up.

There were so many ways Anne could go with this—guilt (do you make a habit of sleeping with other women's husbands?), shame (this is my family; we have children at home), threat (if you come near my husband again, you'll find yourself back in family court)—but they all felt scripted. Frankly, Anne didn't care what this woman did with her life; her only concern was her family.

So, a question for Caroline: Had it really been only that one time? If so, maybe their marriage was salvageable.

"This afternoon," said Anne. "My son saw Hugh kiss you in your driveway."

"Oh, God," said Caroline. She set her mug on the carpet and pressed the heel of her hand to her forehead, as though testing for a fever.

But it was Anne who felt feverish, in the grip of a life-threatening disorder, the end of her marriage.

"You did sleep with him, then," said Anne.

The look on Caroline's face told her all she needed to know.

Anne stopped rocking and put the mug on the floor. She liked water in water glasses and couches you could sit on and television screens you could actually see. She favored books with plots—novels, mysteries—over end-of-times histories more alarming even than her own. Caroline was not a younger, fresher version of Anne; she was a different person, and if this was what Hugh wanted, Anne couldn't give it to him.

She took a deep breath and measured out her exhale. Her entire life's purpose reduced to a single goal: to get out of this house without crying.

"Thank you," said Anne brightly, standing to go.

"Can I—"

"Please," said Anne. She stalked past Caroline to the entry hall, fumbling for her shoes. As she slipped her heels on, Anne looked into the wicker basket, and there it was, the sleeve of her husband's sweater, folded in with the rest of the family's clothes. She started to take it—evidence—then changed her mind. What would she want with it? She needed no reminders of this day.

Anne squared to Caroline, towering over her. "The first thing that needs to happen is that I dispense with this negligence claim."

Caroline ducked her head, listening.

"Until then, there can be no contact."

Caroline nodded, and though Anne had no reason to trust this woman, she also had no choice.

"I'm sorry," said Caroline, and Anne held up her hand but she couldn't stop it, the lifetime of hurt barreling toward her, coming so fast and hard that the walls would break, but what did it matter, and what did it matter? Everything she'd believed in—her parents, her marriage—was already lost, so let this woman see her cry, let this woman see how deadly fucking hurt she was. And be scared, thought Anne. For the last vestiges of her love—Teddy and Julia—she would stop at nothing.

In the driveway, Anne buckled her seat belt and started the car. Sober, focused, calm, she backed into the tire ruts and eased onto Route 166, then set off in silence, wind battering the windows, the reach of her headlights on the road remarkably bright. Twenty years ago she had been after perfection, a husband who would never let her down. Now they were kicking just to stay afloat, and Anne wondered what it would feel like to let go. Was this what her mother had been trying to tell her out at her father's farm, that there was love in the letting go? Anne had believed—how had she believed this?—that her mother would be with her at the end of her own life, that if Anne had come into this world with Joanie, then she must also leave with her, and yet Joanie was gone, and the tears that had eluded Anne at her mother's funeral now sleeted her cheeks, a sob with no end, and it was unexpectedly comforting to finally feel it.

Close to midnight, Anne pulled into the driveway on Susque-hanna Avenue, and if she'd expected Hugh to meet her at the front door, she was grateful when he didn't. Inside, she crept toward the kitchen, leaving her keys on the center-hall table. The house was silent; maybe everyone was already asleep.

Then Hugh emerged from the den with deep red lines impressed on his face: the corduroy couch. She could tell he'd been sleeping downstairs and realized they might never share a bed again. Anne took a deep breath and held it, considering the individual moments of their marriage that had led them here, hairline fissures across their past when she and Hugh had stood on opposite sides of the cracks. If she had been honest with him about her childhood, could they have prevented this, or, like ice floes in the ocean, had they been destined to drift apart?

"I don't think she'll testify," Anne offered.

"What did she say?" asked Hugh.

Anne looked past him to the cavern of their den and saw that he'd already placed a blanket at the end of the couch. A thousand thoughts chased through her mind as she tried to compose a response. "Hugh," she began, but before she could continue she heard footsteps on the back stairs, and Anne looked up to find her father's slippers descending into view.

11

When he slept, he dreamed, and Joanie was there. *Bob*, she said, *I do not have all day. Either make up your mind to mow the lawn or I'll get Ruth Potter's son over here to do it.* She wore a sleeveless dress with a floral print and it looked pretty on her, but he didn't say so. Ruth Potter. Before Bob could stop her, Joanie had picked up the yellow rotary phone and dialed, then Bob listened but he couldn't hear.

In the hallway outside his bedroom: thunder. Clodhopping monkeys, wooden-soled devils, his grandchildren pounding down the stairs. He heard Teddy say something about fainting, but it would take a great deal more than that to get Bob out of bed. He reached for the glass of water Joanie always left him, passing his hand over pill bottles and wadded tissues, a folded newspaper and a pair of reading glasses, his fingers hovering spectrally, then folding into a weak fist as he remembered that Joanie wasn't here.

Bob had aged a year for each of the nine days his wife had been gone. His only solace: at this rate it wouldn't be long until he followed her into the grave. At eighty-six, he wasn't afraid to die but he hadn't

anticipated the pain. A battery of daily pills—digitalis and diuretics
and vasodilators, in blue and orange and white; giant nutlike things
that he could barely choke down—eased the symptoms of his congestive heart failure but turned an unchristian eye on the rest of his body.
When he walked, his joints ached; when he slept, his calves bloated up
like wet loaves of bread. Nausea, dry mouth, incontinence; dizziness,
headache, irregular heartbeat. For every new complaint, Dr. Brash's
pen flew across his prescription pad, until Bob was in possession of a
Russian nesting doll of pills to treat problems caused by pills to treat
problems, all the way back to the tiniest doll, his failing heart.

Bob's bladder was awake again and he had no choice but to tend
to it. He needed those pads but couldn't figure out how to ask his
daughter for them. At the house last week, Anne had found his supply
under the bathroom sink and assumed they were for her mother; now
they were gone, with all the rest of his things.

At the count of three, he pushed off the mattress and grabbed
hold of the nightstand. Dr. Brash extolled the benefits of a walker but
Bob couldn't keep track of his—always downstairs when he was upstairs,
in the bathroom when he was in bed, like a stooped silver man haunt-
ing him through the house, his feet lovingly retrofitted with Julia's
tennis balls.

A series of night-lights lit the path across the rug to the bathroom,
where, without Joanie to reprimand him, Bob had left the seat up
again. Dr. Brash recommended that he sit to urinate, but Bob had a
bit of dignity left, thank you very much. Holding on to the pedestal
sink, he turned his eyes to the mirror, and he could almost believe he
was looking at a photograph of his father: white hair circled the base
of his scalp and made a fan of wisps on top of his head. Whatever
muscles he'd had in his youth had gone the way of his cartilage—he
was a pair of blue pajamas on a wire coat hanger, and it was hard to
believe he'd grown so old when it seemed like only yesterday that he'd
begun to grow up.

Bob shook and flushed and returned to bed, careful not to look at the clock, then pulled the covers up to his chin and nestled in. For fifty-four years, he and Joanie had shared a bed, chasing each other left to right and headboard to footboard across the matrimonial battlefield of their queen-size mattress, and now Bob couldn't sleep without her. When Joanie had been cross, he'd burrowed under her pillow, trying to conciliate her until she'd ceded her cushion and slunk sleepily away. When Bob had been distant, Joanie had cleaved to him while he slithered to the edge of their mattress with his eyes on the window, on the street, on the village and the whole world beyond. Times when Bob and Joanie had fought, they'd shared one pillow, keeping a watchful eye on each other from the center of the mattress while their bodies forked apart, Bob once waking to find Joanie's feet squarely on the carpet, as though she were preparing to run away. Bob couldn't know how Joanie had slept on the nights when he wasn't there, but he had an idea that it was straight across the bed: there had never been a centerline between them.

Bob reached across the nightstand and switched on the light, sending an orange glow over the room. Anne had given him a bureau for his sweaters and cleared a closet for his slacks and shirts, but all his things were still folded in his suitcase at the foot of the bed. Bob needed to believe this situation was temporary, and he hadn't objected when Anne had said he could bring only a few possessions: his beetle collection; his hat stand, though no one but him wore hats anymore; his trombone, which he'd played in the marching band in high school and also in the Navy in Charleston a lifetime ago. Next to the lamp, he'd put up a framed picture of Joanie, her chestnut hair curled at her shoulders and pinned back by two silver barrettes, her lips painted red. They'd been on their way to a dance somewhere, and although Bob didn't remember the dance, he did remember the afterward. Even when he'd wondered what someone else's body might look like in comparison, he had loved his wife.

How horrible to discover, after all these years, that Joanie had kept that book. Bob had been so certain she'd gotten rid of it, a gesture of absolution, forgiveness in their final act, but no, it'd been right under his mattress this whole time, trying to tickle his memory, to force him to look back. After he'd endured for years the sight of *The Sex Cure* flapped open on the coffee table, left on the kitchen counter, winged across his recliner when he came home from work, Joanie had brought it right into their bedroom with them, and Bob couldn't understand it—what did she want from him that he could still give?

Discordant notes of deafening music sounded from his grandson's bedroom next door and Bob dreamed of having the energy to charge over there and jerk the cord out of the wall. There was a disturbing lack of discipline in this household. Not only had Teddy cut school this afternoon and destroyed a thousand-dollar baseball card, he'd stuck his nose in his father's business, where it didn't belong. He was too big for his britches, but rather than reminding the boy of his place Anne had taken Teddy's side and now Hugh was in the doghouse while Teddy was feeling his oats and what Bob wanted to know was, who was in charge around here?

Bob pulled the pillow over his head and closed his eyes. All the pieces of his life were in place except one: ventricular fibrillation or acute pulmonary edema; confined to the ICU or quickly and merci-fully in his own bed? Any which way, Bob was ready. He thought of his friend Roy Lamb out at the nursing home on Beaver Meadow Road, where Joanie and Bob had visited once a month. *Remember Nona Fredrickson?* Bob would ask, stealing a look at Joanie, then run-ning his hands down his sides in the shape of a Coke bottle. *Remember the rope swing we tied to Mr. Wyatt's rotten elm tree?* For one glorious week, they'd taken turns swooping out over the sun-sparkled lake, letting go at the last possible second, then wheeling into the water with satisfying splashes. Roy looked at his Velcro shoes, at his plastic water bottle, at the two people sitting across from him, side by side, and Bob could see that Roy no longer remembered. The mind wanted to forget, it bent toward letting go; it took work to hold on to all these thoughts, and yet here was Bob with a lifetime of memories nipping at his heels.

Bob heard voices in the kitchen and finally looked at the clock—11:57. No chance of sleep now. He located his slippers and shouldered his bathrobe. A light from the laundry room guided him to the back stairs, where he descended by advancing his right foot one step at a time.

"Dad?" Anne peered into the stairwell.

"It's me."

"What are you doing?"

Bob panted softly, blinking against the glare in the kitchen. "I couldn't sleep," he said.

"Well, go back to bed," said Anne.

He stared at her. Add infantilization to his list of complaints. Dementia sounded like a blessing—who wanted to be cognizant for this?

"If you don't mind," he said, "I'll get a glass of water first."

Bob rounded the island toward the sink, nodding to his son-in-law, then paused in front of the first set of overhead cabinets and reached for the knob.

"It's the next one," said Anne. "By the refrigerator. Those are the bowls."

"I'll get it for you," Hugh offered, but Bob waved him away.

Clearly he'd interrupted something. Since the earlier incident, Hugh had changed into pajamas, while Anne had dressed for work. He looked as if he'd been sleeping; she looked as if she'd been on a bad date. It was then that Bob saw the blanket and sheet folded on the couch in the den. He smiled to mask his concern.

"Are you okay?" asked Anne.

"Fine," said Bob. "I'll get there. It just takes me a while."

He had to say something, but what? In a different setting—Sportsman's Tavern, for example—he would've expounded on his theory of the marital law of motion: the temptation to stray and its Newtonian corollary, the equal and opposite desire to return unless acted on by a force. Regardless of what Teddy had witnessed, Hugh was home, and if Anne didn't drive him back out the door, he would remain here.

"That couch," said Bob, nodding toward the den, "isn't suitable for sleeping."

"Jesus, Dad."

Hugh started to speak but Anne hushed him. In four effortless steps, she'd moved Bob out of the way and poured his glass of water. "Here," she said, pressing the cup into his hands. "Drink."

"I'm not saying it's not nice," Bob continued. "Only that it isn't comfortable."

Anne turned to face Hugh, who shook his head helplessly.

Anne spoke softly to Hugh, and Bob angled his body until he was listening with his good ear.

"Are you sure?" asked Hugh.

Anne nodded.

"Okay," he said. "Guess I'm going up."

"Good," said Bob. Putting a man on the couch had never helped anything. "Get some sleep."

When Hugh was gone, Anne pulled out a stool from the island and told Bob to sit.

"Dad," she said evenly.

"It's corduroy," he said. "Who could sleep on that?"

They stared at each other, blue eyes to blue eyes, and Bob had a pretty good idea of what was on Anne's mind. He'd never talked to her about this stuff and he had no desire to start now, but he was genuinely worried she was making a mistake.

"I'm not trying to tell you how to run your marriage," said Bob.

"Yes, you are."

Bob lifted his water glass with trembling hands and took a sip, then licked his lips and tried again. "It's just that Teddy doesn't necessarily know everything there is to know."

"No," said Anne. "But he wasn't making it up, if that's what you mean."

Bob shook his head. That wasn't what he'd meant. The truth was that neither one of them had expected him to outlive Joanie. There should have been more time, time for Bob to make peace with Joanie and, after he was gone, time for Anne to make peace with his memory.

"Maybe I shouldn't have come down," said Bob.

Anne sighed. "Are you hungry?" she asked. "We never had dinner."

Bob admitted that he could eat.

Anne produced a frying pan for grilled-cheese sandwiches and Bob said, "With bacon, if you have it. That's how your mother used to make them." Harvard beets and Hershey pie, Italian spaghetti and deep sea casserole, tomato aspic and apricot Jell-O mold—he wondered if Anne had thought to save Joanie's recipe box; she had been an excellent cook.

Anne rooted through the refrigerator, removing cheese, pickles, ketchup, mustard, and half a tomato, which had bled through its Saran wrap. Anne tossed the tomato into the sink, then returned to the freezer to hunt for bacon. A frosty vapor frothed around her head. She sat back on her haunches and held up a plastic bag. Ice-burned, it could've been anything.

"I'll throw it in the microwave," she said. "See what comes out."

For three minutes, Bob watched the muted light of the microwave pulse in its black box. He was grateful for the white noise, for a few moments without having to make conversation. The smell of bacon filled the air and they exchanged a look, almost affectionately.

Across the island, Anne spread butter on four pieces of brown bread, scraping from a softened stick next to the stove. "How are you sleeping?" she asked. "Is the room okay?"

"It's okay." Bob stole a look at Anne. "I'm up a lot in the night."

"Can't Dr. Brash give you something?" she asked.

Bob sighed. He couldn't say *diapers*. "He's given me enough."

Anne checked the meat in the microwave. The bacon was frozen solid in the center, with its edges cooked to sizzling.

"I don't need it," Bob assured her. "Too much salt."

Anne dropped the bacon in the sink basin alongside the leaky tomato. It still took Bob by surprise how much she looked like Joanie: tall and thin with high cheekbones and a gentle smile. Bob was not often the recipient of the smile, but when he did catch sight of it, his heart happily raced.

Bob closed his eyes and pictured his daughter as a little girl. Forty years ago, he'd taught her to ski on Mount Otsego, helping her up the rope tow, then bracing her between his legs as they snowplowed down. Saturday mornings the two of them sat side by side in the front row of Smalley's Theatre for the cartoon reels, eating tubs of popcorn designed to ruin their lunch. Bob could still see Anne next to him at the sink on Sunday mornings, lathering her smooth cheeks with his shaving brush before shaving sideburn to chin with a butter knife in an earnest pantomime of Bob's routine. Back then she had let him help her, let him hold her, let him offer his hand.

"Anne," he said carefully.

"Dad, please."

She pressed the spatula into the sandwiches until the pan began to smoke.

"I just think—"

"I know what you think," she said. "It all works out. But who does it work out for?" She lowered her voice and said, "Not the kids."

Anne cut their sandwiches into identical triangle halves, then spooned bread-and-butter pickles onto their plates. Bob hadn't realized how hungry he was until the sandwich was nearly in his hands, and he was about to take a bite when he looked up and saw tears gathered on Anne's lower lids.

"Honey," he said gently. It was Joanie's word but Anne cleaved to it, sinking to the stool by Bob's side.

"There might be a lawsuit," said Anne. "A boy fell at the pre-school." She swiped at her cheeks but the tears were falling too fast to catch.

"What can I do?" asked Bob.

She shook her head. "I don't want everyone in town to know."

"No one's going to know," Bob soothed.

Anne stopped sniveling and looked at him.

"Do you really think that—that no one finds out?"

He could've excused himself. He could've pushed back from the counter and announced he was ready for bed. But she was his daughter, and her mother was gone; there was no one left to help her but him.

"I'm not sure," said Bob slowly.

"Well, they do," said Anne.

It had been the gossip that Joanie despised, too, the gossip that she'd wanted him to understand. He had made her the subject of dozens of whispered conversations at the grocery store, the hair salon, the post office, even church, and when *The Sex Cure* came out, it had been Bob's turn to squirm: Joanie had collected every salacious morsel about the scandal that had almost touched him. But years later, when Bob had retired from the insurance agency and Joanie had culled her library to make room for his thousands of work files, Bob watched her throw out that scrapbook without even mentioning its role in their lives the decade before—forgotten, let go.

"Your mother and I were happy," said Bob.

But she had kept the novel.

"Sometimes," Anne agreed.

"Sometimes," Bob said quietly, and Anne regarded him. Bob shrugged. "You were there," he said.

She seemed to be waiting to see if he would take it back, but Anne could have it, the truth that had never really been hidden. "That book," said Bob. *"The Sex Cure."* Bob watched his daughter to gauge her reaction—he still believed it was she who had vandalized the author's home. "Your mother kept it all those years, right under our mattress."

"Under the mattress," said Anne, "not at the kitchen table. She put it away."

"Put it away? If you want to get rid of something, you throw it out. No, it was in our bedroom with us." Bob shook his head. "Then yesterday, Julia came home from school with it." He took a deep breath. "And she had all these questions."

Had it changed the way people thought about one another? Bob recalled the cast lists and the newspaper articles that Joanie had saved, her copy left out for him to see and see and see. To Bob, his affairs hadn't meant anything; to Joanie, they had meant a great deal. And as Julia had stood there waving the book at him, unearthing all the things he'd believed were long since put away, it had seemed to Bob that Joanie herself was reaching out across the grave, asking for the one thing he could never give her: time and all the nights he had already given to someone else.

"I don't know what came over me," said Bob. "I hit her."

"You *hit* her?"

Bob felt sick to his stomach.

"Like?" Anne imitated his backhand, swinging her hand through the air.

He nodded. "I shouldn't have done it," he said.

"No," said Anne. "Tell her that," she advised.

Bob thought of the light-filled days, the warm hours, the cheerful minutes that Teddy and Julia had raced around 122 Chestnut Street, where he'd never once thought to lay a hand on either of them. If Bob's marriage had not been perfect, at least he and Joanie had ended up in a better place than where they'd begun.

Anne slid his plate toward him and Bob picked up a sandwich half. He could almost picture Joanie at the counter with them, taking a bite from the points of her triangle, wiping the crumbs from her mouth. At her funeral, he hadn't been able to cry. He hadn't been able to hear the words that were spoken. He'd shifted anxiously, like a child, until Anne had slipped her hand into his and held on.

"Tell me something," said Bob. "That Halloween."

Anne took a bite of her sandwich and watched him while she chewed.

"Was it you?" asked Bob.

"Not me," said Anne, meeting his gaze. "I was just a kid."

12

Sometimes at night Sam and Carl and I would go down to Council Rock to stare at the lake, at Sleeping Lion Mountain overlooking the Susquehanna Valley, at Kingfisher Tower looming like a grandfather clock over Three Mile Point. And if it was winter, we'd test the ice and slush out as far as we dared, which was usually only a step or two before we heard the frozen water creaking under our feet and shoe-skated back to shore. But tonight, in spite of my dad telling me not to, I went alone, pulled by a tide of shame toward Carl: the note I'd written was looping through my mind on repeat, and the only way I knew to stop it was to confess.

The rooftop outside my bedroom window was slick and I scaled cautiously, one hand palming the shingles, the other jutted out for balance. At the front of the house, I lowered myself onto the metal porch roof, then knelt and slid a leg over until my toe found the railing. Silently, I dropped down, still holding the rain gutter, then jumped back into the grass and wiped my hands on the legs of my jeans.

Moonlight filtered through the tree leaves, crosshatching the front lawn. The only sound was of the wind blowing the porch swing, the right chain whining over a knot it couldn't work out. Sam and Carl and I had abused that swing.

The humid night air had draped itself over my neighbors' lawns, dampening the sidewalks and beading on my hair. I knew every step of this sidewalk, the squares that rose over tree roots and the squares that circumnavigated their trunks; the cracked, the crumbling, and the brand-new squares with handprints and initials stick-etched in. Susquehanna Avenue. On a trip down to Philadelphia, we'd seen what the creek behind our house would become before dumping into the Atlantic, hundreds of miles away, and I'd thought about Teddy and me learning to spell the name of the river, that rhythmic lullaby, *ESSuESS, QUEuEEE, H-a-n-n-A*.

At the curb in front of Carl's house, I brushed a handful of gravel into my palm, then carried it up the driveway to a place just below Carl's window. Maybe I didn't want to wake him: I picked the smallest stones and threw them one by one, hitting first the window frame, then the rain gutter, the drainpipe, the roof. I spent another few seconds reluctantly peppering his house and was about to head home when I heard the back door open.

Carl's mom, ghostly in her white nightgown, leaned out into the night.

"Julia?" she said in her lilting accent. "Is that you, love?"

Her strawberry-brown hair hung in a braid over her left shoulder and she wore fuzzy slippers, but her ankles and calves were bare.

"Are you okay?" she asked. "Do you need Carl for something?"

"Sort of," I said.

"I can get him for you."

What other mother? I looked carefully at her and saw Carl's eyes, his freckled nose. I couldn't help but think that I had sabotaged his mother, his whole world, his only family, and I knew right then that I couldn't tell Carl.

"That's okay," I said. She waited, like she expected me to say more, but there was nothing more to say.

"Do you want to come inside?" she asked after a moment.

I shrugged and she held the door for me. The green light from the VCR clock blinked 12:56. No TV, no music, no lights, but the house didn't seem scary. Just dark.

I sat on the couch by the window, stepping out of my shoes and tucking my feet under a blanket while Carl's mom settled in a rocking chair a few feet away. My eyes adjusted and I saw her pale lips and her long, thick hair. When she didn't braid it, her hair reached all the way down her back, and I wondered if she'd cut it since Carl's dad had died.

"Carl said the two of you are playing a match against each other tomorrow."

For the first time, I let myself wonder who would win. Carl and I typically split sets, but tomorrow, with an audience, I didn't know what would happen.

"I think he's a little nervous," she offered. "He says if he wins, you're off the team."

I rested my head on a pillow. "I wasn't even on it to begin with."

Outside the clouds raced one another across the sky, mottling the moonlight. There were a hundred clouds ahead of the moon and a hundred more just behind, and I watched them chase on, sailing over Cooperstown and beyond the hills, and thought how strange it would be to leave this place one day.

"My dad asked Coach Klawson to give me the exhibition match," I admitted. "It should've been Carl's, but I took it anyway."

She rocked forward and joined me on the couch, pulling my feet onto her lap so that the blanket covered both of us. I curled my body close to hers and soon tears were pooling on my neck.

Of all our mothers, she was the most like us. When she'd caught Sam and Carl and me smoking behind the oak tree in her backyard, she'd taken the pack but left us to finish our OPs, and when she said goodbye to us at night, she told us to get home mayhi safe.

I knew that if the note about her turned up, I would never admit to having written it, which was the worst kind of shame, the kind you cannot even own up to, and the regret I felt then, not only for what I'd done but for the kind of person I was, racked my stomach and squeezed my throat.

"You've had a hard couple of weeks," said Carl's mom, hugging me tight, and she meant Nonz, of course, but what had begun with Nonz was snowballing through my life, no end in sight.

"My dad kissed a woman," I said, testing it out.

Carl's mom was quiet. Backlit, she appeared as a shadow, almost otherworldly. A part of her had died with Carl's dad, which was the kind of love that ruined your life, like the kind of love my parents had would ruin ours.

"There are some things you can't control," she said. "You can't control your parents." She squeezed my feet again. "But you and Sam and Carl take good care of one another."

I couldn't tell if it was an observation or a warning, and I wanted to promise her that we always had and always would, but it wasn't true. We were already shifting away from one another, elbowing for more room.

*　*　*

Back home, I fell asleep sometime after two, armed and ready to dream. Dad was living in Cherry Valley; Mom had pushed Poppy down the stairs. I arrived at CHS with my backpack in hand, but Carl had court papers saying I couldn't come inside and Sam pretended not to see me, standing with Megan V'd between his knees. I chased the note about Carl's mom across every page of the night, but while I was looking for it Carl had already found it, and, even though no one was speaking to me, I still had an exhibition match to play.

When Teddy yanked my comforter off me at a quarter to eight, I didn't even try to fight it—I let him frog-march me to the bathroom, leaning against his shoulder, and I felt a little better knowing he was here.

"Let's go," said Teddy. "Brush, comb. Whatever it is you do in there." He parked me in front of our sink, a petri dish of toothpaste logs—it was our responsibility to clean our bathroom, but neither of us took this task very seriously. I ran the water and applied Crest to my brush.

"If we're late, you won't be able to play," said Teddy.

"It's an exhibition match," I reminded him.

"What?"

I took the toothbrush out of my mouth. "It's only exhibition."

Teddy rolled his eyes, then put a hand on my shoulder like he was the captain of my team. "It's just nerves," he said. "Channel them. They'll keep you alert."

Teddy skipped down the stairs while I went to get dressed. I picked up my jeans and checked one last time for the note. If it was small enough to be lost, maybe it was small enough never to be found.

In the kitchen, Mom handed Teddy cheese toast—a microwaved paper towel with a slice of white bread hardening under a square of Kraft—then asked if I wanted one.

I shook my head and opened the fridge for a Coke.

Mom frowned. "How'd you sleep?" she asked.

"Nightmares," I said. "My eyes feel like sandpaper."

Her blouse was wrinkled, her mascara smudged into two smoky lines. She should've left for work by now but it was nice having her here, seeing us off to school.

"Are you coming to my match?" I asked.

"Of course," she said. "Poppy, too."

"And Dad?"

"Sure," she said. "Of course."

Maybe it was something they'd already discussed: every other weekend and holidays and see you at the match tonight. I wanted to ask her what time they'd be there, and would they arrive together? Would they sit together, would they speak? And what if I lost? And what if I won? Would we go to Gabriella's to celebrate or was this it, the last time we'd all be in the same place at the same time?

I stared into her eyes, trying to divine her thoughts, but her gaze was a cloudless sky, a pool so deep you could drown.

Teddy and I raced up Beaver Street to Delaware and past the elementary school to the CHS bike path. We ran hard and soon my shirt was damp under my windbreaker and I started to pant but kept running until Teddy said, "Slow down. I have a cramp."

For a moment we didn't speak. I cracked the tab of my Coke and took a sip, and Teddy waited for me to put the can to my lips, then tapped the bottom of the can, sending brown fizz over my chin and down the front of my jacket. I wiped my face on his sleeve.

Grass had pushed up through the cracks in the path and dewy water pooled in the potholes. The school loomed close but I kept my eyes on the ground, on Teddy's Air Jordans, which he wore laced but untied, his jeans bagging over the tongues.

"What happened with Dad?" I asked. "Did he really kiss that woman?"

Teddy stared straight ahead, looking older somehow, not only older than me but older than him, not the same Teddy he'd been two days ago sitting cross-legged with his baseball cards on the floor in front of him.

"Don't worry about it," said Teddy, and it wasn't an answer but I heard in it all that I needed to know.

I thought of all the times he'd come to my room when we were kids, too old for babysitters but too young to go out after dark. If I was in the right kind of mood, I'd dog-ear my book and we'd play Surrey, where Teddy had to piggyback me two laps through the house—up the back stairs, down the front, with thirty-second breaks on the guest-room bed and in the laundry room—and I could still see us: me, armed with the kitchen timer; him, sweating down his pencil-thin neck. I'd squeeze Teddy's skinny ribs with my knees, spurring him on, and he'd stagger up the last steps of the back stairs, trying not to drop me. With or without Rick Delaney's Jeep, Teddy would find a way to keep going. Teddy was a mover, a doer—he didn't get stuck. An eye for an eye for Teddy. He would not let us down.

When the homeroom bell rang we started to run again: Teddy out in front, me hot on his tail. I forked my soda into the grass and pumped with both arms, backpack swinging, and I caught Teddy and he let me run alongside him all the way to the front door.

"See you at the courts," he said. He thrust his fists into the air and mock-screamed my name, *Jul-ya, Jul-ya, Jul-ya*, all the way down the hall to his homeroom. I listened until he was gone. I listened until I was alone in the hallway, until the final bell rang, and then I high-tailed it to homeroom.

"Cutting it close," said Sam.

I slid into my seat and ducked my head under my desk to scan for the cubelike note. Nothing. I glanced at Carl.

"What?" he asked. He followed my gaze to his shirt—striped rugby—to his fly—zipped—back up to his copper curls. "What?" he asked again.

I eyeballed the carpet in front of my locker.

"What are you looking for?" asked Sam.

I shook my head.

"Nervous?" asked Carl.

I shrugged. It was as good a reason as any to be edgy around Carl. I couldn't explain that I'd done something far worse than stealing his exhibition match.

"Don't worry," he said, nudging me with his shoulder. "Even if you lose, we can still hang out."

I spent all of math class applying formulas to the probability of the note turning up, but the problem set was infinite. Maybe the janitor had already swept it and bagged it and the note was out of my life forever. Or maybe it was on the floor somewhere, waiting to be found. It was possible that no one would find it or that someone already had, and I thought about all the weeks left in the school year, the never-ending possibility of it turning up.

The day wound on mercilessly—math, keyboarding, English, French—and by the time Sam joined me in the cafeteria line during fifth period, my mind was white static, dead blank.

"Everyone's looking for you," said Sam.

I froze, my stomach swallowing my heart.

"Christ," said Sam. "Are you okay?"

I wanted to go back, I wanted it back, I wanted the note in my hand. I would've eaten it. I would've burned it, then eaten it. I would not have written it. I would not have been the kind of person who would've written it. But it was done, I was who I was, and now Sam would know.

"Where is he?" I asked.

"Who?"

"Carl."

"Carl?" Sam repeated. "Evan. He wants to give you a pep talk for the match."

I tried to swallow, but there was a sandbar in my throat.

"Fucking hell," said Sam. "Pull it together."

But I couldn't stop the tears, and finally he took me by the elbow and steered me toward the choir room, ducking us both into the empty auditorium.

Sam stashed me in row L, then sat in the aisle at my feet. After a minute he said, "I shouldn't have given you the silent treatment yesterday."

"What?"

"I thought that's why you were crying."

I took a breath and my chest shuddered.

"Maybe you should call Claw," he said. "Tell him this exhibition match is filing you over the edge."

"It wasn't his idea in the first place. My dad arranged it."

Sam shrugged, and I could tell by the way he didn't ask any

questions that he'd already guessed. "My dad pays for me to go to Bollettieri camp every summer," he said, "which is basically the same thing. He was probably only trying to help."

The dim auditorium lights shone down in yellow cones, spotlighting Sam, spotlighting the stage steps and the velvet curtain stretching across the stage. I thought of Carl in the cafeteria with his red lunch bag unpacked, his peanut butter sandwich on a paper napkin in front of him. It was hard to believe we'd be playing tennis against each other in a few hours and that an hour after that I might be off the team. I wondered what it'd be like when the three of us didn't hang out every day after school, when Sam and Carl went to practice and I went home to Poppy.

"I did something awful," I said.

"What?" asked Sam.

"I wrote something." But I couldn't say what.

"Are you talking about this?" Sam reached into his pocket and pulled out the note.

Motherfucking shit. I tried to grab it but he stood and switched the paper to his left hand, holding it out of my reach.

"Where'd you get that?" I yelled.

"I was looking for our lunch card yesterday during gym class. I found it in your jeans."

"In the girls' locker room?" I jumped up and reached for the note again but Sam raised it over his head.

"You were outside. The real question is, why do you have it?"

"That is not the real question. And anyway, it's true."

"So? It's nobody's business. Why'd you write it?"

We were so close I could smell his skin, his face moisturizer, and I felt dizzy.

"He was being a jerk," I said.

"You stole his match," said Sam.

"Because you ditched me for tennis tryouts!"

"I ditched you?"

Couldn't he see? The words in my mind were palpable, breakable, and I handed them to Sam. "You kissed Megan. You let Carl have first dibs on me. You knew you were going to make the team, but what about me? Did you even think about me?"

Sam slowly dropped his arm, and I could've grabbed the note but I didn't move. We were face-to-face. The tan line on Sam's forehead had started to fade, but his eyes were bright green.

Sam closed his eyes first, then I closed mine. For a second I thought he might leave me standing there but soon I felt his lips on mine and they were papery and dry and warm. A line of soft stubble brushed my upper lip and my heart bass-drummed my chest. Sam's tongue gently pushed into my mouth and I touched his teeth, his gums. Our bodies were board straight, our hands at our sides, and I smelled the collar of his shirt and tasted bubble gum.

When it was over Sam opened my hand, then closed my fingers around the note.

"Are you going to tell Carl?" I asked.

"About what?" He smiled and held out his hand. "Lunch card, please." I handed it over.

"Sam?" I asked. "Am I a swelfare friend?"

"No." He shook his head. "Hardly ever."

When the auditorium doors clicked shut, I ripped the note into eight pieces, then went across the hall to the girls' bathroom and flushed three times, watching the paper swirl down and away, thinking about how all stories ended—folded up or abandoned, lost or forgotten—making room for things that were just beginning, and I headed back to the cafeteria to join Sam and Carl.

* * *

In the car after school, no one spoke. Sam didn't even try to make me drive. I sat in back and stole glances at Sam in the rearview mirror, and at least once he looked up at me and smiled.

He dropped me off first, then drove Carl across town to get his stuff. My mom's car wasn't in the driveway and a note on the kitchen counter said that she'd taken Poppy to a doctor's appointment: I had the run of the place. I downed a glass of OJ and ate three gingersnaps, then went upstairs to change.

Carl and I didn't have the CHS team uniform, but I had plenty of team-looking shirts from my lessons at the country club. I laid out a navy collared shirt alongside a pleated white skirt, then quickly showered and shaved my legs.

On the porch, I ran into Dad coming home from work.

"Hey, old girl," he said.

I stepped back, retreating until I was a foot above him with the rail between us. In his right hand was the briefcase that Teddy and I had given him for Christmas; in his left, a giant legal folder like the kind Mom sometimes carried.

"Are you heading to your match?" he asked.

"It's not till later."

"I'll be over in a couple of hours to watch you play."

Sunlight reflected off his glasses, hiding his eyes, but I could tell by the tilt of his chin that he was looking at me. On Beaver Street, an ambulance crawled through the intersection on its way to Bassett, and we waited until it had gone by.

"Jules—"

"I don't want to talk about it." I pictured Sam and me in the auditorium that afternoon, his lips on mine. I didn't want to think about Dad having done the same thing with some woman we didn't know.

"I have to go," I said.

Dad started to let me pass but at the last second he collected me in a hug, and I let myself be held.

* * *

The day was sunny, cool, and I ran up the hill to the courts, falling into step with Carl on his way back from the bathroom with the water cans.

"Nice outfit," said Carl, handing me a can. I jounced in my pleated skirt while Carl T'd his arms to model his own uniform. "What do you think?" he asked.

I rubbed the hem of his shirt between my thumb and finger—a soft striped Fila with snaps at the collar—then admired his matching shorts—white with a faux-grosgrain belt. "Where'd you get it?" I asked.

"The attic," said Carl. "My dad's."

I sniffed: cedar.

"And," said Carl. He handed me his second can of water, then fished a red sweatband out of his pocket and pushed it up on his fore-head, ringing his mop of curls.

Carl and I walked down to where Sam and Evan were warming up while the Sauquoit players changed inside Bassett Hall. The rest of our team ran laps around the outside of the fence, Claw yelling at them to keep up the pace.

"Water," I announced, placing Sam's can near the net on Court 2.

"Water," Carl repeated to Evan. "Let us know if you need refills."

Evan waved and Sam said, "Thanks, Jules. Nice skirt," and I felt my pulse speed up.

Carl and I sat on our racket covers on the hill overlooking the courts and noted the order of the warm-up: forehands, backhands, volleys—in a few hours it'd be us, and we'd need to know what to do.

"When do we practice serves?" I asked.

"I think serves are last," said Carl. "It's baseline, then net, then overheads."

I thought about that for a second. I wasn't sure if I even knew how to feed an overhead to Carl without hitting the ball over the back fence.

"Do you want to practice overheads?" I asked.

"No, that's okay," said Carl.

"Yeah," I agreed. "That's okay for me, too."

I glanced at Carl. I wanted to tell him I was sorry, but he didn't yet know what for. I loved him, but I couldn't say that, either. He was my best friend, and I prayed not to lose him.

"I could let you win," said Carl.

"No," I said. "You can't."

Carl shrugged. He wanted to win, too, but he'd needed to offer.

By five o'clock, the hill was a checkerboard of quilts and blankets and folding chairs, and at least some people were there to see Carl and me. Teddy and Kim huddled together under the comforter from Teddy's bed, and when Mom arrived she crossed the lawn to join them. I watched her reintroduce herself to Kim, then softly pat Teddy's head. I looked for Dad but he wasn't with her.

Mom called me over and pointed up the hill to where Poppy was seated on a wooden bench by himself.

"He came to see you," she said.

"Who invited him?" I asked, but she put a hand on my shoulder and steered me up the hill.

I walked to Poppy's bench and sat beside him. A blanket from our linen closet was folded over his lap, a hat on his head. He looked frail but he smiled and I scooted closer to my grandfather, wanting to feel his warmth.

"Hi," he said.

"Hi."

He started to touch my hand, then seemed to change his mind and pulled on the hem of the blanket instead. "Did I ever tell you about the time I won five dollars in a third-set tiebreaker in 1924?" asked Poppy.

About a hundred times.

"Play every point like it's the last one, and don't even think about the possibility of losing."

"I'm not," I lied.

"Yeah, you are." He reached out for my hand again and this time took it. "Is this your racket hand?" He opened my palm and felt for calluses. "Don't let the racket move around. Hold on tight. You hit topspin?" I nodded. "Backspin?" I shrugged. "Use the whole court," said Poppy. "Bring him in. Send him out. Is that Carl?" Poppy squinted and I pointed out Carl in the crowd. "You can buy him a drink when you win. Still friends, but not till after the game."

I smiled and Poppy said, "I'm sorry about the other day. I shouldn't have done that."

"That's okay."

"No, it's not." He kissed my head and I leaned against his bony shoulder. "Nonz would've loved to see you play," he said. And I thought it was true, so I pictured her here on the bench next to Poppy, and I could almost see her: blue apron, yellow dress, the smell of cinnamon in the air. I looked at Poppy and he smiled and said, "Play hard."

Threading my way through the crowd, I passed Evan and Danke Schoen; Teddy and Kim and most of Teddy's friends; Em and her little sister, Maggie. Dad showed up just before I stepped onto the court, waving to me, mouthing the words, *Good luck.*

"Let's go," said Carl.

But I was waiting for Sam.

"One second," I said. "I have to go to the bathroom."

In the dim office hallway I walked to the boys' bathroom, stopping outside the door to listen to the voices: maybe Sam, definitely Doug and Alan. How long could I wait before Carl came looking for me? I counted to thirty, then counted to thirty again.

"There you are," said Sam behind me.

I turned. He was sink-showered, his hair wet but his brow still sweaty from his match.

"You ready?" he asked.

"Not really."

He took my hand and pulled me into the shadows of the hallway and we stood beside a potted plant in the last light of day, then he backed me up against the wall and leaned into me, and I felt his whole body against mine, and we kissed, longer this time, long enough for Doug and Alan to come out of the bathroom and see us there together.

"You better go," said Sam, but I can't remember leaving him. Surely Alan and Doug would've been laughing, catcalling, and probably

Sam and I would've pulled away from each other to minimize the damage, to refute the idea that we were more than friends—but we were more than friends, and in my memory I stayed with him forever, and the match never happened, and Carl didn't drift away from us, and my parents were married for always.

Outside, I joined Carl on Court 1 and it seemed ten times bigger than the court I knew. Above us, the sky was lavender with a full moon already crowning in the east, the pine trees swaying gently in the breeze.

Claw led us to the net and cracked opened a new can of balls.

"Who's serving?" he asked.

I looked at Carl and he spun his racket and I called down and it was down.

Claw handed me the Penns and told us to warm up for five minutes. "Let's get going," he said. "One set. It's freezing out here."

At the gate, he turned on the lights and the purple bulbs began to hum and buzz and glow. The sun was setting, painting the tops of the pine trees orange, and the balls were electric against the court.

I slipped two balls into my pocket and gave Carl the third.

"I'm about to whippoorwill you out of here, six–love," I said.

"No effing way," said Carl.

We walked back to our separate baselines and I started the warm-up with a shot into net, then overhit the next ball, bouncing it behind Carl's head.

Carl restarted the rally and it was a normal feed to my forehand, which I sent back to his forehand, and our warm-up was under way. When the balls were at net, we jogged in to pick them up and I asked Carl if he wanted to practice volleys.

"Let's just start," said Carl.

I asked for two practice serves and Carl said, "Fine, but hurry."

Both of my practices went in so I said, "These are good," and showed Carl the ball.

"Love–love," I said. I tossed up my first serve and spun it into the corner of the service box and Carl returned it into the net, and we were on our way.

It took us a while to find our rhythm—we were nervous, and the night was quickly cooling, and there was a band of tension between us, a humming sense that our lives were about to change. The first couple of points found us standing at the T like beginners, tapping the ball, afraid to hit through. I was focused on the difference between thirty–love and fifteen–all, then I thought about how Poppy had said to go all out on every point: there was no score, just this moment, and the next time the ball came to me I returned it as hard as I could to Carl's deep backhand, wide of the line.

I glanced at the crowd, which was a mistake: my knees wobbled with nerves. I saw Carl's mom seated next to my mom—close, the way she and I had been early this morning—then Dad pacing outside the fence with his back to Mom, and finally Teddy, who had migrated across the hill so that he was standing nearly behind me, his fingers laced through the chain-link fence, Dad's image only closer.

"Fifteen–all," I called and bounced the ball twice, then served to Carl's backhand. He dinked it and I charged the net, my racket open for a volley, but the ball caught the tape and fell back to my side.

"Come on," said Teddy behind me. "You can do this."

I bounced the ball, then tossed it up and let it drop, bounced it some more. I thought of all the bus rides I would miss with Sam if I lost; I thought of him in Hamilton, in Richfield Springs, in Mount Markham without me. I stepped back from the baseline and played with my racket strings.

"Let's go, Jules," said Dad from the sidelines. He'd meant it as a cheer, but it ignited something inside me and I turned and yelled, "Leave me alone!"

After that, not a sound from the hill. I wondered how many people out there already knew about my dad and the woman in Cherry Valley; it wasn't something we could contain. I already planned to tell Sam and Carl, and Teddy would tell Kim, because they were our family, too. I caught a glimpse of my mother leaning forward on her quilt, bending toward me, and she looked like Nonz, almost, and I wondered if I was too old to crawl into her arms. Carl could have the match—it would be victory by forfeit—and I started to walk away, but, just then, out of the darkness came Sam, joining Carl and me on the court as though it were the most normal thing in the world.

"Hey," he said to me. "Hey," he called to Carl.

He picked up a ball that had rolled to the net post and threw it back to me, then sat on the bench where he always sat when Carl and I played.

"Fifteen–thirty," he said. "Let's go."

I stepped to the baseline and bounced the ball twice, finding a cadence; I tossed it up and back and swung hard, my serve kicking over the net and dropping in, and Carl took it on the rise, returning the ball down the line to my forehand, which I hit crosscourt to his forehand. He scooped it up, off balance but still it was coming over, and I moved in on the ball, let it bounce, then knocked it back to his shallow backhand. Carl went for it, got his racket on it, and stabbed it into the fence.

The sound of clapping came on like thunder, a single boom from the dark beyond the courts. Carl showed me the face of his racket, saying nice point, and I backed up to the baseline to serve again.

"Thirty–all," I called, which was to say it was even, which was to say it was anyone's game.

I held and we switched sides near Sam, who handed each of us a can of water. We drank without talking. Carl's face was red; my legs were springy, my muscles loose. I jogged in place, then handed Sam my water can and walked back out to the court.

Carl took two practice serves, then two more. None of them went in. "These are good," he said finally, but they weren't. Love–fifteen.

Carl kicked the fence and I heard his mom shout from the hill, "You can do this, Carl." Someone else said, "Come on, Carl"—maybe it was Em's sister, Maggie—and Carl jumped in place a few times, as if he hadn't been warmed up, then served again.

I was late on my swing and returned it wide into Court 2. After that, Carl held easily, tying the score at 1–1.

When we were still on-serve at 4–5, Mr. Lowry from the *Cooperstown Crier* started snapping flash photos from outside the fence, which wasn't unheard of but had certainly never happened to me. I saw his lens poke through the chain-link, first by Carl's feet, then by Carl's head, then suddenly by my head. I was distracted and Carl's serve got past me four times while I was monitoring the cameraman. Carl held, 5–5, and it was my serve.

Carl knocked the balls over the net to a volley of applause. I looked up, past Sam, to the top of the hill where Poppy was parked on his bench. He had summited the night, high above the valley, a little closer to the sky and a little closer to Nonz. I could see the outline of his overcoat, his wide-brimmed hat, and I waved in case he was still awake, and I thought I saw him wave back, but I couldn't be sure.

I showed the ball to Carl and he nodded and I tossed it up and back. It arced high, then hung still, an ornament on the evergreens, the brightest star. I swung through, brushing the side of the ball, and it kicked up and dropped into the back of the service box. Carl misjudged the spin and tipped it off his racket frame.

I wanted to win and I tried not to think about Carl on the other side of the net, wanting not to lose. We were like spiders on a web and if someone pushed someone else had to get pulled. I could feel the strands under us. The web contained Nonz and Poppy, Teddy and me, my parents' marriage and also their divorce. In six months, they would be separated. In a year, we would bury Poppy in the plot next to Nonz. In three years, the courts at Bassett Hall would be slated for demolition, the nets taken down, the lights dismantled to make room for a new parking lot for the hospital. The lines on the courts were the veins in our arms, and the service boxes were the chambers of our hearts; the divot in the baseline had foreshadowed the end, but we couldn't stop it, we could only slow it down.

Carl and I did our part. I held, he held, and then it was 6–6, and there was no going back. Buzzing lights, and the sound of Sam's voice calling out the tiebreaker score: 1–2, 2–2, 2–3, 3–3. Carl and I were deadlocked, vacuum-sealed in a match we couldn't win or lose, which was the only kind of match for me. Eventually, one of us would stumble. Eventually, one of us would win. But as long as the game lasted, my parents were still married, Poppy was just across the hall, and Sam and Carl and I were impregnable, protected by our words—us on the inside, the world on the outside. We'd had slitters for everything, but never for ourselves.

At 6–7, Carl's first serve floated long and he offered up a paddy ball on his second. I stepped in, taking it on the rise. My return bounced at Carl's feet and he danced around it and got his racket on it, and the ball came off his strings like a comet, tailing up into the sky, above the fence and the lights and the tops of the trees. The stars charted its course.

I tracked the ball with my left hand, rotating my hips and coiling my racket. I shuttle-stepped forward, backward. Blood rushed my ears. I waited until Carl had no choice—until he picked a side, went left toward the backhand court while I shifted right—and then the ball was here, and just like that, I swung.

ACKNOWLEDGMENTS

A tremendous thank-you to my agent, Amy Williams, for her matchless enthusiasm and ardent support, and to my editor, Sarah Bowlin, for her unerring guidance and indispensible insight beginning to end. To everyone at Holt who helped usher this novel into the world, I am genuinely grateful.

Thank you, too, to my colleagues at *Vanity Fair* with whom I have worked these last nine years, especially John Banta and the entire Research Department. If writing a novel is a solitary endeavor, I never felt it.

I have been fortunate to have generous and gifted teachers over the years: Rick Moody, Bertha Rogers, and Helen Schulman, whose encouragement from the time I was fifteen years old has sustained me; Robert Stone, who took me under his wing at Yale; and Ann Beattie, John Casey, Deborah Eisenberg, and Christopher Tilghman at the University of Virginia Creative Writing Program, who supported me then and now—thank you.

For their thoughtful and loving feedback—friends whose careful consideration has helped shape this novel in the best ways—my deepest gratitude to Taylor Antrim, Brian Berry, Kate Berry, Luca Borghese, Alison Forbes, Marnie Hanel, Laura Haverland, Jenny Hollowell, Cassie Marlantes Rahm, Jebediah Reed, Makeba Seargeant, Doug Stumpf, and Lilly Tuttle. For a formative supply of grilled cheese sandwiches and Cokes with a cherry in them, thank you to Bebe and Papa. A very special thank-you to Eleanor Henderson and Mary Beth Keane for their sage advice, and to Molly Cooper, who has read this novel as many times as I have.

I owe a debt of gratitude to everyone in Cooperstown, my oldest friends, who share my memories of the village. To those of you who spoke to me about life in Cooperstown in the 1960s, I could not have put Nonz and Poppy there without your help. To Nick Alicino, tennis coach, English teacher, and friend, you live on in our stories. And to Jamie Bordley and Peter Townsend—everywhere I looked, you were there.

Finally, I could not have written this book without the people who cheer me on every day—thank you to my brother, Stuart, my biggest fan, for always being on my team; to Jenny, Cooper, and Grayson, for making everything fun; to my beloved Gigi, for her faith in me and for her friendship; and to my parents, Peggy and Tom, for their endless love and for moving us to Cooperstown.

About the Author

CALLIE WRIGHT is a reporter-researcher at *Vanity Fair* magazine. She graduated from Yale and earned her MFA at the University of Virginia, where she was a Poe/Faulkner Fellow in creative writing and won a Raven Society Fellowship. She is the recipient of a *Glimmer Train* Short Story Award for New Writers and her short fiction has appeared in *Glimmer Train* and *The Southern Review*. She lives in Brooklyn, New York.